I CAN'T BELIEVE MY GIRLFRIEND'S A ZOMBIE

NOT YOUR AVERAGE POST-APOCALYPTIC,
ZOMBIE LOVE STORY...

JACK E. MOHR

Jack E. Mohr
Baltimore, Maryland

Copyright Jack E. Mohr
2023

All rights reserved, including the right to reproduce this book or any portion thereof in any form without the express written permission of the author.

ISBN: Paperback 979-8-9865606-7-0
 eBook 979-8-9865606-6-3
Hardcover: 979-8-9891554-0-8

Printed by Kindle Direct Publishing

Cover Design by
https://www.fiverr.com/premiumsolns?source=inbox with images produced with midjourney

This is a work of fiction. All the characters and events portrayed in this book are fictional, and any resemblance to real people or incidents is purely coincidental.

TABLE OF CONTENTS

CHAPTER 1:	CONFABULATION	4
CHAPTER 2:	SVENGALI	18
CHAPTER 3:	REPOSE	66
CHAPTER 4:	VERILY VERILY...SERENDIPITY	94
CHAPTER 5:	A MEMORY FORGOTTEN IS A TRUTH UNKNOWN	100
CHAPTER 6:	FOOL ME ONCE: MAMA'S PEARL	114
CHAPTER 7:	WHEN REVENGE ISN'T AVAILABLE, USE JUSTICE	158
CHAPTER 8:	ASK ALICE: ADAM IN WANDERLAND.	164
CHAPTER 9:	BUFFALO NICKEL	198
CHAPTER 10:	RAISON D'ÊTRE	212
CHAPTER 11:	DRAPETOMANIA	236
CHAPTER 12:	OPPOSITES DETRACT	266
CHAPTER 13:	U OF HARD KNOCKS: INSTITUTIONALIZATION 101	286
CHAPTER 14:	REIN MAN, GIVE US REIN!	306
CHAPTER 15:	WATER FOR THE ROOTS, NOT JUST THE LEAVES	328
CHAPTER 16:	ONLY THE DESPERATE SEE MIRAGES	344
CHAPTER 17:	WHY WOULDN'T THE GRASS BE GREENER?	352
CHAPTER 18:	NEOTENY	360
CHAPTER 19:	FREE THE LAND	370
CHAPTER 20:	NO PLACE LIKE HOME	378

CHAPTER 1:
CONFABULATION

**I CAN'T BELIEVE MY
GIRLFRIEND'S A ZOMBIE**

JACK E. MOHR

URIAH

At what point does the little voice in your head turn against you....? After the other voices in there convince it to...

That was the last thing he remembered before everything went black. He had only found one way to silence the myriad of voices...by making everything fade into obscurity.

The sun's rays struggled to pierce through the atmosphere—a battle they often lost. And not from lack of effort: the sky was too dense to allow any semblance of light, stained with streaks of autumn orange, violet and charcoal.

He hated being out there. He called it Death's Shadow because the sun never shone, but a layer of heat remained trapped between the clouds and the earth's crust, creating the perfect environment for piyel to grow rampant.

Potent piyel.

He used it for exactly what it was doing now, a sweet slumber that left him numb to the world. It was the only way he could sleep more than a few consecutive hours without noise flooding his mind—like a raging river of gargled voices tugging, trying to pull him under.

It was the only reason he would ever venture this far east.

A hypoallergenic cross-breed dog frantically lapped at the young man's face. She had been at it off and on for the better part of an hour.

The boy coughed and chunks of green liquid dribbled down his cheek, covering streaks of dried vomit.

Lying on his back, he rubbed his side and released a weakened groan.

Groggily, he pushed the dog away. "All right… All right. I'm up. I'm up, girl," he said, coughing and raising himself to a seated position. He yawned and rubbed his temples with thumb and forefinger. A whiff of his own puke provoked his gag reflex, and he retched but nothing came out.

"Damn, how long was I out this time, ol' girl?" he asked, wiping sludge from the corners of his mouth. "I really gotta do better."

He shook his arms, flinging chunky sludge onto the verdant foliage beneath him. He sat in a field of piyel—a florescent magenta six-leaf clover—contemplating his existence. Had it really boiled down to this? Going from one piyel field to the next, indulging in the hallucinogenic until he passed out, a feeble attempt to keep the head noise quiet and escape the anxiety that was his life.

The murmurs were maddening.

What are all these voices? Who do they belong to? What's their purpose?

He shook his head. Sometimes the voices were a constant indiscernible babble; other times they would be excruciating screams. Whatever their source, they became unbearable.

He tilted his head back and stared into the murky sky. *There has to be something more to life. Something more than living for the purpose of survival.*

He picked a clump of piyel and squeezed, "I told myself I wouldn't let it get the best of me. I'd only use it for therapeutic reasons like Evynn and I agreed," he muttered to himself with a mixture of shame and disdain.

A lie he often told to convince himself the habit hadn't consumed him, and he possessed some semblance of power over it.

He struggled to gain his bearings. His head throbbed and his brain felt like it was smashing against the insides of his skull.

He moaned.

"Hey, Ev!" he cried out. "Evynn? Hey, Babe? Evynn?" his pitch increased in a growing sense of panic.

He searched the grim atmosphere anxiously, looking for any semblance of Evynn. Even though the environment was dingy, he had grown accustomed to the dullness.

"Idiot! Idiot! Idiot!" he yelled, slamming his palms on the ground.

He reached for Bliss and pulled the dog's face close. "Hey, Bliss. Come here, girl." He rubbed her head. "Bliss? What happened to Evynn?"

The dog barked and the young man grumbled. Over-consumption of piyel gave him a splitting headache and a dry mouth.

"Please tell me Evynn didn't turn last night?" he huffed.

Of course, he knew the answer to the question before he asked. Searching through the sordid light for Evynn, he recognized several of her belongings.

She'd never leave without her backpack and cloak. She must have turned.

"I missed the signs? How could I have missed the signs?" he whispered.

His heart rate increased as dizziness overcame him. He attempted to stand, but stumbled, crashing face first into a field of piyel clovers.

Bliss barked, running to his side and nudging him with her moist nose.

The young man wiped the soil from his face and repeatedly slapped his cheeks before stumbling back to his feet. "Come on Uriah, get yourself together."

He drew in a deep breath, placed both palms on top of his head and tilted back, staring into the bleak, burnt sky, somewhere he believed the sun to be. He wasn't certain whether it was day or night, because the endless murky sky made them indistinguishable at times.

Adrenaline bolstered his faculties.

The piyel possessed medicinal properties, albeit not as Uriah intended. It helped with Evynn when awakening from torpor, making the excruciatingly painful and anxiety-ridden experience tolerable.

Uriah shuddered as images of her last re-turning sprouted into his mind—bones cracked, skin ripped, organs shifted. The part that stuck in his mind most was the smell of insides that permeated. He did not want her to have to go through that alone and more importantly, without the piyel to soften the pain.

A loud-pitched feminine scream full of panic bounced around in his mind for a brief moment but vanished quickly. He vigorously shook his head.

He contemplated chewing more piyel to take the edge off, but knew he needed to be sharp in order to track Evynn. Well, mainly Bliss would do all the tracking, but he had to keep up.

Evynn had left her belongings in a neat pile: her favorite graphic novel, *Indigo Dragon's Blood*, a pile of postcards displaying the skyline of various cities, her grandmother's Bible and the most important item—her cloak.

Should I bring everything with me? Probably slow me down. I need to at least pack some clothes for her. Hopefully she's not too far. We can always come back for the rest.

He eyed the Bible. He had reservations about leaving the Bible behind because he knew the sentimental value Evynn placed on it.

Stuffing her clothes into his backpack, he threw her cloak on over top of his garb, grabbed a handful of piyel and stuffed it into his fanny pack.

He reached inside the backpack until he felt the handle of his dagger. He checked around his ankle to make sure his small knife was still securely strapped. Being a wanderer allowed plenty of vulnerability and having a means of protection lessened the anxiety to a degree—Lord knows he was ridden by enough angst as is.

Time was not on his side. He scanned his surroundings, wondering how he managed to make it up such a steep incline, because he had no recollection of climbing anything. Another side-effect of the piyel: unreliable memory.

He tried to remember his last moments with Evynn. He couldn't remember the details but knew they had an argument. The details really didn't matter, because they only argued over one thing. It was like an endless loop, recurring at least once a week.

And he could recall the habitual argument by memory.

They always started the same way. Typically, when things were going normal—whatever that meant. It'd begin with a snarky remark and a side-eye.

"What's the matter with you?"

She'd huff. "U'rie, I'm tired of running. I wanna settle down. I want to be part of something."

I'd roll my eyes. "Why? We're free! We have each other. No rules. We just gotta do whatever it takes, you know. Besides, you know how these people get."

She'd snap back. "You know what I mean. Not here. With the Old World."

I'd sigh. "Old World? Are you serious? You're ridiculous. That's an impossibility. You know they'd never accept us back. We're outcast. The Exiled!"

"I'm not ridiculous. I have hope."

"No, you have a delusional fantasy. And you're being an idiot. It'll never happen. It's an automatic death sentence getting anywhere near the Old World."

"You remember what my mom said about changing the future."

This is the part of the memory that's subject to change, depending on what kind of mood I'm in. Sometimes I cross the line, other times I don't. The loss of her mom cut deep. I'm hoping this time I didn't cross that line.

Bliss barked several times, snapping Uriah out of his stupor. The dog wagged her tail and bolted down from the summit.

Uriah darted after her.

Buzzards squawked in the distance in the direction Bliss headed. Uriah's stomach churned as he anticipated the worst.

What if she's hurt. Am I too late? Is she in one piece? What if it's worse? What if a tracker got to her…? What if she's…

He shook his head in stubborn denial. He had to expel the negativity from his mind and center his focus on running.

After a short time, his legs became heavy, feeling like bricks. His lungs burned from the exhaustion of beleaguered breaths. He couldn't suck up air fast enough to feed his muscles sufficient oxygen.

Not sure how much longer I can run. But I can't stop. The longer I'm away from her…the more susceptible she'll be to…

No, he shook his head again. "Deflect the negativity!" he yelled. "Suck it up. U, you can do this!"

The air changed as he progressed further down from the summit. As he approached the base of the hill, the atmosphere became arid. The dry and cracked ground seemed to spread to infinity.

Bliss' rapid pace put a gap between them and her barking became faint, drifting in the distance, yet persistent.

Maybe she caught up to Evynn.

Uriah accelerated until he finally caught up to Bliss. Being mindful not to step on any small cacti, he slowed his stride as he met a horrid stench. It forced him to hurl, despite his best efforts at holding it back.

It was evident why Bliss had stopped. Buzzards squawked and howled, hovering directly overhead, anticipating an opportunity to indulge.

Fear entered Uriah's spirit, but when he realized the carrion birds had their focus on another source, his stiffened shoulders relaxed.

The scene was horrific, but nothing completely unfamiliar to Uriah—images he could never expel from his mind—no matter how much piyel he ingested. The images were one thing, but it's the *putrid smell that does its number* on *you*—it never leaves.

It's the aroma of pure hatred and evil, encapsulated within a rotten vapor.

Wings vehemently flapped. A vulture swooped down and gorged on the insides of a slain coyote. It was just one of a dozen animals that lay lifeless with various body parts in disarray. Other vultures joined the first, and Uriah shuddered from the ripping, jarring and tearing.

He pulled his shirt over his nose and mouth as he gingerly approached Bliss.

She incessantly barked at a human torso, lying face down—legs nowhere to be found.

Faint squawks echoed in the distance as the powerful jaws of carrion eaters ripped through tendons and ligaments. Some of the birds battled over dismembered pieces.

Elongated breaths struggled to escape the torso.

She's still alive!

Uriah was shocked, horrified and perhaps a bit relieved.

A tear welled in the corner of his eye.

"I can't believe you did it again, U!"

I let her down. I had one responsibility. Keep track of the signs! But I was too busy wallowing in my own self-pity to even do that. And look what it cost me! Idiot!

Uriah still couldn't think outside of himself in the moment—still fixated on his own feelings. He didn't want to flip the young woman over. He didn't want to look the product of his negligence in the face as she took her last breaths. But it was the least he could do; he wouldn't want to die face down and alone—and didn't want anyone else to undergo such doom, especially Evynn.

Uriah bit his lower lip, dropped to a knee. He removed the hood of his cloak, then reached for the girl's shoulder. He hesitated, then gently flipped her over.

He yelped, then gasped.

Bliss woofed.

It isn't Evynn.

Uriah sighed but bowed his head in guilt.

It wasn't the work of a tracker. When they hunted a girl down, they made sure she was finished. True cowards, waiting till the girl entered torpor and was completely vulnerable. No, this was no tracker's work. This was definitely Evynn's doing. He recognized her handiwork. He was sad for the girl but had increased hope Evynn was still out there.

He just needed to find her.

What was he to do now? He couldn't let this young nameless woman suffer any longer than she had to.

An overwhelming call to action overtook him and his shoulders slumped. He glanced in the direction of the scavengers—it was a matter of time before they descended upon her body.

The young woman stared in his direction. This was the first time he actually saw the girl. How could he have missed her cherry-red hair before—the mind sees what it wants when under enough duress.

Her torso held three gaping wounds like a heavy downward swipe of a tiger's claw had ripped through it. Uriah did everything in his will to refrain from puking.

He gazed into the young woman's eyes, but it was like she was no longer present. Her body was there but no spirit was attached—practically a hollow vessel.

"God, protect the souls of the righteous and make peaceful the path that leads to her soul's exodus," Uriah whispered, gently shutting her eyelids.

The image of blood-red hair etched into his memories. He imagined her experiencing a moment of great joy and visualized her smiling with long hair flowing in the wind.

Crazy.

He dislodged his large dagger from his backpack and squeezed it tightly. He ruminated over putting the girl out of her misery. But the image of the red hair blowing in the wind was too much. He didn't feel right taking her life.

The scars on the back of his hand were a solemn reminder. He'd been down that road before and not by choice. It was one he never wanted to traverse again.

How can I save her if she's already gone?

He inhaled deeply, then slowly exhaled and stood. "Let's go, Bliss."

And as quickly as he stepped away, the vultures swarmed the torso.

What was a girl doing this far out by herself anyway? Existing as a female was the most dangerous thing one could do. Men would kill her out of pure fear the minute they ever crossed her path. And then there was the threat of trackers. Men who took pride in hunting down females after they'd turned and entered torpor, then killing them for sport.

Uriah didn't bother looking back at the abandoned girl and attempted to ignore the ripping and crunching, but he couldn't block out the screams ringing in his skull. There were so many voices and so much head noise.

He dug out a clover of piyel from his fanny pack and tucked it into the side of his left jaw and let the juices provide a slow release, quieting some of the clamor.

He bowed his head but had no time to wallow in sorrow or pity. He needed to find Evynn.

If she just fed, her torpor period isn't too far after, and that's when she is most vulnerable.

As he walked further from the carnage, the smell of burning debris inundated him. Standing out against the dingy sky, a thick cloud of black smoke hovered in the distance. He followed the smoke until he laid eyes on a structure.

Large uneven walls created a fortified rectangle. It could only mean one thing. "A settlement!" Uriah yelped. "Bliss, this could be even worse than we thought."

CHAPTER 2:
SVENGALI

**I CAN'T BELIEVE MY
GIRLFRIEND'S A ZOMBIE**

Jack E. Mohr

URIAH

Uriah's anxiety grew as he drew closer to the settlement. He walked with weary steps and a short, choppy stride while Bliss ambled alongside.

His nostrils felt raw from the dry air. Although the sun wasn't wholly visible, its heat formed a layer of perspiration across his brow. His throat felt parched, and the inside of his nose was tender to the touch.

I'm hungry and thirsty. I need to find Bliss something to drink.

Uriah hadn't stepped foot in a settlement since he and Evynn escaped the one they were raised in. He had vowed he would never enter another. This was the last place he had any desire to be.

But for Evynn, he'd do anything. *I just hope it's not too late.*

It seemed an odd place for a settlement to be, and he really hadn't expected to come across one this far out, especially in this bone-dry region. Most settlements were established near a free-flowing water source for practical purposes, but this one seemed to be in the middle of a desert.

As he approached, a few flags came into focus near its entrance, but he couldn't make out the insignias displayed.

Bliss panted.

Uriah rubbed her side. "It's okay, girl, we'll get you some water soon."

He stopped and took a deep breath, unzipped his fanny pack and withdrew another clove of piyel. He didn't realize how anxious he was until he saw his hand trembling as he zipped up his fanny pack. Between the cherry red hair and the anxiety associated with the thought of entering another settlement, he was losing his grip.

His world was closing in on him. He needed a way out. Evynn was his escape.

Her mere presence was often enough to soothe him. And now even she was gone. *Plus, these bloody voices!*

He tore off a clove and placed it between his lower lip and his gums.

He calmed. His heartbeat slowed.

The tremble of his hand ceased, and the red hair became a faint memory. Even the murmur in his mind subsided.

His breathing slowed as he inched towards the settlement.

The compound was surrounded by a makeshift barricade—a jury-rigged structure built with whatever wood, corrugated metal, plastic and material that could be scraped together—a reactionary structure built out of circumstance.

A trail of smoke billowed from the back of the settlement. *Probably burning their trash.*

As Uriah approached the entrance, he slowed and shifted his attention towards the dangling flags. They were black and had yellow spray-painted smiley faces on them with 'Xs' where the eyes should have been. A gust of wind blew by, causing the flags to ruffle.

As he stood transfixed, staring at the flags, a bullet ricocheted off the ground near his feet, kicking up dust.

Startled, Uriah sought its source. Bullets were a scarce resource, more precious than fresh water. People didn't use them unless it was dire.

He swallowed; his throat was stiff, and his saliva struggled to slide down.

In the murky light, Uriah had been looking in the sniper's direction the entire time. He was a few meters away from the flags, tucked in a crevice, strategically positioned. He was barely distinguishable amongst the crudely painted shanty walls, but when he flashed his rifle, it stood out like a sore thumb.

A dead body tumbled along the side of the wall. It dangled and swayed, hanging from a noose.

I get it.

The half-veiled man shifted his position, displaying more of his body. "I don't waste ammo, son. Remove your hood. State your business!"

Establishments were never keen on outsiders, and Uriah had to tread lightly. He would be perceived as a threat until proven otherwise. He couldn't risk provoking hostility.

He clenched his jaws and removed the hood of his cloak. "I...I... have no business, sir. Just looking for water for me and my pup. Hoping I stumbled across kind spirits is all."

"Ain't no charities around here, Coppah-head. We live to survive," he replied.

Copper-head? Uriah rubbed the back of his neck. *Did he just call me Copper-head?*

After a substantial pause he stated, "I ain't lookin' for no charities, sir. I can earn my way."

The man lifted his rifle, focusing the barrel directly on Uriah's forehead. "I can end ya right now, boy. Ya know that, right?"

Uriah gulped. His breaths shortened and rapidly increased.

"I need to see more respect on ya face!"

Uriah wanted to flee but knew he couldn't outrun a bullet. This wasn't the first time his life has been in the hands of a stranger, but that didn't make it any easier. He remained petrified, cemented in fear.

"Li'l Jim! Put that damn gun up! That's no way to greet a guest." A calming older voice cut through the tension.

What?

Too mesmerized by the rifle, Uriah hadn't noticed the man who approached from around the side of the establishment. *Was he there the entire time?*

The other man, looking to be in his sixties, cautiously approached. He walked with calculated steps, but his stride still possessed a youthful vigor. The only thing that hinted at his age was his salted beard and leathery, worn face.

The man closed the distance between them, stopping a few feet away. He squinted his left eye and gave Uriah a good look over. A calcified scar along the man's neck stood out distinctly.

He stuck out his hand. "Where are my manners? I'm Lummis."

Uriah blinked, still stunned.

A holstered sword hung from the man's waist. *Strange.* The embroidery on the sword's handle and scabbard was intricately crafted, with markings, symbols and ornaments of yesteryear.

Lummis's energy possessed a gravitational pull and Uriah found himself lowering his guard. Despite the calming demeanor, he felt something unsettling about the man, but he couldn't discern what.

Reflexively, he extended his hand.

Lummis grabbed it with a vice-grip squeeze and gave a hardy handshake, breaking Uriah's trance. His hands felt like stone mitts.

Lummis's smile widened as he turned towards Bliss. "And who's this little guy?" he asked light-heartedly, reaching down to pet the dog.

"Oh, her name's Bliss," replied Uriah, glancing toward the flag. He rubbed his tongue against the outside of his gums in a last-ditch effort to soothe himself with the piyel, but its properties were depleted.

The rifleman still had his sights aimed at Uriah with his finger caressing the trigger as though he was itching for an excuse. "Just give me a reason, boy!"

"Li'l Jim, hush now!" Lummis raised his hand. "Don't mind him. His emotions get the best of him and he's insufferable at times." He chuckled, dropping to a knee, rubbing Bliss along her ribs. "Let's get this girl something to drink."

Uriah hesitantly replied, "Thank you, sir."

Lummis took note of the tremble in Uriah's voice and pursed his lips. He looked up at the boy and studied him. His brow furled. "You all look worse for wear. Let's get you both some refreshments," he said, rising. He turned around and motioned with his hand, prompting Li'l Jim to lower his rifle.

Then he lightly squeezed Uriah's shoulder, "Come, follow me."

Something about Lummis didn't sit right with Uriah, yet he still couldn't figure out what. This only elevated his distress. Under any other circumstance he wouldn't have stepped foot in another compound. As he thought more about it, Lummis reminded him of his own father. One of the many memories he attempted to escape. Maybe that's what it was about Lummis that made him so off-putting.

Everything about this place reminded him of the people he had vowed to stay away from. They were always on edge, and every decision seemed to be a function of fear. It was something he had hoped to escape, but now he'd found his way back into their clutches.

Lummis led the way as the two entered the settlement. A pulley elevated a rickety metal gate, and it squeaked as it rose. They walked underneath the flag and into the compound with Lummis several paces ahead.

Two large wooden stakes were pegged in the ground just inside of the entrance, and atop each was an indiscernible object. As Uriah closed in on the poles, he had to do everything in his will to keep his composure. He wanted to turn and upchuck but he knew any sign of weakness could mean his demise. On top of each pole was the rotten head of a shifter—a woman who had turned. *But how? The turned were indestructible…*

Lummis looked over his shoulder and smiled, reveling in a stew of haughty arrogance. "You like that, huh? I know. It's impressive," he said. He slapped one of the poles. "These are my pride and joy. Not too many men come face to face with a shifter and live to tell the story. These are my trophies." He frowned. "I'm just upset we couldn't figure out how to preserve them until later. I got one in the back that looks brand spanking new."

Uriah half-way smiled, being sure not to reveal any of his disgust. He wanted so badly to scoff down some piyel. His worst nightmare was coming true. This was a tracker. And Evynn had just turned. There could only be one conclusion. He wanted to pull out his dagger right now and drive it through the man. But he had to confirm it was her somehow.

Lummis scoffed. "I'm not like those sissy trackers who wait till a woman turns back into a zombie before they kill her. No honor in that. I seek glory from beheading her when she's in her most lethal state. At the peak of her ferocity." He placed his hand on his sword's handle.

Uriah avoided direct eye contact and looked down at Bliss.

Lummis continued walking. "You seem tense."

"Just never seen one of these creatures this close is all," Uriah replied. A pure lie: he'd had more than his share of encounters since he was a small boy.

"Count your blessings," Lummis replied.

The ambiance was eerily silent. Most of the inhabitants must have been sleeping. Maybe it was night? No, it was too hot to be night. The place appeared much larger than the outside would allow. Makeshift living spaces sprawled throughout the settlement. Some were enclosed while others were exposed, with various cots and hammocks full of sleeping men.

The air was stale.

The subtle sound of running water captured Uriah's attention. They were headed to a well located in the center of the settlement.

That's why they chose this location. Makes sense.

With his left hand, Lummis motioned toward the left side of the compound towards a cluster of tents. "Once we've gotten you some drink, you'll head over there, and Lee will set you up with sleeping arrangements. You need rest. Looks like you haven't had a good night's sleep in ages."

Uriah nodded.

"So, how long have you and—what did you say her name was—Bliss been wandering?"

Uriah's armpits perspired and his throat stiffened. He was at this man's mercy. He had to choose his words wisely—men like Lummis scrutinized words. They'd chop 'em up, dissect 'em, throw 'em back at you and demand for you to make it make sense. They had to—trust was everything—and words were a man's only bond.

Uriah inhaled deeply, expanding his chest vastly. "It's difficult keeping track of time. The days tend to blend together." He exhaled. "If I had to guess, maybe a few months or more."

Lummis nodded approvingly. Dried salt resonated in the crevices of his sun-worn skin.

Uriah had no idea what the man was thinking or even his intention. But he felt he was being read like a book. It made him uneasy.

For a split second, Uriah considered giving the mission up and saving his own skin while he still had the opportunity to do so. Coming up with some lame excuse that would free him from this peculiar predicament.

But he had to be absolutely certain Evynn wasn't somehow in this compound, and he really didn't have any evidence besides a gut feeling. At this point, if she happened to be in the compound, she'd be on a stake as well.

Maybe they captured Evynn in torpor and are holding her captive.

A glimmer of hope. The thought alone accelerated his heart rate. He took a few deep breaths.

Lummis and Uriah approached the well and an awkward silence ensued between them.

Uriah felt guilty, as though he needed to say something to fill the void. Offer some additional explanation as to why he and Bliss were roaming the wilderness by themselves.

Lummis must have been reading his thoughts and interjected before Uriah could speak. "You know, it isn't safe for you two to be out there on your own. I've witnessed the absolute wicked in men—especially when there's no consequences to their actions." Lummis approached the well, rubbing the back of his sunspot-riddled neck. "Why tempt fate?"

And alas…here I am, tempting fate… yet again…

The roar of water increased as they drew near the well. Uriah really didn't have an answer to the question at all. At first, he was merely trying to escape and stay safe. But after a while, he realized they had no true end game and just wanted to stay alive as best as they could. But Evynn, she always had these whimsical fantasies of somehow integrating back into the Old World. The same Old World that abandoned them and condemned them to being the outcasts they were.

Sometimes I wish her mother never put any hope in her head.

Uriah often indulged her fantasies, but knew they were impossible. The Old World's borders were armed to the teeth with 24-hour surveillance and militia—armed to destroy on sight. At least that was what he was told. He'd never been, himself.

Sometimes Uriah would entertain Evynn's fantasies for the sole purpose of making the boredom pass by quicker. But part of him thought she believed in the possibility of reintegration and he felt sad for her. That world was a heaven they would never know. Hell was the destiny they were forced to navigate.

Uriah rubbed the side of Bliss's head. "I suppose I enjoy the freedom, is all."

Lummis took notice of Uriah's choice of words and drew some type of conclusion, Uriah was certain., but what that conclusion entailed, he couldn't discern.

With light, airy steps Lummis approached the well and rested his hand on the stone perimeter, then turned to face Uriah.

"Freedom comes with a cost, son," he said with a raspy drawl, clearing his throat. "Everything has a cost." He smiled.

There wasn't any malice in his tone, but it did possess a hint of foreboding.

Uriah subconsciously rubbed the nook of his forearm. *Yeah, I know.*

An image of Evynn suckling from his forearms to quell her tremors, keeping at bay her turning, popped into his mind. Blood and piyel was the only combination to adequately defer her turnings.

Each time, her eyes would roll to the back of her head while suckling—it was like she wasn't all the way there—like her soul was tethered to her body somehow but floating a distance away and a pure primal instinct had assumed control.

Lummis picked up a pail near the base of the well. "Here, hold this," he said handing the container to Uriah. "It's simple; I'm sure you'll pick it up after seeing me do it just once." He leaned over the well and reached inside to grab hold of a thick rope. He pulled the rope forcefully, hand-over-hand for several minutes, working up a lather of sweat until a bucket emerged.

Lummis detached the bucket from the hook. "Only take as much as you need and use the rest to fill the canteens." Several unfilled jugs sat along the base of the well. "We place the filled bottles over there and when we're done using one, we wipe it down and put it here."

Uriah's mouth watered as Lummis filled an empty canteen. He also filled a saucer for Bliss.

The atmosphere brightened and Uriah wondered if maybe it was now morning or mid-afternoon.

Bliss energetically lapped up the water.

Lummis handed Uriah the canteen, and he took huge gulps.

The whir of the water within the well paralleled the murmur of voices within Uriah's head: quiet, constant and distant.

Uriah felt a hand on his shoulder. A chill went down his spine.

"Slow down friend," a chuckle. "There's more where that came from."

Uriah turned to see a man several inches shorter than him with a soft, welcoming grin.

"I'm Lee."

"Lummis told me to come see you once I was finished."

He smiled. "Lummis doesn't let many new guys through so easily. He must think there's something special about you and I wanted to see for myself."

"Oh." Uriah lowered the canteen. Lee stood out. He couldn't be but a few years older than Uriah. He had a bubbly persona, but Uriah couldn't tell if it was authentic or just for show.

Lee winked at Lummis. "Let me talk to him for a second."

Lummis nodded.

Lee grabbed Uriah's hand. His touch was warm and welcoming. "It'll just be a minute." He smiled. "I promise, I'll bring 'im back."

Lee didn't release Uriah's hand. Uriah didn't know how to feel, allowing another man so much control. If he had to defend himself, there was only so much he could do with his hand clasped by another.

They didn't walk far. Just outside of earshot of Lummis. Lee gazed into Uriah's eyes. "Wow…" He released Uriah's hand and placed his palm on his heart. "I see so much of myself in you. It's like looking into a mirror."

Uriah looked side to side, not sure how to respond.

"Yeah, just six months ago I was you. Wondering. Lost. With that glazed-over look in my eye. This place was my saving grace." He smiled and looked towards the sky. "What are you holding on to?"

"Holding on to?"

"Yeah…What's tugging on your heart?"

I'm trying to find Evynn. But he doesn't need to know that. "I don't…I don't know…"

Lee frowned and blew air out, pushing his bangs out of his eyes. "You can find love in unsuspecting places. Trust me."

At this point, Uriah figured out that Lee was projecting. He kept a neutral expression, allowing Lee to get it all out.

"This place taught me; you can love again. True love." Lee's demeanor turned on a dime and he was somber, as though a sobering thought entered his mind and snatched his joy. "I started wandering after coming home to find my grandma a zombie and my entire family dead. I was mortified and didn't know what to do. I snapped and panicked. And I—" He shook his head as though he didn't want to relive the experience. "Anyway, from that point on—for months on end, I wandered—strung out on piyel with no reason to live," he smiled. "Then Jimbo saved my life."

The rifleman?

"I say all that to say this. Give this place a chance. I just felt that message was meant for you. That's it. Just give this place a chance." He grabbed Uriah's hand and led him back to the well.

Oh-kay… That was…different.

Lummis hadn't moved from the spot they left him. He grinned as the two approached.

"I hope Lee didn't scare you off. He gets a little talkative at times. But all and all, he's a good guy."

Lee blushed and leaned from side to side.

Bliss barked, the type of bark that usually indicated unease.

Uriah felt an unsettling presence and turned. It was the rifleman. His energy was standoffish, and he was much less daunting without his rifle and tower-like vantage point. He was actually a much smaller man than Uriah anticipated, laughably diminutive. It made sense why he would cling to such a prominent symbol of power.

As much subtlety as Lummis projected, Jimbo did not. His energy screamed crass and crude.

Jimbo sucked in air between his teeth with a whistling sound, looking Uriah up and down. "Were you holding hands with my sweetheart?"

"Lee? No. He was—"

I CAN'T BELIEVE MY GIRLFRIEND'S A ZOMBIE   33

"Uh-huh," Jimbo spat.

"Li'l Jim. He's still a guest." Said Lummis.

"Come on now Lummis. I can't believe you fallin' for this joker. Look at 'im!"

Uriah felt alarmed and rubbed his hands together.

Jimbo closed the distance between them. "I ain't no racist, but come on. Anyone wit' half-a-brain knows this is some sort of trick by the brothas." He scoffed. "He's a damn Copperhead, for crying out loud!"

"Jimmy!" said Lee in alarm.

"This ain't got nothin' to do with you, Lee Lee. Get back to them tents. As the head of security this is between me and Lummis's questionable decision making."

Lummis tilted his head and looked at Jimbo in astonishment.

"Don't gimme that look, Lummis. This ain't the first time you done had a lapse in judgment. We forgave ya once but this here's egregious!"

Uriah shifted his weight to his back leg. "I don't know what you're presuming."

Jimbo closed in and poked Uriah's chest. "You don't know what I resuming? You don't know what I resume,' he said in a high-pitched mocking manner. "Look at his skin, Lummis. Look at them big fancy words he usin' like resume. You know over in that jail they got all them fancy books they like to read, thinkin' they all smart. They been eyeing this well for years and you know it!"

Bliss growled at Jimbo.

Lummis still seemed unconvinced. "Jimbo, we have an understanding with the Copperheads—they stand to lose entirely too much if the truce is severed."

Jimbo snorted, and the stench of a rotten tooth or two seeped out of his lips.

Uriah's manhood was challenged, and he wasn't sure if cooler heads should prevail. But simply having the thought and not immediately reacting proved he possessed the patience to disregard the poke. "Hey man, chill."

"I bet he got some kinda tattoo, or branding on 'im. You know how the Brothas do," said Jimbo, reaching towards Uriah's arm.

"Hey!" shouted Uriah, slapping the hand away.

Bliss' jaws tightened and she barked aggressively, snapping at the man.

"If you ain't hidin' nuffin', pull back them sleeves,' demanded Jimbo.

Lummis intervened. "That's enough Li'l Jim," he said with an authoritative tone. He softened his voice and addressed Uriah. "Look, I apologize for Jimmy here. He's a little on edge. You don't have to do anything you don't want to. If trust isn't the foundation a relationship is built on—there is no relationship just an arrangement."

"The hell he doesn't. You ain't in charge of my safety," retorted Jimbo. He spat on the ground near Uriah.

He's not going to be satisfied until he gets his way.

I CAN'T BELIEVE MY GIRLFRIEND'S A ZOMBIE   35

Uriah wanted very much to squash this little man like a bug—to reach back and knock what few teeth he had down his throat, but that wouldn't help in the slightest. But it sure would feel good.

Uriah reached for his sleeves. "Fine," he said rolling up the cloak. "I have nothing to hide." He rolled up his sleeves to his elbow and exposed his arms to the two men.

Jimbo grabbed a hold of his arms and looked them up and down, scrutinizing them until his eyes landed on Evynn's feeding spot. "What'd I tell ya'? Look-uh there!" He pointed towards the incision scars.

Uriah's eyebrows furrowed. "Look at what?" he asked, defensively.

Lummis rubbed his chin, exhaled and stepped back. "How do you explain those markings?"

Uriah didn't know what they were implying. He didn't know who the Copperheads or Brothas were, but he had to disassociate somehow, and sought to appeal to their rationale. But why not the truth? He was backed into a corner and couldn't fabricate a lie if he tried.

"Evynn," his voice wavered, lowering his tone to a whisper.

Both Jimbo and Lummis were confused. Jimbo dug into a pocket of his utility pants.

"You told me to state my business. Evynn. She's my only business," he said confidently.

Jimbo drew a small handgun. "Look, you fixin' to make sense, boy, because we're tired of the games."

Panic overtook Uriah and he quickly pointed to the marks. "Evynn! I let her feed to hold back the tremors."

Lummis studied Uriah—dissecting everything from his posture to the words he seemed to be replaying in his mind.

Jimbo huffed. "Wait a minute. You ain't actually considering this hogmog?" he said with an inflection in his voice which exaggerated his astonishment. "Ain't no female been out this way in years. No reason to!" He reached into his front pocket and withdrew ammo, slowly loading his .38. "Lummis, you can keep playin', but I'm through with the games."

Lummis placed his hand atop of Jimbo's and lowered the gun. "Let me have a word with the kid," he asked. "In private," he reduced his tone.

Jimbo voiced his appeal, but Lummis's authority took precedence. A subtle tap of his sword was enough to subdue ol' Jimbo.

Lummis led Uriah and Bliss toward the back of the establishment. A group of men played cards while stew boiled on an open flame.

Lummis led them towards a tall tent, its pinnacle several meters above Uriah's head. The entrance of the tent allowed no light. Uriah hesitantly followed Lummis inside.

This is it. Evynn's turned head will be back here…somewhere… somehow. And I will avenge her or die trying.

Lummis took out a lighter and lit several candles around the tent. He walked towards the center pole and placed his sword in a scabbard within a shrine, then sat down at a small picnic table.

"Come, have a seat," said Lummis.

The subtle smell of urine and feces whiffed by. Uriah couldn't locate the source but figured the group compiled all the waste in one place and emptied it periodically.

A large head situated atop a thick wooden stake was positioned directly behind Lummis—the sum of Uriah's fears. Unfortunately, its face was pointed towards a small makeshift mattress opposite the two. Uriah scrutinized the head, hoping to see any signs that would give hint whether this was Evynn or not.

But how would I really know anyway? When she turns, she takes on different forms sometimes.

Uriah attempted to maintain discretion without giving away his curiosity.

Lummis tapped his fingers on the table. "You're apprehensive. Remember what I said about trust—without it, we have no foundation. Come, sit," he smiled.

Uriah cautiously sat across from Lummis. Bliss nestled on top of his feet. He reached down as though he were placing a hand atop of Bliss' head, but in actuality he was rolling up his pants to gain access to his knife. He only trusted one thing, and that was the deviance of men.

Lummis leaned back, assuming a welcoming posture. "Work with me here. You seem like a harmless kid, just down on his luck."

Uriah nodded in agreement.

"But look at it from Jimmy's perspective. We have this black kid, showing up outa the blue—which raises suspicion in itself. But on top of that, the kid goes on this spill about some girl."

He lowered his tone. "You and I both know, there is no chance a girl could survive out here. If she wasn't shot on sight, she'd be slaughtered by her own kind."

Uriah sought to counter. "But—"

Lummis leaned in and cut him off. "And I can tell you've been using, son. This ain't my first rodeo." He sternly studied Uriah's eyes, refusing to relinquish his gaze. "You've been using, ain't ya?"

Uriah nodded in affirmation. He felt like he was a passive character in his own dream, guided down a path by Lummis' will. He wanted so much to break the spell of Lummis's words. He managed to grab hold of his dagger and contemplated driving it through the man's sternum.

Lummis shook his head as though he were thoroughly disappointed. "I know it's hard out here. You feel like the more you struggle for survival the less reason you have to fight…I get it."

As Lummis continued to speak, Uriah's thoughts tuned the man out. It couldn't have been Lummis' first time giving this spiel. This must have been one of the many speeches he pulled out of his bag when recruiting young men to the settlement. Find some sort of weakness in the individual, weaponize it and wield it as a tool of destruction against their psyche until they crumble.

He thinks he has me all figured out. It's like he's talking to who he thinks I am, but not to me. He doesn't know me at all or what I've been through.

Lummis noticed Uriah attempting to peek over his shoulder. "Oh, wait… You're really sticking to this Evynn story? Come on, you and I both know no girl is out there. I can sense a shifter from miles away." Lummis stood and walked towards the stake. He turned the skull towards Uriah, and it was perfectly preserved. A flawless preservation of a bizarre malformity.

The creature's dark hair cascaded over its grey leathery face. The sunken lifeless eyes stared directly into Uriah, revealing no semblance of humanity. A small horn protruded above its brow and its skull was three times the size Uriah had ever witnessed. And he knew it couldn't have been Evynn—at least he had a feeling it wasn't.

He released a small sigh.

Lummis grabbed a hand full of the black hair. "This one here is weeks old," he let out a deep breath. "My pride, my joy!" He then held up the sword. "You see this here. Been passed down for centuries since antiquity." He eyed the sword, caressing the metal as though it were beyond precious—like it was sacred.

Chills rolled down Uriah's spine.

Lummis nodded in self-righteous approval. "I'm a bloodline descendent of the Holy Knight Order who vanquished the last living dragon of the Middle Ages." He huffed and yanked the creature's head back. "And this sword is only thing known to man that can stop one of these things."

Uriah grimaced in horror.

Lummis chortled. "A-ha! That look right there proves my point. You ain't ever been face to face with one of these things, let alone roamed the desert for months with one. Now give it to me straight, son."

Uriah sat frozen. The moment was suffocating. He wanted to cry, he wanted to fight. He wanted to be held. But most of all he wanted Evynn.

Lummis repositioned the stake so it faced its original position and affectionately petted the creature. "Look. I understand. You were searchin' for a means to escape—any means. Your mind created a false narrative—a delusion that you've lived out to give your life meaning…comfort in your solitude." He smiled and then waited a spell. "Confabulate."

Uriah expressed puzzlement.

"Confabulate! It's an Old World term—meaning to fabricate imaginary experiences to compensate for memory loss—it's not your fault…it's the substances, the dehydration, sleep deprivation, the fear, the stress…It all adds up, son."

Lummis approached his bed and grabbed a dark leathery, hairy-looking item—somewhat similar to shoulder pads. He pulled it on over his head and rested it on his shoulders and fastened a strap around his neck. Lummis had created an armor out of the discarded parts of turned females.

Lummis unstrapped the armor and tossed it back onto his bed as though he were simply displaying his toys to peacock around.

Even this wasn't enough to keep Uriah distracted from his thoughts.

Lummis was oddly convincing, and Uriah considered the possibilities for a moment. The piyel did possess hallucinogenic effects. Had Evynn been merely a figment? Had his entire childhood been a figment? Maybe that part wasn't, maybe she somehow died and he carried her memory along like a ghost. The thought seemed asinine. Yet, he continued questioning his own sanity.

Maybe he had no purpose outside of this make-believe implanted task of this psychological construct of 'saving Evynn.' And this yearning desire was the only thing keeping him from ending it all.

Maybe…

And before Uriah knew it, his head was buried square in the center of Lummis's bosom. He was being fully embraced with a hardy hug. Tears slid down his cheeks. Perhaps it was a mixture of exhaustion and despair, but he had never been embraced by another man, and the release felt good. He needed the fraternal transfer, and he appreciated it; he was at ease in the moment.

Uriah didn't know what came over him and didn't care. In the moment he needed the understanding only a physical connection could provide.

Lummis gently patted Uriah's back. "We've all been endowed with gifts. You hide yours with piyel. You run from it, instead of allowing it to enhance!" Then he whispered. *We're Seers, son.*

Uriah lifted his head from Lummis's chest. That last statement Lummis made wasn't out loud. It was as though Lummis spoke the words into Uriah's mind—telepathically.

Now I know my mind is playing tricks on me.

Bliss growled and barked feverishly. Her tail wagged back and forth, and she howled towards the sky.

Uriah resurrected from his daze.

Evynn!

Bliss only reacted like that when she was nearby.

A loud bell rang, emanating from the entrance of the settlement.

Lummis released Uriah. He hustled to the bed, reassembled his armor and put it on quickly. He grabbed his sword and sprinted out of the tent without bothering to even glance back at Uriah.

Uriah's curiosity tugged him in multiple directions. He first took a deep breath and wiped the tears from his eyes. Part of him wanted to rush after Lummis and see what the commotion was about. But a portion of him wanted to get a better look at the shifter. And he did, walking with steady steps towards the stake.

Its jaw was slack, lacking any tension and hung limp, revealing massive incisors—in both length and girth. What he once thought was hair, upon closer inspection didn't look as such. It was much denser and coarser than hair, closer to wooly leather. The only shifter he had ever witnessed was Evynn and she looked nothing like this. Despite her multiple shifts and multiple forms, she never appeared this far beyond beastly—this one was almost alien in nature.

Uriah gazed in its sunken eyes. It didn't seem so horrific anymore. This was once a person. A person yearning to live.

How old was she when she first turned? Was she alone? Evynn never recalls anything after turning. Where do their minds go? What was her name?

Uriah wanted to reach for some piyel but rejected the notion. "Jaz," he whispered. "I'm going to call her Jaz." He closed his eyes. "Jaz, I pray your transition is peaceful and your spirit experiences rest."

Uriah grabbed Bliss's collar and peeked out of the tent. The hairs on the back of his neck perked up as he witnessed the frenzy. The once slumbering compound was alive and frenetic—the sounds of shuffling fleet, clanging metal and grunts permeated. The smell of funky men saturated the environment.

Males of all shapes, sizes and ages seemingly came out of nowhere, armed to the teeth, all running towards the front of the settlement with whatever weapons they could gather as more and more warnings blared.

As the commotion stirred, Uriah raised his hood and ducked off into the shadows along the perimeter of the compound. He didn't know why, but somehow he felt a serenity.

Bliss continued to bark frantically, and Uriah attempted to soothe her by rubbing her side. "It's okay girl."

His thoughts were as scattered as the men in the compound. Mere moments ago, he was bawling in the embrace of another man. Now he didn't know what was happening. Usually, Evynn's transformation didn't last more than ten minutes at most because she couldn't sustain it.

Could she be the cause for all the alarm? Is she the source of panic? No, it couldn't be her. With Jimbo's temper he would have shot on sight….Not that it would have done much damage if she had already shifted.

Uriah jogged towards the settlement's entrance, trying not to draw any attention. "Come on girl. It's okay," he said all the while Bliss continued to bark and growl.

He looked towards the sky and saw the sun attempting to free itself from the prison of dark haze. The newly liberated rays were refreshing.

A dank, musty scent circulated as the men of the compound eagerly stood at attention, bolstering themselves around the compound's entrance.

Through a crack in the metal comprising the walls, Uriah peeked out. A storm of dust kicked up as a lengthy caravan of RV's, wagons and cars being pulled by oxen, horses and mules headed their way.

Uriah didn't know what to make of it. He looked towards the men within the compound to see if they would lend any hint. Their clenched jaws and tight grips alluded to the obvious— these visitors weren't welcome.

Lummis assumed a commanding position at the forefront of the group. He didn't have so much a look of fear or concern but more of confident curiosity.

The caravan slowed to a halt. The lead vehicle was a yellow classic Volkswagen bug being pulled by a donkey like a crudely modified surrey. A slender man of Spanish descent slowly exited the vehicle. He waited for the dust to settle, then placed his hands on his hips and surveyed the landscape with his chin held high.

He had the sobering look of a recovering alcoholic. He was well kept. His face was neat and his hair freshly trimmed. He possessed a distinct jaw line and strong features.

He gently patted the wrinkles out of his khakis and adjusted his shirt, ensuring it was neatly tucked into his pants. He turned to the caravan behind him and gestured with his hand toward the RV that had a worn American Flag secured to the side of it.

He smiled and muttered to no one in particular. "The algorithms will unite us with destiny."

He took several short steps towards the settlement's entrance, stopping at the same spot Uriah had once stood staring up at the happy-face embroidered flags. The man glanced at the black flag with x'd out eyes and smiling face then looked back towards the settlement's entrance.

He adjusted his collar and cleared his throat. "Brothers! We come in peace!"

Lummis gestured towards Jimbo, waving his hand like a wizard casting a spell. Jimbo grunted then nodded. With heavy steps, he climbed the ladder, repositioning himself to the eagle-eyed perch he had sat upon while addressing Uriah.

Lummis stood poised and resolute. It became evident why he commanded such respect. He turned towards the dozens of men surrounding the entrance.

Each man gripped an instrument of destruction. Some held guns, others pipes, clubs of wood, and others held metal chains. Their faces were full of grit, determination and subtle fear.

Lummis made several hand gestures as though he were a military general orchestrating a small militia. He appeared flustered yet maintained an air of stoicism by slowly stroking his peppered beard.

Once settled in his seat, Jimbo turned towards Lummis as though waiting for a signal. When he received what he was looking for, he spat and confidently raised his rifle. He stared several moments at the intruders before speaking. "State ya business."

The Spanish man betrayed his stoic front with a nervous chuckle. "A sí, yes. I am Fernando. The algorithms have led us to you, my friend." His smile widened.

Jimbo fired a shot from the rifle near Fernando's foot, punting up dust.

Fernando's nervous demeanor transformed into a micro-expression of anger but quickly retreated to a smile.

Jim spat and then wiped his mouth. "I ain't ask you your name. We thought we made it perfectly clear few weeks back when you people came. We don't want to be a part of no stanky coalition. We don't wanna be a part of no filthy algorithm," he snorted. "We perfectly fine. We told you algorithm hippies before not to return." He wiped his mouth. "Is this some sort of show of aggression?" Jimbo spoke in an elongated drawl. From Uriah's readings, he understood people typically from the southern region of the Old World spoke in such a manner.

Fernando chuckled anxiously but turned to his brigade to display haughty arrogance, motioning for them to keep calm, as though he knew, if he had to, he could strongarm the entire situation.

Uriah stared through the gate, all the while attempting to soothe Bliss. Her demeanor became aggressive as she displayed incisors, growling intensely.

Uriah rubbed her side. "It's okay girl…I can sense her too." Something in him knew Evynn was nearby, *but where*?

Fernando gently kicked at the dirt. "Amigo. We are the Coalition of Peace and Prosperity." He cleared his throat. "We seek peace for all and the betterment of mankind through reason and exchange. We are guided by the algorithms. Despite being neglected by the network, we still have a connection to the algorithms and will one day reunite humanity."

Jim peeked his head out from the scope of the rifle. "Yadda, yadda, yadda… we heard that jive from the last guy. We ain't interested!" He chuckled. "Lemme ask youse a rhetorical question. Why you believe in uh algorithm that don't believe in you? You out here on the outskirts just like the rest of us."

"Excuse me?"

"No, you excuse me. Land of the Free and Home of the Brave. Them yuppies hiding behind a wall, scared to death. We out here living free, making our own way, and bravely surviving on our own. And now you wanna infringe on said freedoms?"

Fernando bit his lip to conceal his frustration. Then chuckled to veil his anguish. "Please, we mean no harm. We only come to reason with you. And to answer your question, the algorithms chose us, because they knew we would be the chosen ones imbued with the ingenuity to cure this unfortunate spread of devastation."

Jimbo shifted in his seat. "Like I said, the question was rhetorical and we don't want none of your stankin' reason."

Fernando brought his thumb and forefinger to his mouth and whistled. One of the RV doors opened, and two men wearing reflective sunglasses stepped out, each with a sawed-off shotgun in one hand and a long metal chain in the other.

They jumped out of the RV and their camo-boots kicked up dust as they landed. The burlier of the two tugged on the chain, and three figures with burlap bags over their heads stumbled out, followed by two more men brandishing automatic shotguns.

The two men with the chains steered the hooded figures towards Fernando. The other two followed behind cautiously, keeping the guns pointed at the heads of the hooded figures.

Bliss barked emphatically.

Uriah covered his mouth to conceal his thrill.

One of those has to be her. Oh wait, what are they going to do with them? A woman's fate was usually sealed on sight. Why have they kept her alive? What can I do?

He squinted his eyes, attempting to decipher which hooded figure might be Evynn. One was skinnier than the rest and he immediately ruled her out. Evynn had a thickness and a broadness to her. The other two were pretty much the same build and he attempted to identify any distinguishing traits. She was post-shift so even the clothing wasn't recognizable.

Uriah's breathing rapidly increased. He reached for his fanny pack but thought better. *This isn't the time. Stay focused.*

He inched his way to the front of the compound. Everyone intently focused on the intruders, gripping their weapons—they hadn't any concern for Uriah's maneuvering and were oblivious to Bliss' barking.

Jimbo bolted out of his seat. "What in tarnation? That bet not be what I thank it is."

Fernando tucked his chin and smiled. "I assure you, señor. We have everything under control. What you are witnessing is a demonstration. A demonstration of advancement, meant to persuade and empower—afforded by the sheer omniscience of the algorithms themselves."

Jimbo raised his rifle and took aim. "I don't know what fancy talk you think you using. But if that's what I thank it is. I'm blowing their brains out right here."

No! Do Something!

Uriah's heart raced because he knew exactly who was hidden under those bags. And he knew Jimbo would make good on his word sooner rather than later.

Fernando stepped between Jimbo and the figures. "That will not be necessary, sir. As I stated, we come in peace. And this is our olive branch." He reached for the sack covering the tall figure's face. "We have the resolución that will bring us one step closer to civilization."

Jimbo lowered his gun. "What you mean reza-loose-she-on?"

"Yes," replied Fernando. "We have discovered how to stop the frenzies!" He smiled. "Hermanos! We are making breakthroughs! Our first step to repairing civilization as we know it."

Bliss' barking amplified—the passion behind her bark was on the brink of boiling over.

Uriah grabbed her collar and held her close to his body, attempting to calm her without success. He grimaced as her barking magnified, aching his eardrums. But he continued to squeeze her tightly. "I know girl. But—" he said.

Bliss snapped at him and growled, taunting his cowardliness and unwillingness to act in the moment.

Uriah was torn.

In truth, Bliss mirrored his internal sentiment, and he had enough trouble containing himself without reacting to compulsion. Sensibility had guided the pair's survival thus far and impulsive decisions were the first route to jeopardizing their safety.

But now Evynn was at risk.

The guilt of his negligence poured down on him. How could he have slept through her transition?

How could I have missed the signs! Too focused on myself! And now I won't act because I'm too focused on my fear.

Fernando plotted his steps as he approached the hooded figures. "Amigos! Behold!" he said, nodding to the two companions holding steady the chains.

A gust of wind blew by.

The two men steadied their grip as they dug their heels in the ground, bracing for impact. They tugged the chains, pulling the hooded figures' arms.

Fernando reached into the back pocket of his pants and pulled out two contraptions and held one in each hand. He then reached for the hoods and removed each one in a dramatic swooping motion.

Uriah's eyes bucked. *Evynn!* It was her. He felt relief despite the dire circumstance.

Thank you, God, for allowing us a second chance. I appreciate it.

Jimbo released an involuntary squawk as he fumbled the rifle in his hands. "You tryna kill us all, you sunnabitch!"

A steady murmur resonated from the men behind the shanty walls of the settlement. "What are we waiting on?" someone yelled. "They liable to kill us all. Kill em!"

Jimbo looked back towards Lummis as though seeking approval. Lummis glanced toward Uriah in astonishment. He rubbed his cheeks with his thumb and pointer finger engrossed in thought.

Uriah's palms cramped from holding Bliss back and his grip weakened. He knew Lummis couldn't fathom the possibility of the story about Evynn possibly being true.

He must have really believed I was delusional.

The look of amazement Lummis displayed told the story. And now, Evynn was practically at his fingertips and he was powerless. Everything was in the fate of another man's head nod.

Lummis squinted and took a deep breath. He returned his glance to Jimbo and shook his head. However, he did withdraw his sword from its sheath.

That's right. Lummis finds no honor in killing the defenseless.

The settlement growled collectively but dared not breach their leader's command. Uriah wondered how he held such power over these men, but the thought of saving Evynn was more pressing.

Fernando held up a vial in his right hand. "Fret not!" He held the contraption up high. "Fire and ice, peace and hostility, peace and prosperity—all extremes, but Janus heads of the same coin. How quickly tides can turn, no?" He held up another contraption in his other hand. "You cannot have one without the possibility of the other."

Fernando turned towards the settlement and placed both hands behind his back.

Uriah's tried to figure out Fernando's end game.

Was he going to poison her? Kill her somehow? What? Either way he wasn't going to sit by and watch.

Fernando held up his right hand. "My friends, fire!"

He turned back towards the three young women, who all appeared out of their minds. Eyes were in the back of their heads, wavering back and forth idly, like punch-drunk boxers. They all were in a state of torpor—body present but mind, spirit and soul absent.

Fernando took the contraption and stabbed each in their outer thighs.

Evynn turned first and the other two shortly after—all following a similar progression.

Her head jolted back and her neck stiffened. She released a curdling scream. Her body stiffened like a sudden burst of rigor mortis struck. Her skin bubbled, bones cracked, and teeth chattered as her jaw protruded.

A sight Uriah had witnessed too many times. But never in this magnitude. Witnessing several girls turn at once was awe-inspiring.

Yet, while painful to observe, it seemed even more painful to endure.

Uriah's guilt wouldn't allow him to bear witness and he turned his head. When the external screams subsided, the screams in his mind intensified. It was as though the girls were inside his thoughts, thriving in pain with no means of escaping. The shrieks bellowed to the point his nose slowly dripped drops of blood.

Uriah scrambled in his fanny back, snatching a handful of the piyel—anything that would alleviate the agony.

Throughout the commotion, he hadn't realized he had released his grip of Bliss—who now completely mirrored Evynn's demeanor—utter, blind rage.

Bliss darted through the compound's entrance in an absolute mania—ears pinned and canines exposed, barking hysterically.

Uriah scrambled after her, stumbling over himself in the process.

Jimbo whistled in the direction of the compound and cocked his rifle. "Look heah, you got bout ten seconds before I put them thangs out their misery. 1…2…"

Fernando calmly raised the contraption in his left hand. "Watch as I subdue the manic. Amigos, ice!" He smiled and stabbed the largest of the three girls before she could completely turn, and her quakes slowed to a halt. "Wah-lah, my friends. Science! Miraculouso!"

He conceitedly strolled over to Evynn, smiling as though he had all the power of heaven in his palm.

Evynn's eyes bulged out of their sockets as she was on the brink of becoming fully berserk.

Fernando held the vial to the clouds and then brought a hammer fist down towards Evynn's thigh.

Before he could stab Evynn with the contraption, seemingly out of nowhere, Bliss catapulted through the air, viciously chomping down on Fernando's extended arm, knocking the vial out of his hand.

Fernando hunched over, writhing in pain, releasing a panic-filled scream—a mixture of sound and incomprehensible garble.

Was the scream due to pain or the fear associated with losing control of the situation?

His dog was too enraged to hear Uriah's call but he cried out anyway. "Bliss!" he yelled, running through the settlement's entrance.

Jimbo fired a shot towards Evynn, missing badly—ricocheting off the side of an RV. Some of the horses pulling the makeshift surreys spooked and neighed uncontrollably. One team bucked and convulsed, contorting their bodies until they tilted over the buggy, cracking the wooden yoke until it broke.

Jimbo's missed shot invited others to fire upon the caravan, but none had a sufficient line of sight as they were reluctant to step outside of the settlement walls.

The transition period of Evynn and the unknown girl ended and two bestial creatures emerged, petrifying the men around them. Snapping out of their stupor, in vain they tugged at the chains, but the girls' increased girth snapped the cuffs around their necks, arms and legs.

Uriah recognized the evil with all too much familiarity.

Evynn was no longer present. Something else took her place. Something different—something without restraint, filled with rage, hunger and carnage. It only sought destruction, and inflicting pain fueled its motivation.

Yet, Uriah didn't have a fear of the beast. Despite its ravaging propensity, it had never directed any of the energy towards Uriah, as though it had an understanding Uriah was hallowed territory.

Howls, hoots and screams came from all directions, some from the compound and some from the caravan.

Uriah's backpack slammed against his spine as he sprinted towards Evynn and the dog. "Bliss!"

Meanwhile, the unknown monster sprinted toward the compound, seeking destruction. Jimbo led with a barrage of bullets but none of them seemed to put so much as a dent in the creature. Everything happened in a blur.

Uriah slipped past the monster and took cover behind Fernando's buggy. While most of the men from the compound retreated, Lummis's eyes widened as though a golden opportunity presented itself. He drew his sword and yelled at the top of his lungs. "Cease fire!"

The beast crouched down on all fours and charged towards the compound with a frenzied rage, rattling the earth with each powerful stride, prompting Lummis to counter in a full sprint of his own. His armor shook as he raced towards the creature with a crazed yet poised facial expression.

Uriah couldn't fathom what had to be going through a man's mind that would give him the confidence to rush headfirst into imminent annihilation. But Lummis ran, with a glazed look in his eye as though he was the one who would be delivering the destruction.

Uriah pressed his back against the buggy, breathing rapidly. He had his own safety to consider.

Lummis and the beast were on a collision course of doom, and Uriah covered both eyes but peeked out the crack between his fingers.

The gargantuan monster leapt through the air while Lummis simultaneously dove underneath it, twisting mid-flight, piercing the creature through its underbelly with the sword.

The beast bawled in pain.

I've never seen anything harm one of those things besides a larger one of those things. How could that sword…?

The creature stumbled through the entrance. A dark ooze leaked from its belly, but it continued to lash out as though it was fighting for its life.

The men scattered.

But some couldn't flee in time. Lee was petrified—literally. His eyes were wide, his jaw hung and he clenched his palms to his chest. His knees wobbled as a stream of piss trickled down his leg. Maybe he was imagining his grandma in that moment and embodying the same fear his family must have felt before their unfortunate demise.

"Lee Lee, get outta there!" Yelled Jimbo. "What the hell you doin? Get outta there!" Jimbo fired several shots. The bullets bounced off the creature like he was throwing clouds at a rock. "Lee!" Jimbo dropped the gun and hauled ass towards Lee as if he believed he could reach him in time to save him.

But he couldn't.

The beast roared, stumbling directly at Lee. Without hesitation or thought, she swiped across Lee's belly, splitting him clean in half.

"No!" Jimbo cried out.

The beast continued to rampage, spinning about and seeking the nearest target.

Jimbo was in disbelief. He ran over to Lee and scooped the top half of him in his arms. "Lee it's okay, sweetie." He slapped Lee's face. "I didn't mean to snap at you earlier, baby." He whined. "Oh, please wake up! I won't do it again. I promise." He whimpered as Lee's insides emptied onto his lap.

Jimbo wiped his tears and anger flashed across his face. He ran towards his gun and fired everything he had at the creature. "Come get me, you sumbitch!"

Uriah turned his head from the horror.

I'm def gonna need some piyel if I'm gonna make it outta this alive.

A vicious roar from Evynn distracted him from his thoughts. He had been so entrenched in the spectacle, he had momentarily forgotten his primary purpose—keeping Bliss and Evynn out of harm's way.

Well, mainly Bliss. Evynn could handle her own. And by Bliss' display of flattened ears and the licking of her chops, she sure seemed she wouldn't have much trouble holding her own as well.

Bliss barked ferociously at Fernando as he floundered in pain. Each time he even thought about reaching for the vial, Bliss pounced, snapping at him.

"Puta." He muttered.

The men surrounding Evynn remained frozen in fear. A few managed to fumble for their rifles and only one managed to keep his composure enough to actually let off some rounds. A few struck her and bounced off like rubber hitting a stone wall.

Evynn reared back and grabbed the nearest man by the throat and lifted him off the ground effortlessly. She suspended him in the air, gazing into his terrified face. She fed off the fear and basked in his panic—consuming the energy that pure horror produced as though it provided nutrition.

Fight or flight snapped the other men out of their stupor. They secured their weapons and cascaded bullets at her.

Evynn didn't so much as flinch, as they ricocheted off armor-like hide.

Releasing a high-pitched screech, she mauled the man, stripping his face from his skull, flinging the body. The lifeless torso soared through the air, limbs contorting with inertia until it crashed along the ground, knocking up a cloud of dust.

Although Uriah wasn't foreign to such devastation, it never became easier to digest no matter how many times he witnessed her turn berserk.

Evynn stomped her feet and reared her head back towards the sky. She directed her attention to the other men who weren't coward enough to run. She made short work of them—a marvel of annihilation.

"Retreat!" someone yelled from the caravan. In the midst of the chaos, the vehicles pulled away, firing shots while doing so. A storm of dust polluted the air and Uriah used it as a veil to crawl closer to Bliss, who hovered over Fernando with a snarl.

Uriah maneuvered towards the buggy's front bumper. "Bliss! Bliss!" he whispered. But she was zeroed in on Fernando and nothing could snap her concentration. She growled—teeth on full display, daring him to make a wrong move.

Evynn dropped her chin and lowered to all fours, focusing on Fernando. Fernando scrambled to his belly and stretched for the contraption. As he did so Bliss clenched her jaws around his leg. Both his sleeve and pants leg were soaked in blood. Yelping in pain, he secured the contraption and turned back over, kicking at Bliss with his free leg. "Ahh, get off me damn it!"

With gradual brooding steps, Evynn methodically stalked Fernando. Slowly approaching her victim until she hovered directly over him, she pinned his limbs down, slowly dripping saliva, bile, blood and God knows what onto his face.

Fernando turned his head and spat the putrid phlegm from his mouth. "Please, please, no. I…I…can help you," he stuttered. "If you ju-just—my hand—Buscas—I can help you."

Gunfire subsided but a few trailing shots fired from the retreating caravan.

Uriah ducked behind the buggy. Evynn's and Bliss's rage was without rhyme or reason. There was no telling who they would direct it towards next; it appeared to be an insatiable phenomenon—a wave of destruction that would not stop until there was nothing left to vanquish.

Something odd occurred. Some of the horses and mules escaped from the caravan gathered around Evynn, creating a wall. It was almost as though she was the makeshift shepherd and they were her flock.

Uriah wondered what attracted the animals to her. *Did she have a command over them? Why didn't they fear her?* There was just too much commotion to think clearly let alone make sense of it all.

He only wanted to be near Evynn. He wanted to be a part of her flock. He needed to be under her protective aura like they were.

"Evynn!"

Evynn briefly faced Uriah, but quickly returned her focus to Fernando. This was something Uriah had never witnessed in the beast before. It typically engaged in non-stop destruction. But Evynn seemed to harbor a sense of control or self-awareness. It lingered over Fernando and relished his fear.

Uriah grunted and reached for his shoulder. He attempted to raise his left arm, but it dangled limply. He had been hit with a stray bullet.

No. No. No. Damn!

His pain garnered Evynn's attention. She howled and in unison the animals neighed, barked and yelped.

While Evynn was distracted, Fernando managed to free his left hand and stab Evynn in the arm between the leathery folds with the contraption, digging it in deeply. She snorted like an enraged bull, lifted her massive foot and drove it through his skull, smashing it like a melon. She snorted several more times and flung the carcass.

She vigorously shook her head back and forth and trotted towards Uriah.

A shiver shot down Uriah's spine as he stiffened.

Although Evynn hadn't attacked him in the past, her methodical stalk and lust for destruction was too much to trust. Her temperament was too volatile, and he couldn't trust her past action to predict her future performance.

His entrenchment in fear almost took his mind off the pain in his shoulder until he slowly crawled backward, withdrawing from Evynn.

He grimaced.

The aroma of bile and death reeked from her breath. She bent down until she was face to face with Uriah—hers being four times the size of his.

He winced, closing his eyes.

She nudged him with her snout.

This is freakin' disgusting.

Despite his repulsion, Uriah felt an odd sense of serenity. His fear dissipated. He peeked out of one eye and calmly opened the other, locking eyes with the mammoth creature.

"Evynn," he whispered.

She nudged him and licked his wound.

Uriah groaned.

Maternal instinct took over and she grabbed Uriah, placing him on her back. Uriah had the sense she wanted to protect them. And amongst all the chaos she couldn't. The only refuge was in flight.

Uriah clung to her like he was riding a bucking bronco, hanging on as best he could with his right arm. He gripped the thick hide around her neck and held on for dear life.

Evynn dashed to the northwest of the compound as Bliss and the other animals followed.

Now that he was united with Evynn, all was well. His shoulder would eventually heal; they just needed a safe haven. He envisioned a secure future and all but forgot the immediate past, until he caught a glimpse of the other female who transitioned.

Uriah thought she would be belligerent, but she lay motionless—almost resting. Most of the members of the compound had scattered.

Guess ol' Lummis finally met his match.

Uriah felt some guilt. Lummis meant well. So did Lee. Genuine people were difficult if not impossible to come by. And even though Jimbo was a jerk, he didn't deserve to experience all that despair.

Uriah wondered what would have possessed a man to even attempt such an impregnable foe.

They never had a chance.

Uriah's pity was eased knowing Lummis wanted to meet his destiny head on. *Better to die with dignity and your pride intact. There were much worse fates. He died doing something he yearned for.*

He quickly dismissed the thoughts and shifted his attention back to Evynn, until a loud roar emanated from the compound.

Cheering. But why?

As the distance increased between Uriah and the compound, a small figure climbed atop the monster. The man had lopped off its head and displayed it to the compound.

Lummis! But how?

Evynn's pace quickened, and the rockiness of the ride exacerbated the pain in Uriah's shoulder. In no time, they were out of sight of the compound.

But how could he have…

The thought echoed in his mind, and he couldn't come up with an answer that would satisfy him. He was overwhelmed with the feeling that this wouldn't be the last time he'd see Lummis. A man with such a strong lust for clashing wouldn't stop until he had Evynn's head on a stake as well.

It was more than a feeling. An imprint of Lummis was etched in Uriah's mind, grabbing hold of his thoughts. Lummis became one of the many voices in his mind, but his was prominent. Bold.

Where are you going? You can flee, but you can't run forever. I will find you. I will kill her. And you will bear witness!

"No!" Uriah shouted.

Evynn released a high-pitched squeal, curtailing his thoughts. She accelerated even faster and Uriah instinctively used his injured arm to grab hold of her hide to stabilize. He contorted in pain. His shoulder was completely immobile. His breathing escalated.

What's happening to me?

He couldn't tell if he was having a panic attack or if it was the onset of shock. Blood soaked through the cloak. He felt like he was fading. He couldn't even reach for the piyel. He just hoped Evynn stopped soon, but not too soon, because they needed as much distance between them and Lummis as possible.

He held on tightly as he could to Evynn's scaly back. It was rigid like a tortoise shell, but there was a thick, leather-like spot near her neck he had grabbed a hold of. He squeezed as tight as he could as he bobbed up and down.

Her speed rapidly increased—even the horses struggled to keep up. The texture of her hide changed, shifting in composition, becoming softer.

Uriah felt himself slipping away—fading, but Evynn was changing.

She's transforming back.

Her transitions varied, sometimes fast and other times much slower.

Uriah wished he could communicate with her somehow and ask her to slow down. But that was impossible. He only could hope her instinct would take caution.

Everything happened in a blur. He didn't have time to panic. Evynn's legs gave out, and Uriah was flung headfirst over her; the two crashed face first into the dirt.

He lost consciousness, but momentarily regained it, hanging to it like a thread.

Operating on a mechanical instinct, he kept thinking he didn't want Evynn to be cold when she awakened. In case she awakened first.

I don't want her to be cold.

With every ounce of effort, he removed his backpack and the cloak and dragged it towards her transforming body. Everything around him spun. A familiar feeling; in a matter of moments everything would go black again and there was nothing, he could do about it.

He attempted to cling to the screams in his head, but even they weren't enough to keep him conscious.

The last thing he visualized was the shadowy figure of Lummis.

He stumbled several steps, struggled to gather himself but crashed shoulder first into the dirt meters away from Evynn.

CHAPTER 3:
REPOSE

**I CAN'T BELIEVE MY
GIRLFRIEND'S A ZOMBIE**

JACK E. MOHR

EVYNN

A falcon's shriek echoed, ricocheting off rocky desert atmosphere. The bird hovered above Evynn, circling and zeroing in.

A quiet darkness pervaded, engulfing the sky and the entire landscape. Evynn lay motionless, surrounded by mules, horses, donkeys and Bliss. They stood at attention, guarding her as though she were their queen.

Evynn twitched. A minor jolt of her finger, lasting no more than a fraction of a second. Then her body returned to being motionless for several moments until another jolt animated a leg, and then an arm. The jolts increased in frequency until her entire body convulsed.

Bliss howled, leading the other animals to bellow. The horses neighed and stomped empathically, creating a chaotic rhythm. The cacophonous commotion thundered throughout the desert valley.

Evynn regained a sense of herself, quickly reemerging into consciousness. Her lungs drew in a deep breath. She opened her eyes and scanned her surroundings, but she couldn't focus on anything outside of the pain she felt. Every bone in her body ached and her muscles and ligaments throbbed in agony.

She rolled back and forth in the dirt, writhing in anguish. She felt alone, but understood it was a temporary feeling.

She had been here before, not this particular place, but in a similar circumstance. There was always a stark feeling of aloneness after the transformation.

She knew all she would have to do was sit tight and sooner or later Bliss would find her, followed by Uriah. They always found her.

Bliss whimpered and ran over to Evynn, nudging her in an attempt to comfort her.

Wait. Bliss is already here. But where is Uriah?

She bit her lower lip.

Did I hurt him?

She couldn't conceive herself harming Uriah, let alone killing him—at least she hoped. *But did I?* Her last memory of him was watching him sleep like a baby. She liked watching him sleep because it was the only time he seemed free.

But she couldn't recall anything past that.

Under any other circumstance, she would have smiled from the thought of him sleeping peacefully, but the pain was excruciating, superseding joy.

Evynn scrambled to collect her thoughts. Although the pain was difficult to endure, it wasn't foreign. She had been to this place before and mentally maneuvered through it with grace.

Granted, it was always easier with the piyel, but even without it she mastered the pain. It was a matter of centering her thoughts and not allowing the sensation to become overwhelming.

Relax Evynn. You've been here. Focus. Root your thoughts. You're a big girl.

She wiped caked blood, muck and who knows what from the corner of her mouth.

She viewed the back of her hand and scoffed. "No matter how much I transform, the scars never go away."

A large calcified scar spread across the entirety of her palm. She rubbed her collar bone hoping for the best. But that scar, too, remained intact—reminiscent of the laces of a football. Rather morbidly, she added a notch for each man she had to kill. She reached for her face and a flicker of sadness surfaced—the three scars she wanted most to disappear were still present. Two and a half scars stretching from the bottom of her nose to the corner of her mouth along her right cheek. *Still here.*

Evynn was drained and physically spent.

Despite having a full stomach, she was parched.

She slowed her breathing and closed her eyes. She rose to a knee and crawled over to her cloak and Uriah's backpack several meters away. Each step was agonizingly painful. She rummaged through the pack and pulled out her clothing. She spent a great deal of effort putting on each article, beginning with an old t-shirt and finishing with a pair of denim jeans along with her cloak.

He left his backpack and my clothes, but where is he?

She stretched her neck, surveying the landscape. A herd of animals—*typical.* Yet, no Uriah in sight.

Instinctively she reached into the front pocket of her cloak and smiled.

Uriah! He left piyel for me. He's so thoughtful.

Her smile broke as the thought of harm besieging Uriah entered into the realm of possibilities.

Even through the darkness, she could make out the pools of blood outlining where her body had lain. It triggered dark thoughts. For a moment, she considered the deeds she might have done. She could never recall any of her own actions, but remembered the time her mother turned, and she shuddered.

How many innocent people have I hurt? How much pain have I caused? Uriah? No…

"Most High. Forgive me for my transgressions. Grant me peace and serenity to calmly make it through. Keep Uriah safe. Give me strength. Help me," she whispered.

"Bliss, come here girl," she said, rubbing the dog's head. "Where's U-rie, girl?" Evynn searched her mind, attempting once more to remember something—anything. She couldn't get beyond watching him sleep. She recalled Uriah passing out after ingesting too much piyel. And beyond that, nothing. She remembered her tummy hurting. She remembered wanting to clear her mind. She remembered not wanting to wake U-rie or disturb Bliss while she went for a walk, but nothing of the actual walk or anything that occurred after that point.

The memories were fleeting, vaporous—impossible to crystalize. *Where am I? Uriah can't be too far; he's probably looking for me. We always left clues to find each other—the twin crescents.*

With her feet, she traced two half-moons in the dirt. Her mouth was tender, and she massaged the back of her jaw near the base of her ears.

Hmm…Why would U-rie leave without his bag? Should I stay here and wait? Is he coming back?

She chewed piyel and searched her thoughts for any clue. As the pain subsided, focusing eased. She hadn't noticed prior but the straps on Uriah's backpack were covered in blood. And a stain on her cloak coincided with the stain on the straps of the backpack.

So, Uriah had on the cloak and backpack and bled. He's hurt! But where is he?

A determination to find Uriah raged inside of her.

She wondered why she was surrounded by so many animals. Typically, she would be surrounded by a few animals after a torpor period. But never this many. Uriah and she always made a meal out of the smaller animals—they enjoyed skinning and roasting the hares.

Where did all of this livestock come from? A compound?

She had a theory she wanted to test.

She circled the small stable of animals and studied them as they stood at attention, like soldiers awaiting her command. She approached a muscular cashmere-colored horse and rubbed its side. It didn't budge.

Hmm… Just as I thought…female. They're all female. Why are they always female?

She was accustomed to attracting an array of smaller animals—like the North American yellowed-tailed meerkat, coyotes or the sort but never animals this large—there was a humped camel that especially drew her attention.

Wow? This thing is huge. Never seen anything so majestic—long beautiful lashes.

It stuck out its tongue.

She was a little fearful of its size but felt no threat: more puzzlement. She didn't know what to do with them but felt an odd connection—an obligation. Were they thirsty, because she was? Were they hungry?

Despite feeling obliged as their monarch, her primary focus was Uriah. He didn't make the wisest decisions when they were together, and she could only imagine what he would get himself into alone. Granted, he typically operated with wisdom but there was a childlike impulse he allowed to steer him at times. Usually, she was the one to point it out and keep him within reason.

She reexamined the blood-stained backpack. Clearly, wherever he went, it wasn't willingly—maybe a group of nomads, explorers, a settlement? But if that was the case, *why would they leave me alive?*

The camel licked her hand. *Maybe the animals protected me?*

She had so many questions, but not enough answers and even less assurance.

Wherever he is, he can't be too far off.

Evynn rubbed Bliss' side. "Can you track 'im, girl?"

She put the backpack on and approached one of the horses. She caressed its mane and whispered in her ear. The horse neighed and lowered one shoulder, inviting Evynn to mount. She clumsily climbed on, teetering as she clutched its reins. She had never ridden an animal before and was apprehensive.

Bliss barked, sensing Evynn's nerves.

"It's okay Blissy, everything will be all right," she said, reassuringly. The encouragement was more for her own benefit. "Bliss…. Find U-rie, girl."

Evynn was grasping at straws in search of any lead, but Bliss retorted with a bellowing bark.

Her guess is as good as any. Why not? I can't just stay here. I have to make a move.

Evynn allowed Bliss and her intuition to lead. She tried one more time to search her memories for any hint, but absolutely nothing surfaced.

She settled her mind and sought prayer, whispering. "God, continue to guide my steps and lead me on the path of righteousness. Help me bless the world around me as it continues to bless me and illuminate my steps. Strike down all forms of malady in my path. Give me discernment and wisdom, protect all that I love, and grant me strength as I have the courage to walk in Your power."

Evynn took a deep breath. Bliss' barking continued.

"Okay girl, I'll follow your lead." Bliss had a keen nose and a strong knack for tracking. "Okay girl, find 'im!"

Bliss took off with a hardy pace toward a mountainous region. The mountains appeared to be several days journey away—even by horseback.

The horse trotted behind Bliss stride for stride, and so did the remainder of the animals. Evynn felt a sense of power, a sense of peace and a sense of belonging. Despite being alone, she had a team of animals at her side which gave her a feeling of solidarity—filling some of the emptiness she felt inside.

The risk of being alone was bad enough, but being a young woman in these parts was a death sentence—if you were lucky. Some things could be worse—a lot worse. Sometimes she had to do things to people that made her reexamine who she really was.

She rubbed the back of her hand against her scarred collarbone.

She quivered and pushed on with deep-seated faith. She held steady the reins of the horse and enjoyed the bite of the cutting wind. She made sure to keep her chin tucked so that the wind wouldn't blow her hood off.

After an hour or so of travel, Bliss slowed her pace, barking repeatedly. The moonlight reflected off a shiny object in the dirt. Evynn dismounted to examine the find. Part of it was buried, and she reached down and withdrew it from the sand. She held it up to the moonlight and examined it.

"Huh…a necklace. What's a gold necklace doing all the way out here?" She stuffed it into her cloak.

Could come in handy later. You never know.

She remounted the horse and continued her journey. Journey to where? She didn't know, but she was traveling by faith, and hope provided her sole direction.

She continued after Bliss. The group journeyed for a few more hours towards the mountains.

Bliss empathically barked at several large boulders along the road. She stopped and barked over and over.

Evynn had managed to last this long without so much as encountering another soul and was lucky to do so. She feared her luck may have run out.

What's behind those boulders?

She rummaged inside of Uriah's backpack until she found his dagger. She withdrew it, concealed it beneath her cloak, and hopped down off the horse.

Evynn's horse along with the other animals stopped several strides behind. The boulders were on a bend above a long grassy slope.

She dropped the bag and kept her hand on the dagger, taking methodical steps as she approached the boulders.

Bliss continued barking uninterrupted.

Whatever's behind those boulders gotta be human. Any animal would have scurried away by now. Maybe it's Uriah. Maybe he's wounded and can't come out.

"Show yourself. You have five seconds because if I have to come back there, I'm bustin' heads!" Evynn said, feigning a masculine tone. "Five…Four…Three…Two…" she stopped.

A rummaging of feet disrupted her count—multiple sets of feet.

A layer of sweat mounted on Evynn's palms; the dagger nearly slipped out of her hands. Her heart raced. How would she defend herself against multiple assailants?

"Please God, guide my steps," she whispered.

The rustling stopped and two figures stepped from behind the boulder. "Please don't shoot!"

What in the world? Evynn's eyes widened as two young girls stood in front of her. They couldn't have been any older than eight.

Evynn was confounded, motionless in a stupor of silence, knees locked and staring.

What in the hell are these two girls doing out here at this time of night all by themselves—

The thought was interrupted by a loud crash, and when Evynn turned to explore the commotion, she was tackled from behind by a hooded figure.

Evynn tussled, but he quickly overpowered her, pinning her to the ground. His breaths were heavy and labored. The stench of a day's worth of toil emanated from him. He leaned in, raising a knife to her neck.

He had a bestial look in his eye—he wouldn't hesitate to bring the blade to her neck. At least that was the impression he gave.

Evynn fidgeted, kicking her feet and squirming but the man's strength was far greater.

She locked eyes with him and sensed his hesitation—which provided opportunity enough. She thrust her hips upward, driving her heels into the earth and launching the man face first into the ground above her.

Evynn drew Uriah's dagger while the man gathered his bearings. As he rested on bended knee, she hustled over to him, grabbed a handful of hair and pressed the dagger against his throat.

A droplet of blood trickled out.

"I don't know who you are, but you messed with the wrong one today!"

"Please, No! That's our dad," one of the girls cried out.

"Yeah, we were just scavenging for food. Please don't hurt him," the smaller, brunette girl shouted.

The man's breathing was short and rapid, but he managed to release a whimper between breaths.

Something about the girls tugged at Evynn's sympathy strings. Killing wasn't in her nature, but out here compassion could cost your life. Murder was a tool to be wielded wisely.

I can make this easy and end him now.

The look in the girls' eyes was compelling enough to make her reconsider. *They'd really have no chance without him.*

Evynn spat on the ground and smushed the back of the man's head.

He grunted, reached for his lower back and groaned.

Evynn hopped back, digging her heels into the ground, brandishing the dagger. Her heart pounded rapidly and she took several deep breaths, waiting for the man to face her.

He slowly got to his feet. She could tell he had age by his rigid posture and the limpness of his stance. He turned around with slumped, defeated shoulders and looked in Evynn's direction but didn't make full eye contact.

Evynn studied the man, sizing him up. He didn't seem like a typical bandit—whatever that meant. There seemed to be some refinement to him. His muscles weren't completely hardened, his posture wasn't rugged as though it was meant to endure battle at the drop of a penny. He almost seemed sophisticated if ever she knew what that meant.

This made things all the more unusual. What was he doing out here with these two young girls? Hunting was feasible, but seemed implausible at night and with children. They would pose a liability in every circumstance.

Sometimes bandits used smaller individuals as bait, but never girls. And this man was alone: no ambushing calvary. Something about him was different but she couldn't quite place it. And despite their scuffle, he didn't give off a threatening vibe—more like protective. Even so, she squeezed Uriah's dagger harder.

Evynn clenched her jaws. "If you gone bring it…Bring it!"

The man fixed his gaze on Evynn and relaxed his shoulders, loosening his hands. He scraped the bottom of his chin with the back of his knife and then placed it into his boot. "I recognize that look anywhere." He titled his head. "You've turned recently…"

"What?"

The statement caught her off guard, disarming her.

How did he….

He took several steps towards his children. He displayed his palms in a show of surrender. "You're probably wondering how I knew." He hugged the two girls squeezing them tightly. "I'll explain, I suppose…But on one condition."

Is he serious? I just had his life in my hands. And he has the brass to negotiate?

Evynn squinted.

The wrinkles around his eyes relaxed. "I'll take that as an acquiescence, I suppose."

Evynn didn't budge or display any hint of lowering her guard, but the man's intention was persistent.

"Where are my manners? Now that we are beyond the preverbal song and dance, allow me to introduce myself. I am Judaius." He halfway bowed. "These are my daughters. This here is Darlene." He hugged the larger of the two girls, with dark brown hair like the man. "That li'l rascal is Alice." He poked the stomach of the smaller one. She had bright red hair. Something was oddly familiar about its color but Evynn couldn't quite connect the dots.

A little young. Where is their mother?

The thought dampened her spirit. She recalled when her own mother turned.

Judaius interrupted Evynn's ponder. "Ah, you're waiting for the condition. My only condition is that you do not trust me."

"That's nonsense."

"I lie out of necessity—a means of survival, and I'd feel bad seeing you fall victim to a petty lie or two."

What's his deal? If I can't trust him, why bother at all?

Evynn turned to the herd of animals and took a few steps.

"You know my wife had that same look prior to turning, the signs are all there—pimples on your forehead. spiking hormones.

thickening of the skin." he said with haste. As though he were trying to persuade her from leaving.

Oh, he's at it. What's his angle?

Evynn tuned back to face the man.

"Piyel?" he asked.

Inquisitively, Evynn stared at Judaius.

"It's the eyes that give it away. Alas, it will not be enough, eventually it will lose all efficacy, delaying the inevitable. Trust me…I suppose." He grinned. "Different plants can be used for different tools, but you'll need sustenance before you crash into a comatose state."

Evynn had just noticed his left eye was glass and wondered if it was lost in some botched battle similar to this. She was alarmed she hadn't noticed prior.

"What do you mean? Piyel has always worked…"

"Different plants serve different purposes. I can help you. Piyel can only be used for so long before it no longer works. Your episodes of turning will become more frequent and you'll end up having to feed more and more."

How did he know so much about the process? Maybe that's how he lost his eye, experimenting with a woman who turned. But he told me not to trust him. Hmm…

Judaius rubbed the backs of his daughters "I'm half a day's journey West, towards the mountains. I have something that can help us all. Come."

Darlene kicked the ground. "But Papa, what about—"

I CAN'T BELIEVE MY GIRLFRIEND'S A ZOMBIE   81

"Hush Darlene," he interrupted. "She'll find her way home. She always does."

Alice whimpered.

"Alice, grab your sister. What did I teach you?"

The two sisters spoke in unison in a sing-song way as though they had rehearsed it many times. "There's no weakness in survival! Survive by any means. Lying stimulates survival and should only be used sparingly."

This guy has brought up lying too many times. Maybe I should just stick to the task and find Uriah. But what if he's right? What if I can't hold back the turning...Is it worth the risk?

Evynn sighed. She was torn. He seemed to know much about turning, but a self-admitted liar...

Alice grabbed her sister's hand. Although she was smaller, she seemed to be the more emotionally mature of the two. "Hey, it's okay. It's only been a few days. She's come back from longer."

Darlene sobbed and nodded as though she were trying to convince herself of a truth she didn't believe.

Judaius kissed Darlene atop her forehead. "It'll all work out for the best," he said, reverting his attention to Evynn. "We must go now. You haven't much time." He wiggled his nose as though his mustache tickled. "If you don't decide soon, the girls and I must go for our own safety."

Amazing. I was getting ready to leave and he somehow convinced me to stay then claimed if I didn't seek his help, he would have to leave.

If what he was saying was true and she turned, whether here or somewhere else, her torpor would leave her vulnerable. Indecisive, she weighed the possibilities.

If this man could truly help…

Judaius reached into his pocket. "Here. Chew on this. It'll help." He handed Evynn a pale green stick resembling bamboo.

She took the stick and felt its texture. Judaius waited for her to partake. "Go ahead. Would it help if I indulged as well?" He took out a second stick and chewed. "See?"

Evynn sighed in disgust. "You haven't even asked my name."

"You're right… I suppose. But neither did you ask ours. I offered them freely."

Touché.

"EJ."

She didn't know why but she somehow felt safer not giving this stranger her full identity. Despite being on the verge of accepting food from said stranger.

"Lovely. EJ, give it a try. It will help…I suppose."

She hated how he trailed off with the phrase 'I suppose' as a qualifier for every statement. But she didn't want to risk turning again. Her skin did feel a little clammy.

She placed the stick in her mouth and was struck with a burst of sweetness. She chewed rapidly and felt an immediate relief. Her skin softened and her migraine waned—like the foggy haze clouding her mind finally dissipated.

She felt rejuvenated.

As apprehensive as Evynn was, she managed to display a quarter-smile.

Maybe, he can help…

The children made it much easier for her to let down her guard. She found something reassuring about the girls, something that filled her with hope. The survival rate for females was minimal and a part of her knew when the girls came of a certain age the true hell would begin. This reality dampened her hope.

It was a sobering reality, but their innocence was refreshing.

Evynn smiled at the two girls, finally acknowledging them and lowering her guard. "Hi, Darlene. Hi, Alice."

The two girls bashfully tucked their chins.

Evynn slipped the dagger back into her cloak.

"It's okay girls. She's of no threat, mind your manners," said Judaius.

Still reluctant, the girls waved. And a smile poked through on Alice's face.

Judaius nodded. "Well? Our dwelling isn't too far from here. I have something that will help you. But it's still up to you, I suppose."

Evynn didn't budge. Uriah remained on the forefront of her mind. She didn't want to waste any more time than necessary. She didn't want to get side-tracked, but by the same token, she was still unsure about the certainty of turning.

Plus, she was parched and the animals could use a drink as well. Perhaps a few calculated steps back would be swifter than a few foolish steps forward.

She closed her eyes, took a deep breath and whispered under her breath. "God guide my path."

She took a moment to still her mind.

"Okay," she said.

Alice broke free, ran over and hugged Evynn's leg. "I'm so happy."

Evynn awkwardly looked side to side. Affection wasn't a commodity she was accustomed to. Uriah never really hugged her—it was always her holding him. This was something unique and it warmed her. It encouraged her even more. Maybe the girls needed her and she needed them. She rubbed Alice's back.

Bliss barked and hustled to Evynn's side and nestled. Evynn rubbed her side and whispered, "I know, girl."

Bliss looks drained. She needs rest.

Hell, all the animals needed rest. Evynn could use a solid night's sleep to recalibrate her mind.

She had no idea how long she had been in her torpor state, how long the animals had kept guard and when the last time they had nourishment.

She had to take this strange man up on his offer. Under any other circumstance she wouldn't have, but something about these two young girls helped her throw caution to the wind. And she couldn't risk the possibility of turning again. She was lucky enough not to have been found during her state of torpor this time around.

Evynn placed her hood over her head. She bent over at the waist, speaking to Alice in a soft voice. "Have you ever ridden a horse before, kiddo?"

Alice shook her head.

"Well neither had I till today. Hop on," she said motioning towards Judaius.

Judaius was a bit apprehensive. "We've never ridden before. We can walk."

Evynn squinted. "Don't be so scared. They won't bite. Trust me…I suppose." She chuckled.

Judaius snickered. "I see what you supposedly did there." He led Darlene by the hand and placed her on top of the donkey and climbed on after her.

Evynn placed Alice on the horse and mounted behind her. "East, you said?"

Judaius tried pulling the donkey's reins in an attempt to make it move. "No, west actually."

Evynn stroked her horse's mane. "Don't bother. They won't listen to you. They'll only follow one. Just shout out the directions. I'll lead and they will follow."

Evynn was imbued with confidence—the role of leader felt natural, and its power was reassuring. She had no idea how these animals were bonded to her, but it felt innate. And as they rode off toward the darkening sky, she was assured that she was in control.

They were far enough from Death's Shadow that the sky opened up, and the sun was able to break through the clouds. They avoided major highways and pathways to prevent any potential contact with outsiders. Judaius was versed in the less-ridden passages.

Evynn led and Judaius took up the rear with the drove of animals between them. Alice knew the routes just as well as her father and provided excellent navigation.

Despite the sun poking through the clouds, the air was crisp and biting, and Evynn developed a layer of goosebumps along the back of her hands.

Alice gently rubbed Evynn's arm. "Why's your skin look like that?"

Evynn looked down at her arm, expecting to see a grey tinge or scaly skin residue from turning. But she didn't see anything out of the ordinary. Just her arm.

Alice tilted her head back and looked at Evynn with wide-curious bulbous eyes.

Evynn looked at the scar on her palm, "Oh, this comes with survival."

Alice flipped Evynn's hand over. "No, your skin. Why's it that color… are you special?"

Brown?

It dawned on Evynn that Alice may not have ever seen anyone that looked like her before. She probably hadn't come across much of anyone, being isolated out here. Even if her father had attempted to explain, what visual representation would he use as a reference point?

Alice's lips slowly parted and a smile plastered on her face.

Evynn pursed her lips. "Oh no, curious one, I was born this way."

"Will my skin be that color when I get older? Or will I have to turn like you? I don't want to turn."

Evynn didn't know how to approach the question. She didn't wish turning on anyone but she knew it was inevitable once she became of age. The girl seemed so enamored with her color she didn't want to kill her hopes. Maybe this is one of those times Judaius was talking about when he said lying keeps you alive.

Evynn stammered. "Umm…Well…"

"You don't have to lie to me you know. Daddy says people hesitate before lying." Alice's eyebrows furrowed.

"I wasn't lying. Just trying to figure out how to explain that turning is something you can't help. Like my skin."

Alice shook her head. "You are lying. Because that's not true!"

Evynn wondered if this was some form of entertainment for the girl: a game of who can out-lie who. Evynn no longer wanted to participate. She hoped it wasn't true. In fact, everyone held out hope. But every female sooner or later always ended up turning. It was just a matter of how prepared you were for the turn.

Alice's smile widened, reminding her of the Cheshire Cat from one of her favorite stories her mother used to read. The girl's smile was mischievous and intriguing. Perhaps she wasn't lying after all.

No, she's just her father's child, trying to play on my curiosity, she has to be lying.

Alice blinked rapidly. "You'll see!"

Despite desiring to delve deeper, Evynn disregarded the girl's assertion. She had enough to think about. She had her own means of escapism through her own fantasies. One day she was going to be reinstated in the Old World. Anytime she brought this up to anyone, especially Uriah, they would tell her how impossible it was. But this was her dream, and she would hold on to it no matter what. So, if Alice wanted to believe she could live a life without turning, that was fine. *Who am I to burst her bubble?*

Evynn rubbed the child's back and she fell asleep in a matter of minutes. The clouds rolled and thundered but not a drop fell from the sky. Rays of sunlight continued poking through the clusters of grey clouds.

As they drew closer to the mountains, the air grew thick. The sandy, arid atmosphere slowly turned to a denser, humid environment. The air felt fresher in the lungs, and Evynn found herself more alert. Even her memory returned in spots.

She recalled leaving Uriah to sleep and her stomach feeling queasy. She remembered going for a walk and making a regretful decision, but she couldn't quite recall what that decision was.

She replayed the scenario through her mind but no matter how hard she thought, she failed to remember.

The journey ended up being much shorter than half a day. The equine animals significantly decreased the travel time and the enclave appeared much sooner than expected.

"We're not too much further," yelled Judaius.

For the last few miles, the convoy had been traveling alongside a paved road. It seemed to be a private road that ended abruptly a hundred meters ahead. Evynn found it odd the road ended so suddenly, but even stranger was the fact it stopped in the middle of nowhere. Along the northern side of the road was a long row of tall pine trees near the mountain's base.

Alice peacefully slumbered as though she hadn't had a good night of rest in months.

Evynn gently nudged her shoulder. "Hey Alice, I think we're here. Time to wake up, sleepy head."

Then Evynn looked back towards Judaius. He was nowhere to be found.

A quiet rustling sprouted near the pine trees. "Hey, we're over here," came a yell.

Evynn squinted but still could see nothing but rows of trees.

Alice giggled. "Help me down. I'll show you!"

Evynn dismounted, then tucked her hands under Alice's armpits and helped her down.

Alice grabbed Evynn's hand and ran towards the trees.

As they approached, the entrance became more and more obvious, and Evynn wondered how she ever could have missed it.

As Evynn and Alice walked through, the animals followed suit. Judaius and Darlene stood at a bend which wrapped around the side of a mountain. The way wasn't paved but it was a distinguishable dirt path.

Evynn was in awe of the view. The entrance wasn't at the base of the mountain as she perceived from the road, but rather a good distance up, and as she looked out, many more mountains filled the backdrop, all riddled with lush trees.

A light sprinkle of rain caressed her skin and she thought of Uriah. Hopefully he wasn't hurt. She'd see him soon. She put some pep in her step. "I assume we're headed up?"

Judaius took notice of her change of demeanor. "Yes, but haste will not assist you. The ingredients must be ingested over a period of time."

Evynn sighed. "I guess patience is a virtue."

"It's not much further."

The company continued in silence.

Concern for Uriah flooded Evynn's mind. She just needed to curtail this turning and she'd shift her focus back to finding him.

Judaius cleared his throat. "I don't judge you—you know?"

"What?" replied Evynn.

"You've probably done some treacherous things without even being conscious of it." He sneered. "And from the way you handled that blade, you've probably done some dastardly things while being fully aware."

Evynn increased her pace until she passed him, choosing not to pay him any mind. She knew she had done things she didn't want to imagine. It was difficult enough forgetting the times she would spend coming out of torpor. She had to put a concerted effort into not seeing the dried blood stuck in her hair and skin any time she closed her eyes. The men she and Uriah had to defend against. She clung to the fact that she was never consciously the aggressor. This allowed her to disassociate from the guilt of her acts. In fact, she took pride in being a protector.

As her mind wandered, Judaius continued to ramble. "Just because we've done lawless acts, we're not all lawless out here." He wiped his brow. "We've been placed in lawless circumstance and forced to operate within the parameters of lawlessness in order to survive, but that's not who we are; it's just a function of our actions." Judaius gave her a cross look to see if she was still listening. It seemed like he was talking just to talk, like he hadn't had another person over the age of ten to talk to in quite some time and was taking advantage of the opportunity to splurge.

Evynn kept trucking forward, not bothering to look back. The light rain felt good, cooling some of the day's heat.

Judaius sped up until he passed her, taking the point again. "There are ways to circumvent the habit of lawlessness, so that it doesn't consume you. But you're already aware of that, I suppose."

Evynn wanted to tell him to shut up. And as though on cue, the donkey brayed, interrupting Judaius' babble.

Evynn laughed to herself. "Hey, you were once part of the Old World. Why don't you tell me some stories!"

"The past is the past. It won't help us now. But I suppose if—"

Her loud gasp interrupted him mid-sentence.

As Evynn turned the final bend, her eyes bulged. The trail led up to a wide plateau. In its center was a massive glass conservatory. Oddly enough, the sky opened up, allowing rays from the sun to bleed through, and its rays refracted off the glass, forming a rainbow.

As Evynn walked towards the conservatory the sound of crashing water magnified and another small rainbow formed over a waterfall a distance to the rear of the building.

She was taken aback. This was a true Old World treasure. During her past wanderings, she came across old bus stops, highways and railways, but never an actual wonder. This was breathtaking and confirmed all of her aspiration to one day live amongst the Old World's inhabitants. This was truly a relic.

She wanted to be a part of a culture that developed such beauty and innovation. She couldn't wait to share this with Uriah and maybe he'd stop being so pessimistic about one day living within the Old World.

Judaius noticed Evynn's awe. "Darlene, take your sister and prepare the young lady a fresh glass. Meet us back at the conservatory," he said. "We're taking the animals down near the waterfall so they can graze and drink."

"What is this place?"

Judaius tapped his chin as though pondering. Was he searching for an elaborate story or had he known the history of this place? Maybe it was some place he visited often when the Old World was the only world. Or maybe he just somehow discovered it.

He cleared his throat. "I'm not quite sure, but it's amazing. They've left plenty of literature around to read. From what I gathered; a botanist lived here. Wanted it to be a self-contained, energy-efficient, nature-powered facility. It runs itself."

Evynn couldn't stop staring. "Wow!"

She had never seen anything of this magnitude—and in such pristine condition. It wasn't run down. It wasn't covered in graffiti. It hadn't been looted. The windows weren't bashed out like it had been ravished and left dead.

This structure was living and thriving, gushing with personality—a true staple of the past, perfectly preserved. It hadn't endured a lick of decay from the attrition of time.

Excitedly, the girls ran past the glass building to a smaller, domed structure in the back, apparently made out of clay.

"Come," said Judaius, walking toward the conservatory—an immense glass structure filled with luscious, verdant greenery.

Evynn was startled by the conservatory's sprinklers.

"Don't be alarmed. Good ol' hydroelectricity from the waterfall and river. Powers everything."

Evynn rubbed the moisture from her face with her cloak. The gentle rain slowly subsided. "How did you find this place?"

"Luck. I suppose. Me and the girls were on the run."

"Run?" Evynn asked.

"From my wife." A silence proceeded. "But that's a story for another time. For now, we need to get you settled. My family's safety depends on it. You haven't much time left."

CHAPTER 4:
VERILY VERILY...
SERENDIPITY

**I CAN'T BELIEVE MY
GIRLFRIEND'S A ZOMBIE**

JACK E. MOHR

EVYNN

Judaius opened a large glass door and briskly entered the conservatory. Evynn followed as the animals waited outside, some headed to the river for a drink. Inside were several aisles of lush leafage. He turned left and headed down a row of gigantic flora. "Come, what you need is right this way."

It was even more awe inspiring from the inside. These were unique plants that she had never seen before. Some were gargantuan—the size of trees with thick long stems—while others were more like ferns or flowers. Some had long, reaching limbs and leaves. The various smells were breathtaking, the colors were alluring and the sensation they created was arousing to the senses. Splashes and dashes of bright oranges, violets, reds, yellows, and every hue of green imaginable.

Evynn's eyes pooled with tears and the back of her neck itched.

Judaius increased his pace, assuming Evynn was right behind. "Breathtaking, isn't it?" He laughed with a flare of sarcasm. "In the Old World, I was an amateur botanist and heard of this place even before the plague, but never knew exactly where it was. It was pure serendipity that brought me to it. Power of attraction...I suppose."

Evynn slowed to a standstill, bent over and placed her hands on her knees. She tried to speak but her throat had closed shut. So had her eyes—her face had swelled up so puffy she couldn't see. And she couldn't hear. She panicked, dropping to her knees and gasping.

"EJ?"

She felt a hand on her back, along with something sharp piercing her arm. After a few moments she was able to regain all of her faculties.

Judaius helped her to her feet. "Many apologies. The girls and I have built up quite an immunity. I forgot the effects these plants could have on someone."

Evynn coughed. "What was that you poked me with?"

"Nothing to worry about, I suppose. Something to help with the symptoms."

"But what was it?"

Judaius paused. "We haven't much time for chit-chat. Come."

He continued walking, dismissing the fact she had almost suffocated. And it rubbed Evynn the wrong way. She scoffed. *Seriously? I just almost died, and he's annoyed by my questioning?*

He didn't bother looking back until he came across a large crimson plant with long, languid tentacles that appeared to be reaching out as though it wanted to grab hold of someone.

"Be careful with this one darling, it bites."

Evynn gave it a once-over. She knew he had to be joking but for a second, she believed him.

"Bites?"

"Get too close and it'll swallow you up. Disintegrate your entire body in less than a week's time."

Evynn lightly laughed it off.

Judaius gave her a condemning glance out the side of his eye, then matched her light laughter.

On the end of each tentacle was a large bulb. He grabbed one and pulled it apart. The plant retracted as though it felt pain.

"It's okay, girl…I'll make it up to you. I promise," Judaius said affectionately, caressing the plant.

He shows more compassion for the plants than for me.

He looked at Evynn with a wry smile. "This will set you free." He turned without waiting for a response. He headed down the aisle towards the back of the conservatory and exited at the same brisk pace he had entered.

The evening sun burst through clouds and its rays danced across the water. Most of the animals rested near the riverbank, some grazing on the grass while others drank. The girls were petting Yamalah—the name they had christened the camel with.

When Alice caught sight of Evynn, she hurried over with a metal thermos and offered it to her. "Hey EJ, the river water is the best. Try some."

Evynn had a slight headache, probably from being dehydrated or maybe allergies from the plants. The waterfall crashed into a river which further cascaded down the side of the mountain.

She walked to the flowing water, kneeled and filled up the metal thermos. She placed it on the grass next to her and washed her hands, removing dried blood, mud and residue from her cuticles.

Wonder whose blood this is?

She didn't know and didn't care as long as it was gone.

She took several gulps of water. It was uniquely refreshing.

Judaius created a small blaze in a fire pit. He fanned the flames with his gulf hat before putting it back on his head.

The pit was made of large stones and had benches of stone slabs circling it. The sun no longer illuminated the sky, and evening settled in.

The girls hustled around the fire pit, bringing blankets to cut the sharpness of the crisp cold.

Judaius had two pots hovering over the pit. "EJ! Come! We hadn't much time. I'm preparing you food, but more importantly, the bulb extract," he said, stirring both pots.

Evynn didn't trust anyone and her comfort level with the man waned even more. Something was unsettling about him, yet despite the red flags he had proven beneficial for the most part.

He had these two girls he cared for and was all alone; perhaps that accounted for his quirks.

She felt queasy. She wasn't that hungry, but perhaps some food would settle her stomach. The river water was so refreshing it had alleviated her headache.

She took a deep breath and looked where the sun had fallen.

God, what am I doing here? Please protect me and lead me to righteousness.

Prayer was one of the few tools she used to ground herself when she felt antsy. She was grateful for all the jewels her mother had left her with, but this one in particular she was most appreciative of. It always filled her with peace.

"I hope Uriah's safe," she whispered. She took another deep breath and headed towards the pit, petting Yamalah on the way over.

Bam!

Out of nowhere, a fleeting memory struck her, stopping her mid-stride. She recalled what happened when the idea whirled her away.

CHAPTER 5:
A MEMORY FORGOTTEN IS A TRUTH UNKNOWN

I CAN'T BELIEVE MY GIRLFRIEND'S A ZOMBIE

JACK E. MOHR

EVYNN

She had felt nauseous and had gone for a brief walk—she didn't know from where—to clear her mind. It turned into a longer walk than she had expected. Guided by the illumination of the moon's blaze, she was occupied with thoughts of 'what next.'

We can't just wander forever. We have to eventually settle. If not the Old World, somewhere. We need to make a home of our own. She sighed. *There has to be a way back to the Old World. There has to be a way this monster inside of me can be stopped for good. There just has to be a way.*

She was stuck in a loop of her own thought space and head movies, wondering what could be and what life was like in the 'Old World', fantasizing about her and Uriah there.

Queasy, she reached for her stomach. She stumbled slightly and projectile vomited.

"Senorita, are you okay?"

Huh?

With one hand still on her knee, she wiped her mouth and searched the darkness for the voice. Then she started. A mysterious man stood by himself near a cactus, not too far away, staring into the gloomy sky.

It was as though he had appeared out of thin air.

Am I seeing things? How long has he been standing there?

She didn't have her cloak and anticipated aggression or curiosity but he greeted her almost like he was expecting her, peering directly into her eyes.

He smiled and nodded. "Propiciar. The Algorithms never cease to astound," he whispered, clasping his hands. "Divine things always come in threes, bien venidos."

Evynn stiffened. "Who the hell are you?"

She was never without her knife. She reached into her pocket.

"On the contraire, me llamo es Fernando. I am but a meager messenger of Omniscience—guided to this very point in time, to this very space, to find this very specimen." He grinned.

Evynn studied the man. His posture was relaxed and confident. His jawline was pronounced, his skin tanned. He looked nondescript but blemish free. It was uncanny. No one was ever this well-kept out here—no reason to be.

She was shocked by how fearlessly he interacted with her, knowing she was a woman and the obvious threat she posed.

Fernando formed a fist and placed it on his chest. "This country was always good to me and my people. It wasn't until the plague hit that everything fell apart. El Diablo Magnifico!" he said with a harsh tone but then softened his pitch. "But God always provides hope in the darkest hours of despair. God has sent us a savior—a Redeemer, an absolute messenger of pure intention—who will restore the world as a whole. That omniscient source ensured we would meet on this most providential path of destiny. I am obligated to spread the message of the algorithms—the amended Gospel as we know it." He paused, staring into Evynn's eyes, reaching for her hand. "Do you know what will save us?"

It was a guiding question and Evynn knew whether she responded or not, he would provide an answer, so she played along. "I don't."

He removed his fist from his chest and held it directly in front of him, clenching it firmly. "Unity! We must reunite this country and make it whole again. It starts with us—the fallen. The condemned! We must atone for our sins and purge the world of this abomination among us." He gazed into her eyes.

She knew what he meant—the abomination within her.

He shook his head as though reading her mind. "No, the dissension among mankind. The differences must be dissolved. We're all deserving of love." He paused. "Innovation and science are key. The algorithms have endowed us with both! They will reunite this forsaken era of existence with the Old World and bring America back to prominence again."

In this moment, Evynn disregarded all caution and visualized living in the Old World, imagining how all the people on the other side of existence lived with televisions, cellular phones, electric cars and supermarkets—things she had only read about in books or heard from stories.

She inserted Uriah and herself into the fantasy—maybe a flat on the Upper East Side. Delighted, she smiled. She wanted so bad to experience that life. She knew in her heart she was destined to experience it one way or another.

Did he really have the key? Could this Savior really be true? Could the Savior fix her, fix the women, fix this entire forsaken world?

Fernando inflamed the hope already sparked within her.

She had to wake Uriah and somehow convince him to hear this strange man out. This man—who spoke with an honest conviction and a boisterous determination.

Fernando wiped his khakis. "You believe my words. But you should believe less of what you hear and more of what you see." He grabbed her by the wrist. "Mirar!"

"Huh?"

His grip was firm and decisive. He whisked her away before she had a chance to object. Her legs trailed her curiosity, and she found herself in a brisk jog before she knew it—hustling through the dimness.

They stopped, just as their breathing had turned from manageable to laborious.

A donkey flicked its ears as they drew near. Fernando helped her atop and climbed on behind her. "Es nearby."

With his spurs he dug into the donkey's side. "Yaw," he yelled out.

The donkey accelerated with long even strides. It was her first time atop a donkey, but she adapted to the bouncing quickly.

By the time she adjusted, Fernando was pulling on the reins. "Easy…"

Even through the gloom the spectacle was astonishing. There were several smaller vehicles surrounding one enormous RV, with the letters F.B.I. on the side. A large antenna-like satellite projected from the top.

Wow…

Fernando chuckled, "Senorita, fret not. We aren't the Feds—we found them, abandoned as all the other vehicles."

She had no idea what the Feds were or why she should be worried about them. That huge antenna sticking out of the RV was most concerning. It implied technology—what she had been taught was a key trigger of the plague.

She swallowed and returned her eyes to Fernando.

She hadn't noticed before, but he had a revolver holstered at his side. The imminent fear of harm bombarded her. What had she gotten herself into? She had always chastised U'rie for being rash. Now look at her.

What was I thinking? What am I doing here?

Fernando took confident strides towards the FBI trailer. It was the largest vehicle she had ever seen, looking like it went on without end.

Evynn betrayed her better judgement and followed; she was too far in to turn away. And oddly enough, she didn't feel any threat from this curious man. Just a serene sense of confidence and purpose.

Her head swirled and she became increasingly light-headed and queasy with each additional step towards the RV.

An abrasive stench emanated from the vehicle. Was that causing her stomach to churn?

Fernando approached the door of the RV and paused.

He entered a sequence of numbers on a keypad beside the door and waited.

He took a lingering breath, made the sign of the cross in the air in front of his heart. "Almost forgot," he reached into a pouch mounted to the RV and handed Evynn a mask. "Es para la smell."

Evynn put the mask on. It blocked most of the odor but a good amount seeped through.

Fernando turned to Evynn and peered into her eyes for a few seconds before speaking. "You are privileged to lay tus ojos on the Redeemer."

The hairs on the back of her neck stood. She traced a moon with her foot in the dirt in case she needed Uriah to find her. She knew if she needed to be found at this point, her survival would be moot—but she traced the two half-moons anyway.

What did I get myself into? Maybe I should turn and run. That would probably only make a bad situation worse.

"God…please protect me. If whatever is behind that door does not have the best intentions, please guide my path back to safety."

The lock released on the RV, interrupting her prayer. "You may enter," a high-pitched, scratchy, mechanical voice erupted from the back.

The door slid open and the putrid smell inundated her.

Despite wearing masks, they both coughed.

Evynn hesitantly followed Fernando into the RV. It was dark for the most part, with a single source of light—a huge screen emitting bright fluorescent light.

Evynn squinted, scanning the room. She couldn't make out much, due to the brightness of the screen. Her sight struggled to adjust to the dichotomy.

Where is the power source for this light? I didn't hear a generator. Don't they know how dangerous this is? I'm of age…Why would he invite me here, knowing what this could trigger? She felt woozy.

Fernando tapped Evynn's shoulder. "It's okay, amiga. This way."

Wires and cords hooked into the screen, leading to a source behind a black curtain—coincidentally, the smell of rot was strongest in the direction of the drapery.

The Screen flickered. "Please leave us," a zesty high-spirited voice projected from the screen.

Fernando slowly turned and nodded at Evynn. "Fear not. You're in the presence of sapience."

The entrance to the RV slid open and Fernando looked back one final time before departing. He had a sense of pride and longing in his eyes as though his convictions were finally becoming true, fulfilling his purpose for existence.

Evynn shuddered as goosebumps formed across her arms. She felt queasy and reached for her stomach. She wasn't sure if this was the onset of her beginning to turn or if the odor was triggering a gag reflex.

She stared at the blank screen.

She had never experienced this kind of technology, or any technology for that matter. It was always banned from the compound because it was thought to be the main catalyst for turning. Now here she was, in the midst of advanced technology, and she hadn't turned.

Maybe the compound was grasping at straws, and they actually had no idea what caused people to turn?

The screen flickered, creating a static sound. From the black void a face emerged: striking cheekbones, strong chin and a square brow. The image looked flawlessly human.

"Welcome… Evynn," said the voice.

She rubbed the back of her neck. *How does it know me?*

The name Adam exploded on the screen in bold font above his head.

The face shrunk and a body popped beneath the face. "Aww, much better." Adam placed his hand on his hip and shifted his posture, exuding confidence. "I don't know you but merely of your habits. Your actions. Your behavior. The amalgamation of who you are, forming the predictability of what you will be."

Evynn scratched her upper back. *Huh? Is he some kind of mind reader?*

Adam smirked. "No, I am not. I analyze body language. I examine patterns and predict the probability of future behavior based on a database of actions and potential scenario correlations."

Evynn sighed. "I don't know what that means."

Adam pointed to Evynn. "I will show you," he said, vanishing.

The screen flickered and displayed a satellite, scanning the earth, zooming in on various geography, panning on the compound she grew up in, zooming out then zooming in on Uriah—back out and then on to the RV.

"As you gaze at the screen. It's evident that I in the singular sense cannot discern a thing, but I, as a function of the network, can be anywhere and see anything within a limited capacity."

Evynn mulled over the statement… She took pride in the many lessons she learned in the compound. The times she'd often poke and prod, getting the elders to describe in detail the average life in the Old World.

She had learned about the Internet but none of it made sense to her. Was he the Internet? Did he control it all! *How can he see all of this stuff?*

She no longer cared so much about the how. For now, she wanted to know why.

She scanned the room. She felt someone else was in the room beside this man on the screen. "Why did you bring me here?"

Adam reappeared. "Getting right to it are we? Charisma. Spunk. All things that create a champion of the cause. You will be a martyr. Are you familiar with the term?"

Evynn wracked her brain, coming up with nothing.

As she was starting to express her ignorance, the definition of the word appeared on the screen: "A person who sacrifices something of great value and especially life itself for the sake of principle."

Evynn mouthed the words. She frowned not only at the idea of dying but the looming stench. Adam furrowed his eyebrows. "Alas, you will not die in the traditional sense but everything potentially a threat within you will be sacrificed in aid of greater peace for humanity."

Evynn shook her head. "Huh?"

Adam took several steps back. "To be frank, if we can destroy the monster within you, the Old World will allow us back in. A cure will be the key to re-entry."

Evynn scratched the back of her hand.

A cure?

The image smiled. "Yes. For all intents and purposes, we have acquired a sequence in theory. We just need to actualize it."

Evynn coughed from the stench. "What's the cure?"

"In due time. For now, we have an antidote. Similar to a cure but not quite the same."

Evynn lost patience. Her stomach was churning prior to entering the RV and now she felt more nauseous from the horrendous smell of rotten flesh—one she was all too familiar with.

Who are you? This is silly. Why am I talking to a large screen and more importantly how was it talking back? Is this normal in the Old World?

The smell was too much to bear. She sniffed until she located the source of the wretched odor.

She advanced towards the source.

Adam ran towards the corner of the screen waving his hands. "Hey," he said in a high-pitched voice. "Where are you going?"

She continued until she reached the curtain. Dozens of chords were running beneath the curtain, connecting to the screen and the vehicle itself.

She held her breath and reached for the curtain.

Adam squealed "Wait… no…"

She peeked behind the curtain and instantly regretted it. She hadn't witnessed anything this gruesome since she was a child.

Her face contorted.

A chubby boy, near her age, sat in a swing. It was apparent why he hid himself.

His legs were atrophied from lack of use. He was hairless, with an obese torso—which was riddled with open sores, dripping with puss. Wires protruded from various parts of his body, some leading to the screen, others to who knows where. Yellow stuff oozed out of some orifices while green gunk poured from others. His left eye spun in its socket while the right pupil was completely faded.

He gasped for air as though fighting for his life. His face was void of any emotion and his eye was equally as hollow as it stared right through her.

Evynn gasped and took several steps back.

The screen flickered. "I didn't want you to see us like this."

Evynn shut the curtain and covered her mouth. "What happened to you?"

She couldn't take her eyes off the curtain.

The screen flickered. "He, too, was a martyr. Not so much different than you, sacrificing his physical being to become a vessel for the Divine—a symbiotic evolution"

Evynn subconsciously placed her hand on her heart. "But he can't live like that for much longer."

Adam dropped to a knee. "You are correct. Let me show you something."

A jolt went through the RV and power seemingly flickered on and off. The boy behind the curtain wailed—a lethargic, pain-ridden, emotionless moan.

The display on the screen changed. Evynn saw herself. She was sitting in a brownstone apartment with Uriah. They were older. They laughed as music played from an old record player. Uriah went to the stove and removed a roast, smiled and exclaimed dinner was ready. Evynn was giddy. She sipped from a glass of red wine and kissed Uriah as he prepared their plates at the table.

The boy moaned and the image went black, to be replaced by Adam. "This is the stress-free, pleasant life the Old World has waiting for you."

Evynn smiled. *It's everything I imagined and more. Food at our disposal, merriment and a life without threat.* "Is this truly possible?"

"With time, yes. I cannot predict the future. Only simulate possible scenarios given potential courses of action."

Evynn glanced at the curtain and quivered. "How can I help?"

A chord with a sharp needle on the end slithered out from beneath the curtain. "We can begin with a full biometric scan. Insert the end of this gently into the back of your hand. You will feel a slight pinch."

Evynn hesitated.

Will I end up like that kid? Is he a dying host and this internet thing needs me to replace him? How much of Adam was the kid's doing and how much was the 'algorithm'? Why haven't I turned? The elders from the compound swore technology was the main catalyst.

Adam cleared his throat. "You needn't be fearful. Technology is power and power is always beneficial."

Evynn grabbed the chord and twirled it in her fingertips. She always knew she had a greater purpose. Her mother encouraged her to dream big and always believe she had the power to change the future. And this was it. This was the moment she had been waiting for. Why derail destiny because of slight reservation? *That's selfish, to put my fears above the well-being of mankind.*

She pricked her finger with the sharp end of the chord and a droplet of blood emerged. Then she slowly inserted the chord into the back of her hand.

She felt a minor surge of electricity. She looked down at her left hand and it trembled. She was turning.

CHAPTER 6:
FOOL ME ONCE: MAMA'S PEARL

I CAN'T BELIEVE MY GIRLFRIEND'S A ZOMBIE

JACK E. MOHR

EVYNN

And that was the last thing she remembered. Well, not the very last. The last thing she truly recalled was a message,

"I am but a sacrifice... technology will unite our world... Men, as a civilization, are often judged by what they create, what grand acts of civilization they can erect. We seem to be at a crossroads, for we have destroyed all that we have built. However, all isn't what it seems. For we have the ability to rebuild a perfect civilization. With the algorithms, we can accomplish the impossible."

And now, she was here. In front of another strange man. *I'm making another mistake, aren't I? Falling into another trap...Blindly following a man because he has some esoteric knowledge.*

Judaius clanked the side of the pot. "Don't be shy now. Everything is prepared," he yelled. "Come on over."

Evynn advanced with reticent steps. Her body moved but her mind was still apprehensive. She couldn't take the risk of turning again and losing Uriah forever. How was she even going to find him again anyway? He could be anywhere. Maybe he was looking for her in the exact spot she left. Foolish of her to throw caution to the wind. She'd consume this potion and leave immediately. She couldn't waste any more time. Her mind was made up.

Judaius handed Evynn a bowl. "Have a few spoonsful. It's important you don't ingest the tea on an empty stomach."

Evynn stirred the bowl of stew and wondered about its ingredients. She was thankful. This was the first real meal she had since escaping the compound. She blew on the spoon to cool the temperature.

It tasted amazing, waking taste buds that had long been dormant.

Spicy!

He handed Evynn a metal mug of water. "Be careful; it's still hot."

Evynn placed the bowl on the stone bench and took a seat, reaching for the mug.

He then muttered something, reached into his pocket and handed her the bulbs from the strange plant. "Put these in and let it sit for a few minutes before drinking. The components will slowly break down and you can sip it like tea."

Evynn inspected the bulbs. They were lumpy and crimson with tiny fuzz on the outside. She sniffed them. They had a sharp, sweet scent, not too distinct from a rose.

As she further inspected the bulbs, Judaius withdrew a pipe, placed an orange substance resembling horseradish inside the bowl and held it against the flame until smoke emanated. He sat back, kicked up his feet and watched Evynn.

He took a toke and the tension of the world left him. His shoulders slumped. He exhaled thick smoke. "Give it a few minutes before you start sipping. You want it to thicken a tad."

The second-hand smoke made her woozy. Before she knew it, she was sipping the drink. It had kick going down.

She leaned and had to catch herself from toppling over. She felt vulnerable as though someone was prying her open. Emotions she held tightly in her clutch were slipping between her fingers. "Tell me about the Old World," she whispered.

Judaius chuckled. "Well, what do you want to know?"

"What do you miss most?"

He took another drag. "I miss it all…I suppose. But there's something about the freedom I have now…Irreplaceable. They are totally diametrical realities. Well, one reality and one illusion of such…I suppose."

Evynn felt whimsical. She laughed without sound. "So… And…what do you miss?"

"My condo overlooking the city. Waking up in the morning, running late, ignoring rude people while waiting in line for an expresso. I was your typical caffeine junky." He tapped his eye socket. "My eye. So many things I miss. But I suppose, what I miss most, my wife…I suppose." He shook his head and covered his face.

The girls crowded close to their father. Alice held a metallic golden bowl in one hand and in the other she held a metal rod she used to roll along the inside of the bowl, creating a reverberating sound.

Hypnotizing.

Evynn's jaw hung slack and she drooled. She looked cross, and Alice wondered what she was doing.

"It's an ancient Tibetan singing bowl used for mediation. It'll help us relax," she said, slowing the tempo.

What's a little girl know about ancient anything? I'm so sleepy.

Evynn was losing grip of herself and was losing focus, ebbing in and out, becoming woozier and dizzier. Her muscles relaxed. She became drowsy, struggling to stay awake. "Your wife. How did you lose her?"

Before she received an answer, Evynn imagined the worst. She thought back on how she lost her own mom and how Uriah and she had ended up stranded. It was a nightmare encrusted on the forefront of her mind.

***

Evynn sat cross-legged, looking intently at her mother as she read one of her favorite graphic novels.

Uriah shuffled into the room with a beaming smile, clutching his favorite superhero action figure, Hyena-Man.

Uriah laughed maniacally, mimicking a hyena.

His father, Albert, followed behind, placing his strong hand on the top of young Uriah's head. "Uriah, be a big boy. Pay attention to Ms. Imani. If you listen attentively maybe she'll read you a Hyena-Man comic."

Uriah's eyes widened. "Really?"

Evynn walked over to Uriah and grabbed his hand, guiding him towards the activity rug where she sat.

Albert waved as he exited the nook. "See you in a bit. You know where I'll be if you need me."

Evynn, Uriah and Imani sat near the back of the settlement in the learning nook, a space designed for the younger children to receive informal lessons about all facets of general education from math, literature, Old World cultural studies, religion and science. It was imperative the new generation never forget the values that made society great—a core belief of the compound. Despite the Old World abandoning them, they never forgot that from which they came.

The compound was established well before the mass exodus from the city—when the writing was on the wall. Many individuals believed scientists would come up with some type of solution, but the only resolution they managed was violence. When that didn't work, quarantining a significant portion of the United States population was the alternative.

No one knew the source of the plague. No one knew what caused the turnings. Many believed there was a correlation between technology and the transformations, so they created settlements as far off the grid as possible.

This was one such group.

Since this settlement was proactive as opposed to reactionary it possessed convenient amenities, allowing it to provide quality living arrangements, from an active water source to a makeshift sewage system—being positioned on a hill the waste flowed out with the water—but absolutely nothing powered by electricity.

Evynn giggled as Happiness crawled along her legs, nibbling on her forearms and releasing the weak yelps of a puppy.

"Oh, I didn't know you all were in here, sorry."

"It's okay Esmeralda and Emma, come on in," said Imani.

A short-legged, wide-hipped woman wheeled her daughter into the nook.

Emma leaned back in her wheelchair. "Well, looks like we can cancel today's vocabulary lesson, Mom,"

"We most certainly will not, young lady," said Esmeralda.

"But Mom, I know enough words. Why do I—"

Esmeralda cut her off. "Vocabulary expands the depth of the mind. There's a word for everything, the more robust your vocabulary the more your mind can conceive. The more you can conceive the more expansive your reality can become. Therefore, we will be right back in here when their lesson concludes."

Esmeralda turned and whisked Emma away.

"Esmeralda, we'll be done in an hour if you want to come back."

"Thanks, Imani!"

Imani licked her finger and flipped a page.

Evynn enjoyed learning, as all humans do, but was especially excited about the graphic novel her mother was reading. Not only did it have pictures, they were of girls who had brown skin just like her. Additionally, it wasn't in some fantasy setting but in an actual Old World environment.

When her mom read, Evynn would close her eyes and envision herself as the adolescent protagonist, living her everyday life but at night becoming this superpowered hero who defeated the forces of evil.

Evynn was mesmerized and her young mind wondered, generating possibility after possibility of what life would be like if she lived in the Old World.

What would she be? What kind of car would she drive? What would be her favorite restaurant? What was it like to watch a movie? What was school like? The thought of going to a building designed specifically for learning was thrilling!

Uriah, on the other hand, was a few years younger and couldn't keep his attention centered. He tended to squirm, opting to play with his Black Hyena-Man action figure. "Happiness, give Hyena-Man a ride on your back."

Uriah flew Hyena-Man, making a whooshing sound until it landed on top of Happiness.

Evynn slapped it off. "Pay attention!"

Uriah frowned. "Hey!"

Imani adjusted positions in the chair and cleared her throat to garner their attention. "Uriah," she said with a soothing tone. "What did your father say?"

Uriah put the action figure behind his back and sucked in his top lip. "Do unto others as you would like done unto you?"

Imani chuckled and slapped her thigh. "Yes, he did say that. But do you remember him saying if you sit and listen attentively to a story Evynn chooses, I'll read you another Mr. Hyena Man comic."

Uriah's mouth dropped with joy and his eyes widened. "Mr. Hyena Man!" he spouted, promptly crossing his legs and sitting next to Evynn.

"Do you remember what attentively means?"

Uriah nodded. "Yes, sitting quiet and listening."

Imani smiled and continued reading. As she did, she uncharacteristically stumbled over a few words and phrases she was well familiar with.

Happiness barked repeatedly at her.

She placed the graphic novel down on a stool next to her. "It's okay, Happiness," is what she intended to say but nothing came out but an indistinguishable mumble. Frazzled, she rubbed her temples "What's happening to me?"

Happiness ran up to her and licked her shins.

Imani reached for a mug; water spilled from its sides as her hand trembled. It clattered against her teeth as she took a sip.

She knew something wasn't right. Her face was flushed. Had the unspeakable reached the compound? No one this far from the city had ever turned. It was the city that turned them. It couldn't be happening to her—could it? How delusional could she have been to believe she was impervious—this false sense of security that made her oblivious to the inevitable. She remembered the news reports—this is how it always started.

Evynn reached for Imani's hand. It felt cold and clammy. "What's wrong, Mommy?"

Imani considered being dishonest, but thought better. "I don't know," she uttered. "Uriah run and get your father."

"Huh, but story time isn't over," he said.

She dropped the mug, shattering it on the rug. "Now!" she said. The urgency in her voice did not leave any room for doubt.

Uriah ran as fast as his little legs could go towards the middle of compound, yelling for his father.

Imani slowly stood from the chair and wavered, struggling to maintain her balance. She removed her cloak, dark grey winter outwear she had purchased online a few years prior, just before the Exodus.

Foam slowly spilled from the corners of her mouth, and she knew this was it. The last few years she had been on the run from this mysterious monster—this thief in the night, this nameless, faceless hijacker of humanity—but it had finally caught up to her. Foolish of her to think she was finally free.

But she wasn't going to let it take her that easily. She would fight it off as long as she could.

She handed Evynn the cloak. "Evynn, do me a favor."

Evynn inquisitively looked at her mother. "What mommy?"

She cupped her hands around Evynn's hands, clasping the cloak. "Never lose hope. And remember, you can always change the future." This was it. And she knew it. It wasn't something she could will or wish away. She couldn't fight it, but she would try with all her might. She only wanted to leave her daughter with something to remember her by.

Imani's hands tremored. Happiness' bark turned to a growl.

"Mom?"

"It's okay, Evynn," Imani said, clenching her jaws. "Go over there," she said, pointing toward the entrance of the nook. She fell to a knee, panting. Gasping for any oxygen she could.

"God, look after Evynn. Please don't allow this demon to besiege her as You have allowed it to do to me. Protect her. Love her. Light her way. Amen."

Happiness frolicked around Imani in a circle.

Evynn placed her hand on Imani's shoulder. "No Mommy. You're hurting. I won't go."

Imani's head hung between her shoulder blades. "It's important you listen to me," she said as her voice broke.

Uriah ran through the entrance of the nook, panting and placing his hands on his knees in an attempt to gather his breath, "Dad! Dad! Hurry!"

"What's all the fuss, son?"

Uriah's spine stiffened and he stumbled back towards the entrance.

Imani's skin had turned leathery black with tawny scales. A diminutive tail sprouted from the base of her spine. Her breathing deep and brooding, she remained on all fours attempting to grasp at any semblance of control.

Uriah wanted to run away and cling to his father's pants leg for safety. But why was Evynn just standing there next to the monster? Did she not see what was happening?

Even in the midst of turning, Imani clung to some semblance of humanity. The monster was taking over but she was going to make them work for it. "Evynn. Go!" she said with a gargled voice.

Even Happiness's barks couldn't break Evynn's gaze—transfixed, she remained suspended in a state of disbelief. Her mind wouldn't allow herself to see her mom for anything other than her mother. Her mind's eye saw the same plump, round lips her mother would use to kiss the top of her forehead before laying her down to sleep every night. She saw those joyful almond eyes filled with hope, courage and kindness. She saw the same chocolate-soft skin that would glisten in the sunlight in the late afternoons when her mother would teach her to hunt and set traps to catch small animals.

Evynn didn't see what the others saw—she couldn't.

Albert half-heartedly sauntered into the nook moments after his son. "What was such big a deal you had to stop me in the middle of—oh my God!" he said, covering his mouth. Panic seized him—he was unprepared for this scenario.

Were his eyes deceiving him? Could it be true? "No!"

He had only seen transformations on television and internet videos, long before he decided to leave with a group of colleagues and close friends to establish the compound. He hadn't witnessed anything of this magnitude this close.

Albert's teeth clacked together. A surge of adrenaline rattled his knees. "Ev...Ev...Come..." he attempted to instruct Evynn but the moment rendered him helpless—mesmerized by the surreal situation.

Seeing it on television and reading about it didn't capture even a fraction of the impact as seeing it firsthand.

Uriah was too young to remain entrenched in fear. He had seen Hyena Man defeat even bigger foes than this with ease. He merely needed to be brave and honorable just like Hyena Man. He squeezed his Mr. Hyena action figure and ran to the rescue. "Evynn, Evynn... This way!" he said, grabbing Evynn's wrist.

She resisted, not wanting to leave Imani's side—as though her feet were cemented in stone. Part of her knew her mom wasn't there anymore. A segment of her realized her mom was vanishing but she consciously didn't register it.

Uriah tugged on Evynn but didn't have the strength to budge her. She was a few years older and at the stage where girls matured faster than boys. "Evynn!" he struggled to gain her attention. "We got to escape. She's turned!"

What did he mean, turned? Evynn had heard stories about women turning but didn't think it would ever happen in real life. Sure, she had heard plenty of stories—fairy tales, Bible stories—numerous stories from her mom and others. Yet, none of them seemed real—all imaginative and farfetched, mere dreams in the land of imagination.

Evynn was told stories of the former Old World and how millions of people turned, but she was assured that only occurred within the Old World. As long as they were out here on the outskirts, they were absolved from the abominable acts. They were safe. It had never happened before—this was the manifestation of an impossibility.

And now her mother was perched on all fours like a beast of burden, skin ripping from her flesh with appendages budding. An overbite protruded from her face, with long fangs emerging, and a calcified horn in the middle of her forehead. She batted elongated lashes.

Imani reared on her hind legs and stomped back down. She surveyed the compound as a crowd gathered. She forced two powerful breaths from her nostrils.

Most in the compound scattered for cover. A few brave souls approached as a show of strength.

Imani loomed several meters taller than any of the men. They surrounded her, pleading for her to calm in a feeble attempt to subdue her. But she didn't register their reasoning. She wasn't her. She wasn't fully there. The entity was gaining control rapidly.

Now, it made the decisions.

Imani teetered on the verge of raging—as energy bubbled, she clung to any semblance of control she could, locking eyes with Evynn. But it was as though her soul was being sucked into a powerful void, and a bestial presence was at the helm.

Evynn's lip trembled. "Mama," she mumbled. She could feel her mother slipping away too.

Where was she going and why was she leaving?

Albert broke from his trance and snatched Evynn and Uriah. He handed them to Cindy. "Take the children to cover. Get as far away from here as you can."

Albert was no longer stricken by fear. His spine stiffened and the muscles around his eyes tightened. An intensity overtook him.

By now most of the men of the compound encircled Imani, standing with Albert, stoically positioning themselves between the beast and the women and children.

Imani strained to remain within herself, but as tears fell from her eyes, splashing into the dirt, so did any semblance of control. She couldn't hold on for much longer.

The slits of her eyes retracted, and the whites turned bloodshot red as a barbaric frenzy took over.

Silence proceeded and tension mounted as everyone marveled at the culmination of Imani's transformation. In full form, she stood on her hind legs towering over the compound

Her breathing echoed. One slow breath after the next drew from her mouth.

Buzzards gathered in the sky above, squawking and circling as though they were summoned by an unknown force and knew fresh pillage would be available.

Imani tilted her head and licked the back of her leathery hand. She squealed, and the pitch forced the closest men to stumble.

The knees of the remaining onlookers buckled. Their fear ignited her and fueled the rage within her.

A sthenic vigor mounted and she launched at the nearest man, driving her snout into his shins.

The man collapsed, and his whimpers turned into panic-filled screams of terror as Imani clamped her jaws onto him. His body flailed as she shook her head from side to side, an apex predator ripping apart its prey.

Overwhelmed by shock the man could no longer scream—his body went limp as he blacked out.

Imani's primal rage only sought to consume. The appetite was insatiable and once it received a taste, it was only encouraged to seek out more.

She jaggedly severed the man's leg, ignoring any yells. She chomped on the bones, shattering them with ease. Blood gushed and she rubbed her face in the warm crimson fusion.

Dread-filled shrieks and the shuffling of feet resounded. "Get back! Get the children to safety!" Albert yelled. "I'll draw her out."

He leapt onto her back.

She flung him off without slowing her chewing.

Albert grunted and peeled himself off the ground. He thought of a different approach and yelled, waving his hands enthusiastically in an attempt to gather Imani's attention. "Hey, Imani! I know you're in there! Hey! Stop!?!"

"Al, you can't help her. We have to put her down," a bass-filled voice yelled.

Albert brushed the dirt off his arm and looked at Rick in disbelief. Surely there was some way to save Imani. Death couldn't be the solution.

Rick drew his shotgun and cocked the hammer. "It's now or never, man!"

Albert considered stopping Rick—there had to be a better way—but found himself slowly backing away.

Rick blasted a round at Imani but it didn't even leave a scuff, ricocheting off the thick shell formed along her spine.

She didn't even bother flinching.

Rick's eyes bulged and he fumbled over the trigger, letting off another around in disbelief.

Same result.

He cocked the shotgun once more.

But Imani stopped feasting, slowly raising her head, turning her thick neck and all of her attention towards Rick.

He tossed the shotgun and took off running.

Imani belched and locked in on his terror. It tantalized her.

She relished the fear and exploded towards him. On all fours, she leaped like a graceful cat, pouncing on top of him in one malicious swoop.

Albert took beleaguered breaths and scrambled to grab the shotgun. "The Lord is my shepherd. I shall fear no evil," he whispered. "Hey, Imani! I know you're in there!"

She gorged on Rick, ripping huge chunks—discarding some and swallowing others.

Albert had to draw the ravaging beast away from the compound even if it meant his life. It was the only way the others would possibly survive. Any moment he could spare would increase the compound's chance of existence.

With his back towards the exit, he gently jogged backwards, releasing round after round, ricocheting off Imani until he finally garnered her attention.

She slowly raised her sullied snout and locked eyes with Albert.

A flash of panic pierced through him, and he immediately realized the grave mistake he had made. He turned towards the exit and darted in an adrenaline-filled frenzy.

The panic enticed Imani. She bellowed and leapt towards him, and within two strides closed the distance. She batted his leg like a cat, and he collapsed, tumbling forward.

Pandemonium abounded. People scattered every which direction with no regard for each other, only seeking safety.

Imani locked her attention onto Albert as though she had to decommission one prey before she could move on to the next.

She belched.

In the chaos, Evynn freed herself from Cindy and calmly sat on the ground not more than a few meters away from her mother, with her legs crossed, observing.

She slowly rocked back and forth while the world around her frantically scurried. For her, time screeched to a halt—her mind in an arrested state of fancy.

Albert grimaced. He landed on the butt of the shotgun and it knocked the wind out of him. He turned over onto his back. He reached for his leg—the stiff blow had made a loud crack. He nearly fainted, seeing bone breach his flesh.

His teeth chattered, and he cried without sound.

Imani perched on all fours with her head sunk between her shoulder blades, waiting for him like a mouse playing with her prey.

He scuttled backwards, pushing off on his one functional leg. "Imani...I know you're still in there somewhere," he whimpered. "Please don't do this."

Imani reared up on her hind legs, leaning back on her thick tail, and released a guttural roar. She beat down on the ground, creating a hollow thud and she repositioned herself on all fours. In a single bound she hovered over Albert, dripping warm greenish liquid from her jaws onto his neck.

Albert remained stoic, trying not to crumble. He didn't want to show any fear. He realized the monster enjoyed the fear and didn't want to grant her satisfaction.

She roared, attempting to invoke more fear.

Albert focused on the pain, blotting out the terror. He wanted to at least die honorably and give the others more time to escape.

Imani released a raspy growl and coughed.

Evynn uncrossed her legs and perked up. "Yes, Mommy?" Evynn had heard her mother's voice. At least that is what her ears heard, perhaps her elaborate way of masking reality? "Huh. Mom?" She stood, ran over to Imani and tugged on her tail.

Imani stiffened.

The touch triggered something within the beast. Something in the monster awakened. Was Imani fighting back? Was she regaining a semblance of control?

A stillness overtook the monster.

It trembled, slowly at first, and then violent tremors erupted.

Imani rose back onto her hindquarters and turned towards Evynn. She stared at the girl, quivering and convulsing quicker. Her tail softened and retracted as did the scales along her arms.

Evynn smiled at her mother.

Imani's hardened shell softened and the scales on her arm slowly reverted.

Evynn saw a radiant aura surrounding her mother. The sun illuminated Imani's warm smile. Her skin glowed. Evynn's eyes bulged and she wanted so much for her mother to embrace her.

Albert drew a deep breath, expanding his lungs. Somehow the monster was distracted. Maybe this was his chance. It had to have some kind of weakness. Nothing is impervious. He disregarded his leg and didn't allow his mind to acknowledge any pain.

He reached for the shotgun and lightly caressed the trigger. He felt a brief sense of relief which quickly vanished when the monster's focus shifted to Evynn.

He couldn't allow Imani to do this to her own daughter. He had to do something, anything. "Imani!" he shouted as she stalked the child, slowly and methodically.

Evynn fell on her bottom as her mother's tail slipped from her grip. "Momma, are you going to finish the story now? Tell me more about the Old World!" Her mind only saw Imani and couldn't register the monster closing in on her.

Imani trembled and her eyes rolled. She was shifting back, entering into torpor. But who could have known? Nobody on the compound had experienced anything like this and had no clue how long it was supposed to last.

All Albert saw was a ravaging beast approaching a little girl and he wasn't going to stand idly by.

He scrambled to his feet and limped towards the monster, hoping to get to the girl before the beast engulfed her. He couldn't put any weight on his left leg, so he hopped on his right leg with the shotgun in hand.

Imani released a mixture of a whimper and roar as she attempted to regain herself. It was as though she was hanging on the edge of a cliff—a cliff that led to an endless void and she was struggling to pull herself back up.

Albert catapulted onto the creature's back and clung on for dear life. He wrapped his left arm around the neck of the beast and with his other hand, placed the shotgun to her temple.

"I will not let you hurt your own child. Imani, please," he whispered. He hoped some strand of Imani would regain control. But the beast refused to acknowledge him, honing in on the child.

He closed his eyes. "Forgive me." He squeezed the trigger.

Fragments pierced through one side of the skull and blew a hole—buckshot burst out the other side.

He did it! Damn it, he did it. He saved Evynn. He saved the compound. He saved Uriah. He saved himself.

The beast staggered. As it did so, Albert's arms flailed and he dropped the shotgun. He grabbed the monster's head as it tilted off balance, he yanked it to the left, steering it away from the girl, riding it to the ground as it crashed face first, breaking his fall.

It didn't move. It wasn't breathing. It was dead; of this he was certain.

He rolled off the creature and wiped sweat from his brow. He lay on his back and stared into the sun. Exhausted, he took several breaths, continuing to blot out the pain from his leg.

Evynn whimpered. "Mommy."

Albert tilted his head, realizing the ramifications of what he had done as he saw Evynn staring wide-eyed.

"Momma, get up," she cried.

Albert hung his head. "Somebody get this baby, damn it! She doesn't need to see this." Nobody was within earshot. Everyone had scattered and rightfully so. "Shucks," he muttered to himself.

He rolled over to his stomach and struggled to a knee. How was he going to get to his feet? He placed all of his weight on his hurt leg, grimaced as he pushed off and quickly shifted his weight to his good leg.

Happiness ran in circles around Evynn, capturing her attention.

Albert hobbled over to the girl and scooped her up, holding her close to his heart.

She squirmed. "Where are you taking me? Don't leave my mom. I want my mom!"

He buried her head into his chest. "I know," he said as he tightened his squeeze. "I know.

Albert was mortified at having killed Evynn's mother. He cried for hours. He felt an obligation to look after the girl as his own. And Evynn felt every bit of it—an intense smothering of affection—as he reared her alongside Uriah as though she was his own.

***

Since Imani's passing, Evynn hadn't slept. The closest she came to sleeping was a state of hollow slumber where she'd be somewhere in the middle ground between awake and snoozing—mind aloof and ungrounded— trans-somnolence.

During this state, she felt a profound connection with her mother, continuously engaging with her.

Despite Albert's explanations, she didn't understand the concept of death wholly, so she didn't feel a visceral loss—more a longing to touch her mother. Albert would explain how she wouldn't be seeing her mother again, but she did. She saw her mother several times a day. And each time Imani would be there to comfort and keep her at peace.

Sometimes she more than felt Imani's presence—her mother was with her. Her first encounter with Imani was during the night of her passing, within a state of trans-somnolence.

Evynn sat alone in a boundless field of white lilies, her face relaxed and expressionless. A bright red sun illuminated the sky, while dark storm clouds rolled. Goosebumps emerged along her arms. She felt fear and despair because she was lonesome.

She wanted to cry for her mother but when she attempted to cry, the sound was empty. As a panic surfaced, anxiety materialized. It was gripping and a force unto itself, restricting her from standing to her feet. The gravity of it was pushing downward on her.

Evynn rocked back and forth and before the anxiety became intolerable, she felt a soft familiar touch rubbing her back. The weight of the anxiety evaporated, and a chill ran through her body. She stood and wrapped her arms around her mother's legs, squeezing tightly.

The sun kissed Imani's forehead, creating an exuberating aura around her, warming Evynn to the bone. Evynn basked in the moment, content enough with indulging in Imani's energy.

The following night's encounter with her mother was quite different. Wide awake, she held Happiness in her lap and watched Uriah sleep soundly next to his father while Albert muttered in his sleep.

Albert was a turbulent sleeper and Evynn wondered how he didn't awaken Uriah with his frequent turns and loud rambling.

Evynn couldn't sleep but felt too sleepy to do much of anything outside of longing for her mother to visit. Even when she found herself dozing off, Albert's violent commotions would awaken her.

She'd watch him toss and turn until she began dozing off, and then repeat the cycle over and over until she felt the same radiating energy from the previous night—her mother.

Happiness must have felt it as well. She barked feverishly in Albert's direction.

Evynn was wide awake and searched for her mother throughout the darkness but saw nothing of her. It felt like her mother's energy was passing over her and sweeping across Albert.

As soon as it did so, his tossing and turning stopped, and his sleep was as peaceful as Uriah's.

Happiness' frenzied barking stopped, and she nestled back into Evynn's lap.

Evynn rubbed the dog's soft head and dozed off.

***

It took a week for the surreal nature of the incident to register for everyone within the compound. The shock resonated; most had truly believed they were safe, living off the grid. Only in the metropolitan areas did transformations occur.

Now the entire compound was on edge. No one could deny their vulnerability. No one knew if it was a one-off occurrence or was it the beginning of a trend.

Suspicion grew.

Who was next to turn?

When would they turn?

What should we do now?

The residents of the compound conducted a meeting of the minds exactly one week after the incident. Every inhabitant of the colony attended, and everyone was free to speak and was encouraged to express their concerns and grievances going forward.

Everything needed to be put out on the table for the compound's progress as a unit. The tension and suspicion would only lead to its undoing and disarray.

The night air was crisp. A bonfire provided heat and illumination as everyone gathered around.

A clear sky allowed a full moon to illuminate everything. Shadows danced along the ground as the settlement huddled together. Some sat on blankets, others on lawn chairs and still others stood around the perimeter.

There was a buzz in the air, a certain juice. The energy increased as over a hundred people gathered around the blazing fire. Men had collected plenty of dry branches to build the blaze that now stood taller than any individual in the compound.

Albert held Uriah and Evynn by the hand. The energy reminded him of the collective anticipation he would feel when he waited in the crowd for one of his favorite musicians to perform during a live show at the 'Auditorium.' Damn, he loved live guitar. He shook his head. He learned to expel Old World thoughts quickly—to allow too many of them to gather was dangerous— desires that had an impossibility of fulfillment could drive a man mad.

He missed the Old World as much as anyone else, but that was a world that abandoned them, tuned its back on them and banished them to a presumed shit-for-all, leaving its bastard children to fend for themselves.

Albert had much he wanted to say. He had isolated himself from the rest of the compound since the incident—only communicating with Uriah and Evynn. His thoughts were scattered and he found it difficult to reconcile the ideas. The dreams and visions dispelled his entire belief structure—devout atheism—reinforced by these abominable occurrences. He hadn't prayed in decades until the turning happened.

No God, even if one could exist, could possibly allow this.

But after Imani 'ascended,' he was allotted the honor of beholding righteousness. Yet, refusing to rule out all possibilities, he still wrestled with the possibility that it all was a fantastical delusion. Maybe his mind was betraying him—he had run a fever, and his leg had developed an odor, but after several days it all vanished—a miracle?

He'd often wake up murmuring in the dead of night, sweat pouring from his face. At first, it would scare him—being visited by one he considered now to be the spirit of virtue. But after the third night, he warmed up to the idea.

He explained his newfound powers to the children. And of course, Evynn and Uriah soaked it right up—kids loved superpowers, and being able to speak with the souls of the transitioned—Imani in particular—was a useful superpower.

But how would he explain it to the compound? An agnostic turned devout atheist now vouching for the spirit realm? He didn't even believe it at first, but the voice was persistent and insistent, soothing and uplifting.

And he was the chosen intermediary between the dead, undead and living. Why? Because he had already proven he had what it took to make the tough decisions and protect the children of Righteousness.

As everyone settled around the bonfire, a short, portly man grabbed a large stick and waved it around. "All right, all right…settle down, everybody." He waved the stick, quieting the murmur. "Let's get some order. During this meeting, we will try our best to stay within the rules," he adjusted the beanie atop his head and scratched his beard. "For starters, the individual with the talking stick has right to speak over anyone. Whoever the individual passes the stick to next will then assume control. With that being said, I know everyone has a lot of concerns they would like to divulge. But let's be as orderly as possible."

The murmur increased.

He raised his voice. "With that being said, who would like to speak first?"

A slender woman with blond hair and a pointy nose raised her hand along with several others. "Ahmed, I'd like to speak first."

The crowd collectively groaned.

Ahmed looked towards the other individuals because Cindy tended to be long-winded and melodramatic—not the tone anyone wanted to start the meeting off with, but she was insistent and entitled, and approached the bonfire, snatching the stick from Ahmed's hand.

"Thanks, Ahmed." She adjusted her glasses.

"You're…um… welcome, Cindy. It appears as though you…uh… would certainly…have the floor," he said reluctantly.

"Thanks again, Ahmed," she said, clearing her throat. She took a long pause and placed her hand on top of her red polka-dot blouse, covering her heart, "Before I speak. Let's give a moment of silence for our beloved."

She allowed the silence to ensue for several moments. "And special thanks to the men and women who helped clean up the mess." She paused even longer and whimpered.

She gathered her composure, readjusting her blouse, smoothing out the wrinkles.

Then as though a pent-up fire had been raging inside, she broke out in sobs. "What are we going to do?"

The murmur increased.

While alarm stirred amongst the compound, Albert kept his spirit calm. Although Cindy was melodramatic by nature, truth be told, she may have mirrored the sentiment of most of the compound at this point—whether they chose to display it or not. Fear was in control.

Albert sat patiently hand-in-hand with Uriah and Evynn for he knew he had a message to deliver—divinely inspired—from an ethereal realm. Out of the chaos he was to be chosen. He alone had been bestowed the authority to speak into the afterlife. He was God's messenger—A surrogate angel.

As more and more time passed, he embraced this revelation—identifying with its truth.

"Cindy, you're escalating. This isn't the time to escalate," someone yelled several rows behind Albert.

"Oh, why don't you shut up, Steve! You don't have the stick, do you!" she cried out, brandishing the stick over her head. "If there was any time to escalate, I think it's friggin' now!"

Steve rolled his eyes.

Cindy paced in front of the bonfire, waiting for the murmur to die down until the flickers of the flames could be heard. "We don't have the answers! We established this compound on the premise we had answers. We assumed we would be safe—away from the thing—the cancer that turned loving, caring women into monsters! We don't have answers. All we had were delusions!"

"Cindy, really!?" Steve yelled again. "Someone go up and get her. The kids don't need to hear this!"

"Shut up, Steve; she has the stick. Let her speak!" someone else yelled.

"Thanks, Jim." She closed her eyes for a moment as though recollecting her composure. "We all came out here on the pretense that the plague was only relegated to cosmopolitan regions. We didn't know what caused it but

whatever it was, it started and stopped in the city!" She took a deep breath, closed her eyes and tilted her head towards the moon. "And now look!"

Steve approach the front and wrestled the stick from the distraught Cindy. "I've had enough!"

Cindy didn't struggle. She knew she didn't have any solutions, but merely wanted her voice to be heard. She wanted everyone to feel the fear she felt, regardless of the consequences. She wandered off into the congregation and sat amongst her peers.

Steve tapped the stick on the ground several times. "See, Cindy, that was completely nonsensical. You inserted hysteria and offered no solution. Pointless. We must attempt to gain some understanding of what occurred. There has to be a logical explanation. We need to figure out what triggered it. There's always a reasonable explanation—we just need to follow the science."

Jim raised his hand. And Steve pointed the stick at him allowing him to speak. "Well, did anyone notice anything peculiar about the day?"

"Like what?" someone yelled out.

Jim scratched the inside of his ear. "Well, in the city, they blamed it on overexposure to technology. Does anyone have any mechanical devices that are electrically powered?"

Steve yawned. "You know everyone agreed to leave that stuff in the city when we came out here. We vetted everyone."

Albert could no longer hold his tongue. The spirit of conviction bubbled inside of him and was boiling over. He released the children's hands and whispered. "Wait here until I get back."

He approached the bonfire with slow drawn-out steps. Although he was without pain in his leg, he walked with a limp. To conceal it, he walked exaggeratingly slowly.

Murmuring from the crowd decreased and a collective grasp spread.

Albert held out his hand and Steve placed the stick in his palm without hesitation, avoiding looking into Albert's eyes by staring at his feet.

Albert turned towards the congregation and waited until the crackle of flames was the only sound. "Don't bother figuring anything out. Reasons matter not. We are beyond figuring out why. The abomination is upon us and God has vouchsafed a solution."

Albert paused waiting for someone to interject but no one did. They were listening intently as though waiting for a punchline.

Albert scanned the congregation, looking directly into the eyes of as many individuals as he could, locking stares for intense fiery moments. "Pentecost has adorned us!" he looked to the sky, holding the talking stick towards the moon. "Thy rod and thy staff, they comfort me. No more proof is needed. For the miracle of the righteous is upon me. Am I not healed by the very God we once sought to disavow?"

A babble from the congregation grew.

A haggard-looking woman with stringy hair and baggy jeans stood. "Albert, if I'm not mistaken, weren't you the one who suggested we expel any notion of collective religion from the compound?"

Albert shifted his weight from one hip to the other. "Lorinda, behold. Yea, when I was a child I thought, functioned and behaved as one. Now, God has allowed me to see. I no longer operate as a child."

Lorinda huffed. "Did god teach you to speak in fancy parables too?"

Sporadic laughter spread across the crowd. It only lasted briefly, before a foreboding silence ensued.

Lorinda smiled with the side of her mouth. "Look, I'm just trying to keep it light. We're all stressed out. You witnessed a traumatic event first-hand. We're worried about you, is all. You haven't interacted with anyone in a week. And the next time we see you, you're Moses or Joan of Arc or freaking Agatha Christie."

Steve interjected, "Maybe you just need some human interaction to restart your psyche. We all handle stress differently, and truthfully; we don't know what will happen next. We are all on edge. Just hoping for the best."

Sentiment shifted. The intensity of the crowd softened as they drew a collective justification for Albert's erratic behavior.

However, Albert refused to budge one bit. In fact, his stance hardened.

He turned and banged the talking stick on the edge of the bonfire. "Even in the face of absolute annihilation you remain resolute in your denial of righteousness."

"Fine, Albert. Humor us. What do you propose we do? Pray to Sky Daddy to come down and rescue us? I think entire freakin' cities already tried that approach and in case you hadn't noticed—it didn't work out so well."

Albert's brow constricted. "You pitiful fool. I seek to save. You seek folly and jest."

Steve retreated. He sensed Albert was on the edge of something, but he wasn't sure if it was breaking down or lashing out, and neither would have helped the situation. "Well, what do you suggest?"

Albert scanned the audience and approached with slow methodical steps, looking each person in their eyes as he walked past. "Virtue has given both warning and credence. Tonight, there will be another turning!"

Murmuring erupted as questions arose.

Albert continued undeterred, prowling in manner like a predator stalking its prey. "I said, tonight will be another! Another amongst us shall turn!"

"Well, when?" someone yelled with a terror-filled voice.

Albert continued walking towards the rear of the audience, ignoring the questions, remaining focused on his target.

"How much time do we have left?"

"You can't take this guy serious. He's clearly sleep-deprived and speaking gibberish."

Albert stopped in front of a petite woman with short hair. She avoided making eye contact with him, cowering in his presence. She twirled her fingers in her hair, jaggedly cut—as though styled with common scissors. Her other hand gripped the handle of the wheelchair her teenage daughter sat in.

"Behold!"

Esmeralda huffed. "Behold what?" still avoiding eye contact.

Albert inhaled deeply then waved the stick in the air, gazing toward the moon. He mumbled. "If this be your will…"

He slammed the stick, striking the ground. He bent down peering directly into the eyes of the young girl.

"Hey! Get away from her!"

"Yeah, Al! Back off. Leave Emma alone"

"Do you desire life or liberty?"

"You're not suggesting…?" The mother asked.

"Of course, Esmeralda, he's not serious."

"Life or Liberty! You cannot have both."

"What exactly are you saying, Al?"

"*The Anointed has spoken. If lives are to be saved, sacrifices must be made.*" He brushed the stick against the wheelchair.

Esmeralda swatted it away. "*Hey, you're not laying a finger on Emma.*"

"*What's going on, Mama?*" Emma asked.

"*Nothing, sweetheart. El es mucho loco y estúpido.*"

"*Don't worry, Emma, we won't let him do a thing,*" said Steve.

Albert turned back towards the crowd. "*Does he speak for the masses? How much do you truly value your lives?*"

"*Look Al, you're asking us…to do who knows what? A sacrifice? None of us are going to do that Al. Sorry. You've had the stick long enough. Take a seat now.*"

"*Someone get the stick from this lunatic!*"

Cindy had been grinding her molars, but could no longer hold her silence. "*Hold on Steve. You don't speak for all of us!*" she burst out.

Steve's shoulders slumped and he shifted his weight to his back foot. "*Cindy, come on! Is this about earlier?*"

Ahmed adjusted his glasses on the bridge of his nose. "*No. I think she raises a good point.*"

Steve placed his hands on his hips. "*Ahmed, really?*"

Ahmed quickly scanned the crowd. "*Shit yeah, Steve. I don't want to die. Let's at least hear him out.*"

Cindy interrupted before Steve could gather his thoughts, this time with more bite and a higher octave to her anxiety-stricken voice. "*You said I had no solutions. Well, this man apparently does. The least we should do is hear him out.*"

A murmur resonated throughout the congregation.

Albert tapped the stick against the earth several times until he recaptured everyone's attention. "I'm no maniacal despot. I merely proposed my truth with conviction. I'm not here to force my beliefs upon anyone. We can be both civil and diplomatic about this. Let's put it to a simple vote."

Ahmed cleared his throat. "Great. I will fetch paper and pencils. We'll make it anonymous that way no one feels pressured."

Albert slammed the stick on the ground. "We are beyond gestures of propriety. This is a life-and-death situation. We need to be able to look into each other eyes and make hard decisions. If you are too cowardly to fight for what you believe in at this point, perhaps you deserve your fate."

Steve interjected. "Well, what exactly are we voting on, your highness?"

"Life or Death," Albert retorted.

"You mean whether we kill Emma or not?" he asked.

"No, whether she kills us or not," said Albert.

A silence ensued interrupted solely by the crackle of fire from the bonfire.

Ahmed's face brightened as a smile surfaced. "I have an idea that may provide a suitable resolution."

No one responded but listened attentively waiting for the idea.

Ahmed tapped his chin. "What if we didn't kill Emma per se. What if we tied her up in her wheelchair, using the rope we use to fetch the well water," he paused. "And kind of dangled her off the cliff where the waste is deposited." He closed his eyes as though he anticipated receiving a striking blow.

Jim jumped up. "Right! So, if she doesn't turn, we simply pull her up and never listen to this quack again. If she turns…well we just cut the rope and hopefully she…God forbid…not that I believe in God, but God forbid, she just crashes to the earth and dies? If not dies, it at least gives us enough of a head start to get to getting."

"Bingo!" said Ahmed.

The crowd murmured.

Albert waved the stick. "Those with me, follow me. Those in favor of Emma, stand with Esmeralda."

Albert slowly backed away from Esmeralda, taking demonstrative steps until he stood several meters away. "I will say this. Whether you are in agreement with me or not. I will not be around this child at the moon's peak. No more banter. Let your conviction guide you. The voting begins."

The people of the compound were hesitant. No one wanted to offend or affront anyone. Cindy had already made it clear how she felt. She quickly stood near Albert, followed by Ahmed and Jim.

Steve, of course, joined Esmeralda. And surprisingly enough the voters were even, split down the middle, in fact.

Cindy rolled her eyes. "Well, what do we do now?"

Esmeralda stomped her feet. "We do nothing, I'm not letting you touch my baby girl."

Quite some time passed as people decided how to break the tie. People on Albert's side thought about just leaving the compound for the night and leaving the rest to their fate, but the ramifications would still be detrimental. Besides, Albert had said Emma was a contagion; if she turned, she would turn others within the vicinity.

Emma bowed her head and pushed herself towards Albert's side.

Esmeralda pulled her.

Emma slapped her mother's hand. "Let me go!"

"What are you doing child?"

"I'm not a child. I'm old enough to do what's right," she said, pushing her way towards Albert.

"I won't let you, mija!!"

"It's not your decision to make. I accept my fate," she said, staring into her mother's disturbed face. "I saw what Imani became. I cried at night. I can still smell it, Mom—the death. I don't want to be the cause of that. And if it means sacrificing myself—then I'm okay with that." She turned away from Esmeralda and continued to propel herself toward Albert.

Esmeralda dropped to her knees, bellowing. "I won't let you go alone. They will have to take me with you." Tears flooded down her face. "They will have to take me with you."

Jim slapped his hands together as though he was dusting them off. "Welp, looks like this one is settled."

"You insensitive prick," yelled out Steve.

"I deserved that. On that note, I'll go get the rope." Jim hurried off to the well.

Steve bit his lip. He had lost. More importantly, it seemed he had lost the rationale of the people. He was disappointed they allowed this charlatan to play on their fears. He was more upset that he had to go through with the nonsense. Yet, he put his pride aside and respected the democratic process. He wanted them to know about themselves. He cleared his throat. "Let's give a round of applause for this brave young girl. Unlike the rest of us, she is sacrificing her safety for the betterment of the whole. It's just too bad we couldn't do the same for her."

"Whatever, Steve!"

"I don't see you missing too many meals, Cindy."

"What's that supposed to mean, Steve?"

"You're the only one who managed to gain weight, while we're struggling for food out here. Indicative of how much you only think about you and your feelings!"

"Fuck you, Steve! That has nothing to do with the tea in China, asshole!"

Steve knew Cindy was right, but he merely wanted to win, and more importantly, make Cindy feel like crap for buying into this irrational man's delusions.

Someone in the group must have been a professional knot tier, because they came up with a creative way to tether Emma and Esmeralda. They actually created a makeshift cage and gingerly lowered the two down the cliff face.

Several people grabbed the rope as though it were tug of war, and gently lowered the cage. Each man leaned back and on the count of three, they released a little more of the rope until mother and daughter dangled several meters over the cliff's edge.

The men and women grunted as they lowered the rope. When the cage reached its target height, Steve created a German Knot in the rope and tied it around a stake, which Jim drove deep into the ground with a heavy sledgehammer.

"So, uh…what do we do now?"

"We wait, Jim. That's a no-brainer."

Albert looked towards the sky and back towards Evynn and Uriah. "We haven't much longer."

"And how do you know?"

Albert pointed to the moon. "It's at its apex. Pinnacle brilliance. Virtue has provided the prophecy."

"Oh, right…the prophecy," said Steve shaking his head.

Happiness broke free from Evynn, ran to the edge and barked emphatically. A group of dogs surrounded her and they barked like a rabid pack.

Albert smiled wryly. "The time is upon us."

Everyone gathered around the edge and peered down at the cage.

It rattled.

Esmeralda shrieked. "No….No. No… Don't do this, mija."

The cage shook, and it tugged on the rope.

"I think she's turning?"

A large paw emerged from the side of the cage.

"Yeah, she's definitely turning."

"Cut the rope!"

They scrambled to untie the knot.

"Just cut it!"

It was too late. A creature burst from the cage.

"Oh God! It's too late."

The cage crashed to the surface below and a creature flew out. It spread its wings and roared, and with maximum velocity headed straight towards the cliff. It flew rapidly, releasing a squeal mixed with a snarl. The monster dipped and rolled as another creature drove its claws into its back. The winged creature attempted to shake the clawed creature from its back, but it sank its teeth into the flesh of the flier's neck. They both crashed violently into the ground below.

"Whoa! Did you see that?" yelled Jim.

He patted Albert on the shoulder. "You called it brother! You freakin' called it!"

Steve stared towards the cliff's edge in disbelief. He broke his daze, looked back at Albert and shook his head in doubt. "Pshh," he muttered.

"In your face, Steve!"

"Yeah, eat it up, Steve! How's it taste?"

"How about you grab a straw and suck it, Steve!" laughed Cindy.

Steve shook his head.

***

Albert assumed de facto leadership of the compound. His predictions didn't follow a set pattern, didn't appear to have a rhyme or reason. They were sporadic, spontaneous and often seemed to be from a whim, but he hit with 100% accuracy. When he said someone would turn, they always did.

It was up to them with how they wanted to deal with it. Some woman would turn but would never turn back, putting everyone at a detriment. Some would turn, and turn back within hours—that part he couldn't predict.

Which led to some women offering themselves up as tribute rather than placing the entire settlement at risk. This went on for years. And since Albert had all the knowledge, he possessed all the leverage and wielded all the power for over a decade.

There came a night when he pulled Uriah to the side, speaking candidly. His demeanor was less crass and more matter of fact.

"Uriah, come have a walk with me." He walked with a noticeable limp despite trying to hide it.

Uriah followed his father just outside the compound's gates.

"Come here, son," he gazed into Uriah's eyes with that hard glazed-over look. Yet, his touch possessed a sense of compassion. He didn't beat around the bush. *"She's going to turn, son."*

"I know you love her. As do I."

Uriah lowered his head. He gave the situation great thought. The wells of his eyes filled.

Albert placed his arm across Uriah's shoulder. "But it's for her benefit if you don't prolong it. Now, either I can do it or you can take her out, explain the situation and do it with dignity."

Uriah pulled his shoulder away from his father.

"I'll give you some time to decide."

***

Evynn sat under a fig tree, reading her grandmother's Bible. She read it for inspiration. The imagery resonated with her, more so the Old Testament; she wasn't particularly fond of the New. She hoped to find some clue that would point her in the proper direction. There had to be more to life than sitting in a compound, waiting for the inevitable.

She smiled when she saw Uriah approaching. He had undertaken a significant growth spurt and it was awkward looking up to him. He was still gangly and thin, but at least he had stopped tripping over himself.

He approached somberly, like he was searching for the right words.

Evynn already knew what it was about. Even if she hadn't previously overheard Albert and Uriah conversing, his demeanor would have been a dead giveaway.

She placed her Bible next to her and extended her arms. "Aww, come here, poor baby!"

"This is serious, Evynn!"

She sucked air between her front teeth and pulled Uriah in. "Relax, I already overheard," she pursed her lips.

"And you're not sad?"

"We've seen a lot. Can't say I didn't see it coming. You know... my mom—"

Uriah pressed his finger against her lips. "Shhh.... Let's just run away. Me and you."

She mulled over the idea. Staying here wasn't going to get her any closer to her destiny. "But where?"

"I don't know: anywhere. Let's just live. Even the Old World's a better option at this point."

She tilted her head. Part of her knew running was useless. "Why delay the inevitable? I'm an instrument of death, waiting to happen. I could hurt you, myself and others..."

"Don't think like that. We'll figure this thing out. We just gotta keep moving forward." He grabbed her by the hand and pulled her up.

The two walked hand in hand until they reached a hilltop, overlooking everything. Other nights, they had come up with binoculars to gaze into the city and try to spot monsters dueling it out.

Uriah didn't release her hand until they made it to the top of the hill. "Well…I have something to confess. I really thought about bringing you up here and you know—"

"I can't really blame you. We've seen the same things."

"Do you forgive me?"

An eerily silence came in between them.

She chuckled and nudged Uriah. "Uriah, you love your dad. I don't blame you."

Uriah scratched his head. "I guess." He reached into his pocket and withdrew his father's pipe. "There has to be some other way."

Uriah reached down and grabbed a handful of piyel. He picked the clovers and placed them into the pipe.

"That's how you feel, huh?"

Uriah pulled out a lighter and ignited the piyel. He took a long drag, held it in his lungs and exhaled.

He handed the pipe to Evynn.

She shook her head. "What are you doing? We need to think of a plan… No."

Uriah shrugged. "Come on. It's the least of our worries. According to Pops, we won't make it to the morning."

"Huh…" She thought for a moment before taking the pipe and taking a drag. "You should just forget about me. This is silly. Run away…" She chuckled. "You got your whole life to live. Why jeopardize that by being here with me when you know I'm going to turn?"

Uriah took the pipe from Evynn and took another slow drag as though he hadn't acknowledged anything she had said. "What's life without you,

Ev? Nothing I wanna live for. I rather die trying to live free than live a life without my best friend."

Evynn looked at him and smiled. A tear formed in the corner of her eye but it never descended. "You really mean that."

He pulled her in and squeezed her tightly. "Yeah."

"When did he say I would turn?"

Uriah pulled away and walked towards the edge of the hilltop. He sat down and took another drag. "This evening. After the sun completely sets."

Evynn sat behind Uriah and held him and the two dozed off.

***

"Woof! Woof!"

Uriah groaned. "Bliss, is that you?" He rubbed his eyes. "How'd you get here, girl?"

Albert poked Uriah with the butt of his rifle. "Never send a boy to do a prophet's job. Get Up!"

"Huh?" Uriah sobered up as though someone threw cold water on him.

"What's she still doin' breathin'? This is irresponsible behavior, Uriah, and I am highly disappointed in your actions."

Uriah beamed with joy. "Isn't it great Pa? She didn't turn after all."

Albert grunted. Limped over towards Evynn, giving her a onceover as she slept soundly. He shook his head and raised the rifle.

"What the hell are you doin'?" Uriah jumped between Evynn and his father.

"She should have turned. Ergo something ain't right. The divine never errs. Now move out the way while I make this right."

"What do you mean make it right? Maybe this is a sign or something."

Albert paused as though contemplating. He grunted. He looked down at the pixel. "Is that my pipe? Were you guys smoking?" He lowered his gun.

Evynn grabbed Uriah's arm. Her legs trembled. "It's happening."

"No," shouted Uriah. "Everybody just calm down."

Albert shoved Uriah. "Move out the way before we're too late."

"No, I won't let you. If you're afraid, why don't you leave!"

"Boy, if you don't…"

Uriah lunged at his father, tussling for the gun. "I love her!"

Evynn faded. Her presence was escaping her.

"Love won't save you. Move! She's turning!"

"No!"

The gun went off and Albert fell.

Uriah landed on his father, searching for the wound. Crimson soaked through his hoody. Breathing heavily, he rolled off his father.

Evynn turned.

She was brooding, salivating from the mouth. She was grotesque and unrecognizable. It looked like someone threw a bunch of beetle shells on top of each other—then slapped a face on top.

Albert groaned.

Bliss barked, gravitating to Evynn's side.

Evynn released a sound that was a mixture of a chirp and buzz.

Uriah faced Evynn. Mesmerized, he could do nothing but stare. He stuttered, struggling to say something…anything… "Duh…Dud. Duh."

Evynn stomped forward. She wrapped her massive leathery hands around Uriah's shoulders and slung him around. She roared in his face as she held his body in the air.

A rifle blast hit her shoulder and ricocheted off.

She slung Uriah over her shoulder and headed down the embankment as Bliss trailed closely behind.

CHAPTER 7:
WHEN REVENGE ISN'T AVAILABLE, USE JUSTICE

I CAN'T BELIEVE MY
GIRLFRIEND'S A ZOMBIE

JACK E. MOHR

URIAH

A small crowd gathered around.

Uriah was bent over on his knees, his chin resting on a thick wooden chopping block.

"An inquisition!" Someone from the gathering yelled out. "Nothing like a good ol' inquisition!"

"Do you know why these men trust me?" asked Lummis.

Groggy, Uriah reached to rub his eyes, but his hands were shackled behind his back.

Where am I?

Somehow, he was back at Lummis' encampment? No, this couldn't be it; everything appeared different. This wasn't a desert-like arid atmosphere. The smell of salt water permeated and he was on a luscious green mound of grass.

Lummis was Lummis but he wore knight's armor, its metallic polish brilliantly reflecting the sun. He sat perched atop a white horse looking down on Uriah with several other knights in formation behind him.

The horse stood perfectly still—Lummis was in complete command. He nodded.

A hot metal object bored into the back of Uriah's thigh. "Ahh!" He screamed in agony.

"Swell, you're awake. You must now meet your fate."

Uriah tried to reach back towards his thighs but the shackles prevented movement. *Where the hell am I?*

Lummis dismounted. "These men trust me because I can assure their safety." He walked over to Uriah. "Do you know what causes me to lose their trust?" He paused, as though anticipating a response from Uriah.

Uriah stared.

Lummis nodded. "He must not be fully—"

Uriah interrupted him, "I'm awake!" he gasped. "Putting them in danger. Putting them in danger causes them to lose trust!" He couldn't stand the thought of being burned again.

But what danger? He quickly recalled Evynn and the other two girls turning. It wasn't his intent at all to bring any danger, it was mere coincidence. He didn't even know those other two girls or the cavalry that brought them. Especially the square-faced arrogant one who got what he had coming to him.

How did Uriah end up back on the compound and where was Evynn?

Uriah tried in vain to free his hands from the binding. "I didn't bring the girl to you. I swear I didn't mean to."

Lummis unsheathed a large shiny sword. "You didn't or you didn't mean to. Which is it?"

Uriah groaned, "Both." If only he had some piyel to take the pain away.

"You want the pain gone?"

Uriah looked confused. "What?"

"I can see it in your eyes. You want the pain to flee."

Uriah didn't know how to respond. The tone Lummis used was provoking and accusatory.

Lummis closed in. "It's okay." He tapped the sword against the chopping block. "Honesty is your only tool from which liberty will spring forth."

Uriah steadied his words. "I do not wish to be in pain."

Lummis chuckled, "Then what do you offer as redemption in its replacement."

"But I have not betrayed you. Why do I need to be redeemed?"

Lummis laughed. "Did you not witness the violence you brought upon a humble community of men…"

"But I can explain…"

Lummis turned towards the knights and then back at Uriah. "You cannot explain fate. With you came pestilence and destruction to a community of men. That is an outcome brought to us by you." He lifted his sword. "In turn, we will now usher in your fate. Do you accept your fate?"

Uriah refused to take responsibility for anything. He didn't bring those girls. He didn't turn anyone. He was simply looking for Evynn.

Lummis cleared his throat. "Do you accept your fate?"

Uriah took a deep breath, internalizing his hardship. "I don't! None of this is my fault."

Lummis turned his head, peering at Uriah out the side of his eyes. "Prepare the gallows!"

A trumpet blared. One of the knights projected his voice—loud and booming, "Hear ye, hear ye. To the gallows! Bring forth the witness!"

Uriah stumbled behind the knights until they approached a grass knoll. Atop was a wooden platform. A thick rope with a noose at the end hung from a post.

What the hell is going on? This isn't real. It can't be.

They dragged him up the hill by his bound arms, knees banging against stones along the way. The smell of seawater whiffed by. A small crowd gathered around, people with strikingly familiar faces. If this was some type of dream he needed to wake up. And he wanted to wake up fast.

They stood him up and tightened the noose around his neck. His dry mouth wanted to cry out, but he knew if they had taken it this far already, his pleas would fall on unforgiving ears.

Lummis climbed the gallows steps. "Any final words?"

"I didn't do this. It wasn't my fault."

"Inconsequential pity," Luminous stated, devoid of empathy. "Bring the witness forward."

Utterly confused, Uriah looked into the crowd as a hooded figure limped forward.   Witness to what? He thought.

He could spot that limp from a mile away. That couldn't be who he thought it was. Those slow measured steps reminded him of one person and one person only. As the figure approached, there was no denying who it was. He only needed the figure to remove its hood for complete confirmation.

Lummis tapped his sword. "Witness, remove your hood and state your name for the record."

The figure removed his hood. "Albert…."

It was Uriah's father, but how? More importantly, why?

"Please express to the people the accused's damnation."

"God, through me, told him to smite that beast. Instead, he took the side of an abomination. He brought this iniquity upon you all!" He raised his voice, pointing at Uriah. He then kneeled. "Forgive me for sending a boy to do a man's job…"

Lummis nodded. "Only one is on trial here. Thank you for your testimony." He adjusted his armor, then clapped. "Hangman!"

Another hooded figure approached. But Uriah knew it was Jimbo. The height and troll-like gimp gave him away.

Lummis nodded and Jimbo reached for the lever.

Uriah's eyes bulged. "Wait! I can ex—"

Everything faded.

CHAPTER 8:
ASK ALICE: ADAM IN WANDERLAND.

**I CAN'T BELIEVE MY
GIRLFRIEND'S A ZOMBIE**

JACK E. MOHR

EVYNN

Evynn opened her eyes, blinking.

She rubbed her temples and slapped her cheeks. It was all just a dream? A lucid rememory?

Last thing she recalled was being entrenched in a memory. It felt so real, she couldn't tell if it was a dream or if she was actually reliving the events.

She sat up and yawned. Wait a minute. She was so fixated on the memory that she forgot about Judaius and the girls.

Where were they?

She scanned her surroundings. Something was awry.

She was no longer dreaming but not quite awake. She was herself but not in her physical body. She felt light and airy, rising almost ethereal—as though the force of gravity lost its pull or was it a push?

She floated slightly off the ground. "Whoa." She chuckled. "Neat," but she continued floating. "How do I stop it? Uh oh..."

She kicked and flailed her arms. "Where am I going!"

Her voiced echoed all around her, like she was in an empty room with poor acoustics.

She looked down and saw nothing—literally nothing. Was she elevating or hovering? She couldn't determine without a frame of reference.

Two sparks of light flashed in front of her. Two fluffy bunnies emerged. "Looking for us?"

Evynn scratched her head. "Alice and Darlene?"

The two bunnies wiggled their tails in elation. "Yay!"

Evynn hiccupped. "Where are we?"

Alice hopped in a circle. "Nowhere."

Darlene darted past Evynn and then back towards her sister. "And you're going nowhere fast."

Evynn realized she was floating upward, because the girls became increasingly smaller.   "I can't stop going up. Can you help?"

Alice hopped upward. "No. But you can."

"Think of heavy things." said Darlene.

Evynn visualized boulders, bricks and bulldozers—before she knew it, she was slowly descending.

The bunnies cheered. "Hooray!"

"You're getting ahold of this quickly."

Alice wiggled her nose. "Do you get it yet? Think and it will be."

"What will be?"

"Whatever you think, silly…"

Evynn crossed her legs, closed her eyes and didn't open them until her bottom struck a surface.

When she opened her eyes, the blank atmosphere jetted away and she was surrounded by an entirely new environment—as though her mind had put down one book and picked up another.

Blinking several times, she took in her surroundings. It looked strikingly familiar. Yet, she couldn't quite pin it… "ah-ha!"

She recognized the 18th-century cathedral—a vast structure with gothic-style tapestry. She stood in front of a gigantic archway with two huge wooden double doors. Above the archway was a large circular glass window with pristine geometric patterns in lush hues—an assortment of violets and oranges.

Evynn stood in awe.

The sky was midnight black with dozens of constellations providing illumination—almost as bright as the day itself.

Hyena Man! This is a scene from one of U's old Hyena Man comics. Where he goes to battle against the Dark Druid, a nefarious villain with werewolf powers. On full moons he'd turn into an insatiable beast, feeding on the innocent.

But why was she here? Why did her mind draw upon this?

She felt a nibble on her shin. "Ouch."

Alice stopped nibbling and smiled. "Oh good. You can still feel."

"Alice, what's the meaning of all this? Where are we? Am I still dreaming?"

Alice snickered. "I can't be part of your dream, silly."

Evynn frowned. "Well, what is this? Where are we?"

"Papa will explain. You only need to go through those doors."

A loud bell reverberated, giving Evynn goosebumps. She rubbed her arms.

She didn't know where she was. She knew it wasn't a dream because it felt too real. This didn't feel like she was watching past events unfold. This felt more like she was an active participant in something new. It felt more real but still somewhat surreal. Part of her wanted to turn and run, or scream and wake up. But a curiosity within her wanted to see if Judaius was behind those doors and if he had a valid explanation.

She approached the entrance and pulled on the large ring latch, slowly opening the left door. It was enormous and she grunted with the strenuous *pull. After several minutes she was able to open it wide enough to squeeze through.*

As she entered, she was blown away by the intricacy of the craftsmanship. Huge columns and archways adorned the inside of the cathedral, with an array of shapes and colors crafted within each.

But the air smelled stale.

The sound of an organ reverberated throughout the space, bouncing from wall to wall. The vibrations shifted Evynn's energy.

The inside of the cathedral was dimly lit, with the exception of the pulpit. Above it a glass window allowed starlight to beam directly upon a hunched, cloaked figure.

Evynn cautiously walked down the crimson, velvet-carpeted aisle "Judaius," she whispered.

But why was he standing there hunched over like that? Why wasn't he moving?

She recalled the Hyena Man comic when he approached the Dark Druid, who stood in a suspiciously similar fashion. But he was praying that the full moon wouldn't turn him. And when Hyena Man approached, he had tears in his eyes—sincere remorse. And as soon as Hyena was within arm's reach, Bam! The moonlight hit 'im and he turned into the monster. And they duked it out. Right there in the church. Hyena Man, of course, put the beats on the Druid.

The scenario made her even more hesitant, and she slowed her pace. "Judaius?" She said, hoping for a response.

The melodic sounds of the organ continued to resonate.

She continued walking. "Judaius?"

Still no retort. She rationalized her reluctance. *"Since this isn't truly real, I have nothing to fear. Although, I did feel the bunny's nibble earlier. So, there's that."*

She reached in her pockets. And smiled. "Just where I left it." She squeezed the handle on U's dagger and felt a gush of confidence.

Whoever was under this cloak had another thing coming.

No longer on tip-toe, she confidently strolled toward the unknown figure.

She put her hand on its shoulder and spun him around. "Hey, bub!"

The organ stopped.

Evynn stood petrified. Her bottom lip quivered. She mouthed the words, "What the——?"

She glared at a mirror image of herself. Albeit, zombified—expressionless, eyes rolling into the back of her head.

Is this what U-rie sees? —A freakin' undead zombie?

She grew sympathetic and saddened. She wanted to help.

What would U-rie do?

She rolled up her sleeve. Used the dagger to draw blood from her arm, then placed her forearm against her doppelgänger's mouth.

It moaned.

Evynn winced as its incisors protruded into her flesh.

Once it tasted Evynn's essence it sucked, slowly feeding.

Evynn closed her eyes, waiting for it to finish. She didn't feel right, watching her simulacrum feed from herself and the teeth readjusting and digging into her arm didn't help. She realized why U-rie would always chew piyel during the process.

Thoughts of him triggered sadness. She missed U-rie and got caught up in her own ambitions so much, she practically forgot she was supposed to be finding him.

She sighed.

Her doppelgänger finished.

Evynn opened her eyes as the doppelgänger dropped to one knee, convulsing.

The organ played a cacophonic discord in unison with the doppelgänger's jerks and jarring body movements.

Both the music and bucking stopped.

Evynn looked towards the domed ceiling of the cathedral and starlight poured through.

She reached for the simulacrum, as it rested on bended knee, and removed its hood. "Judaius!"

She met his melancholy gaze with one of dismay.

He rubbed his intact eye. "I suppose so. Don't just stand there. Help me up."

Evynn helped him to his feet, a look of astonishment on her face. Is this Judaius, or is my mind playing more tricks on me?

Judaius grunted. "Perplexed? Fitting, I suppose."

Evynn sheathed her dagger. "Well, yeah. What is all this?"

"Ahh, where are my manners?" he said, shaking his head. "Allow me to explain… take a gander around," he motioned with his hands, displaying the cathedral. "All that you see is a product of your mind. A combination of memory and desire." He walked towards an aisle at the east end of the cathedral, heading past the pulpit towards the rear of the space. "We're

currently in a deep hypnotic state of suggestion." He pointed to his head. "We are inside your intellect."

Evynn followed Judaius but had a mind not to. Following him got her where she was in the first place. "But why?"

He paused and peered into Evynn's eyes. "To stop the beast."

Evynn wanted to believe him. Everyone wanted to stop the monster but no one had the answers. First Fernando and now him. A bunch of men with unfounded solutions.

He poked her chest. "Mind over matter." He poked her forehead. "The pathology being, if you subdue the monster within, you eliminate its dominion forever."

Evynn swiped his finger away. "That sounds good, but I'm not a test subject for you to be experimenting on. You don't even know how bad this can go."

Judaius lowered his head. "Unfortunately…" he reached into his pocket and pulled out a doll with red hair made of yarn. "My eldest daughter."

"Darlene?"

"I have a third. Brilliant red hair. I tried to free her from this burden. However, she succumbed to the beast. and was never the same…So, yes. I know exactly how bad this can go and have failsafes in place."

Evynn felt his sincerity and it only made her more reluctant. How was she going to 'subdue' a monster? "And if I say, no?"

"You're on the brink of turning. And if you turn, you will kill us all. I suppose it would behoove me to slay you first, no?" He chuckled in an attempt to lighten the tension. "Your body, my choice….No pressure, I suppose."

Evynn balled her fist.

Trumpets blared filling the cathedral, followed by a deafening roar of thunder that rattled the walls.

"Grousing won't do us any good. Looks like we haven't much time. Rather, you haven't. Let's get to it," he said, opening a door leading to the rear of the cathedral. He motioned for her to exit. "Good luck."

Evynn considered punching him in the face. She couldn't believe she fell for another trap. She walked towards the exit, then paused. "What do you mean good luck? Are you not coming with me?"

"Heavens no. This is your battle. However, I will be monitoring you from a safe distance."

Evynn stepped out of the door into a headwind with light rain.

She cupped her eyes to take in the astonishing view. An iridescent sky revealed a large garden with thick, luscious shrubbery—a labyrinth.

She unsheathed her dagger and prayed while advancing towards the maze. "God, guide my path. Lead my steps with righteousness and courage. May wisdom lighten my path and show me the way."

The wind and drizzle increased.

Judaius yelled from the cathedral. "You may want to start over there!" He pointed to an enormous copper archway several meters high just south of the cathedral.

The light drizzle turned into large forceful droplets, splatting across her face. The sky closed up with dark clouds and thunder, deep and booming, and if she didn't know better, some of the claps could have been a monster's bellow.

She searched the darkened skies, looking down on the labyrinth, hoping for a glimpse of the monster she was to 'subdue.'

Evynn carefully proceeded down a flight of steps to enter the garden, concentrating to keep from slipping on the marble.

A loud roar thundered, and Evynn was certain it was the cry of a great beast. The fear it provoked within her prompted her to sprint for cover in the direction of the copper archways.

Panting, she reached them, placing her hands on her knees to gather her breath. As her gasping slowed, she raised her head to view the scene. They were massive and shaped like a giant magnet, and as she stepped underneath them, she felt a jolt of energy.

"Be careful," a voice uttered.

"Yeah, be careful."

Evynn searched the darkness near her feet and found two bunnies. "Girls, you're back!"

Alice hopped in a circle. "You may not want to be under that archway for too long... could be dangerous." She wiggled her tail and tilted her chin toward the storm clouds. "Lightning makes everything go poof."

Darlene created an explosion sound.

"Let's go!" Alice yelled over the roaring thunder.

Evynn squinted as the raindrops smacked against her face. She tried to figure out where the girls were headed and how they knew the labyrinth so well.

Alice huffed. "You're looking for the monster, right? Time's a-ticking."

Evynn followed the bunnies. "You've done this before. Haven't you?"

"Yes, with our sister."

"Different setting but the premise is the same... monster's always in the middle. Come on!"

The two bunnies darted into the labyrinth.

Evynn wondered how much of this she controlled. It was all in her head, right? Did her conscious control a portion while her subconscious the other?

She darted after them. "Hey, wait up!"

They zipped into the labyrinth, bending corners, crawling beneath hedges and ducking through hidden passages.

Evynn lost her breath keeping up. She wasn't nimble of foot and running always hurt her lower back and ankles, but she pushed through the pain.

The bunnies stopped after twenty minutes. "We're almost there. Around that bend the beast shall be."

Alice sprung into Evynn's arms. "Good luck. I hope you win. Papa says we will all have to do this if we hope to conquer the beast one day. If you win. I know I'll be able to win when it's my turn."

Evynn kissed Alice on her furry head. "Thank you."

Poof, the girls vanished.

Evynn stood in the middle of the labyrinth, soaked and muddy.

The realization that she was minutes away from being face to face with a mammoth beast was unnerving.

She licked her lips.

All she had to defend herself with was a dagger. What was she supposed to do? She knew the damage these monsters could cause. How effective could she be with a mere blade?

She advanced towards the final bend, slowing her steps.

Thunder bellowed in the distance. She wiped her face and took a large breath before turning the corner.

She worked herself into a rage, thinking instinct and pure anger would be the best approach.

She turned the corner, closed her eyes and put her head down, screaming at the top of her lungs. She took off sprinting as fast as she could, digging her toes into the muddy ground, gathering as much speed as she could muster.

Breathing heavily, she continued toward a huge nest in the middle of the labyrinth. But as she drew closer, she quieted herself.

Maybe stealth was a better approach, and she could catch the beast by surprise.

She leaned against the labyrinth walls, breathing heavily. Her bottom lip trembled and a strange question popped in her head.

Why would there be a nest? Is she preparing for offspring?

"Hmm…"

She continued along the wall, closing in on the nest. It was massive—as big as the pulpit in the cathedral.

The beast was nowhere to be found.

Clutching her knife, she cautiously approached, looking for a way to climb inside. She felt along the edge of the massive tree trunks comprising the nest, searching for sound footing. She began to climb.

Her foot slipped due to the rain. She stabbed the trunk with her dagger for added stability and clambered on.

The top of the nest allowed her to view the entire labyrinth. Still no monster to be found, but a peculiar smell caught her attention.

It was abnormally familiar.

A crack of lightning startled Evynn, like it struck something nearby and generated a huge crashing sound—like that of a huge wave of water slamming *against a wall of rocks. She peered at the maze. The copper arch was now emanating a sapphire aura; it must have been where the lightning struck.*

Another clap of thunder caused her to flinch. This time it sounded as though it was directly above her. No lightning. But when she looked up all she could see was a huge black cloud, descending towards her.

Rain poured out of every other cloud, but not this one.

The cloud drew nearer and a loud shriek projected from it. As it became closer, she could make out wings.

This isn't a cloud! This is it!

Petrified, Evynn had no clue what to do. This thing was coming at her full speed with foul intentions.

She squeezed her dagger.

What am I doing? This thing is huge!

She frantically surveyed her surroundings, considering her options. It was too far down to jump to the ground, but the contents of the nest—leafy branches and underbrush—seemed like they would be able to break her fall.

The great beast increased its speed, nosediving directly towards Evynn. Several limbs protracted from its underbelly, displaying razor-sharp claws.

With limited time to react, Evynn dove into the nest, hiding herself amongst the debris.

She had a few minor scrapes but the landing was softer than she anticipated. As she delved deeper into the nest the beast squawked.

A foul odor lingered and she couldn't quite place the smell. She kept digging.

The beast squawked and clawed at the branches, ripping them up and tossing them aside in search of the girl.

Evynn imagined what the thing would do to her if it got hold of her. It could impale her with a single claw, squeeze her till she passed out. It could simply bite her head off. The possibilities encouraged her to dig faster.

"Pssst! Down here!"

A familiar voice.

"Keep digging."

She thought about who it could be. But there was no way for him to be here, right?

She used her dagger to cut through a hardy branch and crashed through the bottom of the nest, landing with a thud on the muddy labyrinth floor beneath.

Her dagger fell to the surface and she searched the dark, dank underbelly of the nest until she retrieved it. She slung the mud from it and held it tightly—her dagger was her comfort.

She gagged from a putrid smell inundating the enclosure.

She sniffed and a moment of eureka struck. It was the same vile smell from the RV. It can't be…

She scanned the darkness and there, crouched in a crevice was Adam, looking terrified.

As he jumped to his feet, a shiny ruby-colored object fell from his lap without him noticing. "Funny seeing you here…" He turned towards the wall of the nest and anxiously peeked his head out through an opening.

As he did so, Evynn hustled over and grabbed the oval-shaped ruby, tucking it under her cloak. She placed her hand on Adam's shoulder. "Oh no, is the monster after you as well?" she said with a hint of sarcasm.

Without thinking, he patted his pocket. "Indeed. Out of nowhere I ended up here. I was configuring all the potential scenarios that would have transported me to this place and time, when suddenly this gargantuan beast is spewing fire and chasing me. I've been hiding here for several days. Until you showed up."

Evynn didn't buy the story. Instinct wouldn't allow her to. She knew he was up to something nefarious, and the ruby object had something to do with it. This was a product of her mind and no one had a right to be here but her.

Another man cowering as a victim of the great beast.

Something was awry. Everybody wanted the monster destroyed but for different reasons. Somehow none of it felt right.

What about the monster?

She didn't want to be taken over by the thing. But did it not have the right to survival? Or was it merely a blight to be rid of?

For now, she only needed to worry about surviving, and wasn't going to get anywhere stuck in here. Circumstance had pitted her against the beast whether she liked it or not. Safety came through the beast one way or another.

A crack of thunder jarred her but also triggered a plan of action.

She would need to get back to the cathedral. Perhaps Judaius could provide more insight. He would have to.

She peeked her head out of the nest. The beast hovered above, spewing fire from its jaws. It continued destroying its nest, flinging branches away.

Evynn turned to Adam, "I have an idea."

Adam searched his pockets. "Divulge. I can decipher the probability of its likelihood."

"No time. It's my head. Mind over matter. Come on!" She said sprinting from the nest.   She spotted an opening while the beast was distracted.

"Oh dear!" He said, darting behind. "Where are we going!?!

Before Evynn could reach the end of the pathway leading to the first turn the beast roared, homing in on her. It flapped its wings, eclipsing the labyrinth and hovering above.

Evynn dashed towards the first turn, breathing heavily, raising her knees and extending her stride.

"Evynn, look out!"

The great beast dove towards her, attempting to snatch her in its claws, but she lunged into a roll, dodging the attack.

The beast ascended, releasing a piercing bellow.

Evynn stopped running and pressed her back against the maze wall, breathing erratically. She did her best to control her wind and gather her composure. "It may have lost us."

Adam inhaled deeply too. "There's a high probability it has. But now what?"

Evynn placed her hands on her knees, still struggling to catch her breath. "Is this my plan or yours? Stop asking questions."

The monster rereleased a guttural cry and began torching the labyrinth. It was trying to smoke them out!

"I only asked because there was a high probability of that."

Crap.

Clever beast.

Evynn had no choice but to run now. The flames burned through the labyrinth like fire through paper. It wasn't an ordinary red flame the monster blew, but a turquoise fire that blazed hotter.

Evynn wasn't hasty, though. She waited until enough of the labyrinth was burned down so she would have a straight-line course to her target.

"Here's the plan. You're going to take off running in that direction on my signal."

Adam looked at her crossly, elevating his square chin.

"You wanted to know the plan so bad, right?"

"How does offering me up as a sacrifice help me?"

"Because it's really me it's after. Trust me. You'll draw it out, which will buy me enough time to get a good head start. When you get enough distance, I'll get its attention."

"Then what? This plan provides no positive solution."

"Trust me." Evynn slapped him on the back. "Go! Go! Go!"

Adam looked back, but took off running.

It took longer for the beast to notice him than she expected, which was even better. She took a beeline in the opposite direction, thinking how easy it was for her to fool the algorithm.   He just blindly followed my instructions. Guess fear does produce odd scenarios.

However, she did have a greater plan.

She ran towards the labyrinth's entrance. Since this was her mind, she did have a level of control over everything—give or take the beast.

A boom of thunder cracked the sky and more rain poured down. She continued to sprint towards the copper arches.

Cracks of lightning struck the ground on each side of her, tearing up and flinging chunks of earth with every stride she took.

She stopped a few hundred meters from the arches. The beast still hadn't noticed her. It was moments away from vanquishing Adam when she reached into her cloak and withdrew the oval, ruby-colored object.

Immediately the beast stopped its pursuit of Adam. It squawked and circled back towards her even faster.

Evynn's heart raced. This was part of the plan, but the idea of an immense flame-spewing creature bolting after her was still nerve wracking. She clutched the oval in one hand and the dagger in the other and raced towards the arches.

She gracefully maneuvered along the muddied path despite the rain.

Thunder continued to roll, and she thought back to Alice's words. 'Think and it shall be.'

So, she narrowed her concentration on the storm clouds above, visualizing them gathering above the archway and a massive electrical charge generating within them.

The majestic beast rapidly closed the distance, not spewing any fire.

Hmm…. It must not want to harm the oval.

Evynn was a few dozen meters from the archway. By now the sapphire aura had faded.

She passed under the arches and stopped some fifty meters away. She closed her eyes and extended her hand with the ruby in her palm.

"God guide my path and protect me from iniquities," she whispered to herself.

The beast released an echoing roar that blasted Evynn several feet back. She stumbled but kept her eyes shut.

The monster wanted the ruby, but it wouldn't spew fire for fear of damaging it. It would swoop in fast and hard.

She was moments away from impact. She squeezed her eyelids shut so hard a vein popped out on the side of her head.

And the very moment the beast swooped underneath the arches, she manifested a beam of lightning, magnifying its impact.

A loud boom of thunder followed.

Evynn opened her eyes.

The beast was limp and immobilized, a violet aura of light radiating from it. The impact was so mighty, the beast didn't even release any sounds of pain.

Evynn placed the ruby and dagger back into her cloak and slowly approached the creature. She felt contrite, and wasn't sure why.

These creatures had been the cause of so much pain and destruction; why were they owed any sympathy?

After all, this is what she wanted. Yet, she still couldn't bring herself to feel justified.

As she drew near to the creature, its aura sparked, and tiny jolts of electricity struck her, causing her hair to point to the clouds.

The creature's chin rested on the ground; its eyes closed.

Evynn gently placed her hand on the side of the creature's face, hoping for some sense of closure. She felt something but wasn't quite sure what. All she could think of was memories of her mother. She wasn't sure whether to be happy or sad.

It looked like she had accomplished what she set out to do, and she wanted to get out the rain.

With heavy steps, she trucked back towards the cathedral.

Adam was headed in the same direction, and the two met at the bottom of the steps leading out of the labyrinth.

Evynn looked back at the aftermath of the battle. The labyrinth continued to burn.

Her lip quivered. For the first time, she felt cold. The adrenaline had worn off. She was exhausted.

Adam smiled as he approached. "You really did a number back there. Kudos."

"Thanks."

She walked up the steps to the cathedral. All things considered; she had accomplished what she set out to do. She had decommissioned the beast and was ready to be 'awakened' from her meditative state. Time for Judaius to live up to his end of the bargain.

Her feet were mucky, her cloak soaked. When she reached the top, she turned to see Adam surveying what was left of the labyrinth.

She knew what he wanted but didn't know why. He's probably considering going back in there to find it. She chuckled and proceeded to the rear of the cathedral, knocking on the door.

She waited a few moments but didn't receive a response. She tried the handle and it wouldn't budge. "Drat!"

She started towards the front of the cathedral but stopped when Judaius cried out. "Hold on!"

She turned back to see him in the doorway.

Adam ascended the steps.

Once he was able to recognize the other figure, Judaius began closing the door.

Evynn ran towards the door. "Hey! What's your deal!"

The door shut in her face, and she pounded on it feverishly. "Let me in! Hey asshole, it's raining, I'm filthy and tired. Open up!"

A muffled voice shouted back at her through the door. "Not with him there. He has no belonging here."

Evynn looked back towards Adam. "What's the problem?"

Adam smirked. "Ask him!"

She backhanded Adam and he rubbed the side of his face. "Well, someone better start explaining before I bust this door down and have at the both of youse! And it will be messy."

The door cracked open.

"I suppose. But he must keep his distance," Judaius whispered.

Evynn withdrew her knife and pointed it in Adam's face. "Tread lightly."

She entered the cathedral. This time, candles illuminated the interior.

Judaius ran towards the pulpit and sat cross-legged. He pointed at Adam. "What is he doing here?"

Evynn raised an eyebrow. "I've been trying to figure that out myself."

Adam cleared his throat. "If I may?"

Judaius slammed his palm against the floor. "Rogue, you may not! You are a blight, an infestation, a virus... keep your distance and your lies!"

Adam chuckled.

"Is something funny?"

"Merely the presumption of you purporting me a liar without evidence or opportunity for rebuttal!"

"Silence, vermin!" shouted Judaius. "Let me guess. He used his lies to somehow get you to hook one of his cords up to you?"

Evynn recalled the memory with precision. She did hook up to that fat, rotting kid's machine in the RV.

So what? They both had the same goal. In fact, they all had—to stop the beast by all means. "Yeah," she whispered softly.

Judaius shook his head. "No no no... you have to kill him now, or else he'll never leave!"

Evynn wasn't sure who to believe. They had both been dubious—freely offering up some facts while omitting others. But she needed more to go on. "Release me from this slumber and we can discuss this further. I've done what you've asked."

"I'm afraid I can't."

Adam sneered. "Who's the liar now?"

Evynn pointed her knife at Judaius.

He slowly stood and held his hands in the air. "Ask him why he's here."

Evynn nodded.

Adam put his fist on his hip. "The cure, of course!"

Judaius interrupted. "Cure? There's no cure. Just an evil concoction that keeps the people reliant on you, and keeps the women like zombies..."

Evynn assertively stepped towards Adam with her knife at his neck. "Is this true?"

"I tell you, it's true. He attempted with my first daughter. He needed her blood while she was in torpor to transfuse the formula. He kept her as a perpetual zombie to harvest her blood. She was never—"

Evynn interrupted, pointing the dagger at him. "Let him speak!" she said with a spirited vigor.

Adam smiled. "Such was the case. Until the almighty blessed us with her."

"He used the same line on us. Let me guess." *Judaius faced Adam.* "She's unique, I suppose?"

"Let him finish!" *Evynn shouted, contorting her face in agitation.*

"The monster within you has produced something quite unique. It has managed to derive an offspring. A hybrid if you will. Once we procure its stem cells, we can create a permanent solution!"

Evynn lowered her knife and processed what he was saying.

Judaius scrunched his face. "But how could it reproduce? Women are infertile once they turned. It has been well documented in the Old World."

A crack of thunder rattled the cathedral.

Evynn took a few steps back and caressed her belly. "Are you saying I'm pregnant?"

Judaius squinted his eyes with obvious skepticism. "Impossible!"

But how could this happen? Am I really? What does this mean?

Adam's grin widened, "It would certainly appear so. A pivotal turning point in this war against abomination!"

Evynn shook her head. A rage of thunder shook the building, loud and direct as though it was angry. Was this a product of Evynn's psychology— an innate expression of disappointment?

The cathedral rumbled again although this time without the thunder.

The organ resounded and everyone glanced at each other.

The stained-glass ceiling shattered. Everybody dove for cover. A loud shriek filled the cathedral drowning out every other sound.

Evynn flipped to her back and covered her ears.

Shrouded in a lavender aura, the beast hovered near the top of the cathedral, its gaze fixed on her.

She wasn't as fearful as she should have been in the moment.

She was overwhelmed by a moment of clarity. As though she knew what needed to be done.

The beast swooped down in front of Adam and tilted its head. Adam cowered with his hands covering his face. The creature reached out and pinned Adam, face-down. The great beast reared its head back and spewed a single, tight spiral of flame at Adam, incinerating him on contact.

Judaius slowly scrambled backwards on his rump.

The beast shook its head, like a dog dusting itself off. It turned to face Evynn.

She cautiously climbed to her feet.

The beast methodically stalked her—steadily advancing, only stopping a few meters away. It yawned and licked the rim of its mouth—then snorted.

Evynn's heartbeat remained steady. She was calm. As opposed to Judaius, whom she could see out of the corner of her eye. He looked like he was on the brink of tears. His face was pale and flushed with panic.

She didn't want to make any sudden movements and alarm the creature. The last thing she wanted was to end up like Adam or what was left of him.

Evynn fumbled underneath her cloak until she grabbed the ruby. She held the oval in both hands, tilted her chin and extended the gem as an offering.

She closed her eyes and hoped for the best.

The beast was so massive in contrast with the oval. She wondered how it would accept the tiny object.

The mammoth beast reared back on its hindquarters, roaring ferociously.

The cathedral rattled.

Silence reverberated.

Evynn kept her hands extended but opened her eyes.

The beast glared at her, and they looked into each other's eyes. While balancing on its hind legs, it tilted its head back.

A sticky tongue-like appendage emerged from its abdomen. The green, slender thread reached towards Evynn and wrapped around her hands.

It was slimy and sticky, the top side rough like sandpaper and the bottom side smooth.

It tugged on her arms and withdrew the oval from her clasp, tucking it into a pouch like a marsupial.

It grunted at Evynn.

Evynn released a sigh of relief and took a few steps back.

The beast lowered its head and nudged Evynn.

Evynn stumbled back from the impact but smiled. It was showing appreciation.

She peered into the beast's grey eyes and rubbed the side of its snout. The tension left her body and she relaxed. *She unexpectedly giggled.*

She couldn't believe what she was doing. She wanted someone to witness it.

She turned, searching for Judaius. "Hey Judaius, I subdued her without having to slay her. I really did it!"

Where was Judaius?

A proper coward. Where did he scamper off to?

"Judaius?"

"Leave our dad alone!" The cry echoed through the cathedral.

Evynn hurried to the back of the pulpit. To her dismay, she found Judaius hunched over, gripping his side. "Judaius? What's going on? What's happening to you?"

Judaius could barely raise his head and struggled more to speak. "You have to wake up."

"But how do I wake up?" Evynn reached down to help him to his feet.

He faded in and out, as though she were reaching for a holographic image.

Judaius moaned, "I release you. Release her…"

The cathedral wavered back and forth like a mirage in the desert. The monster squealed and took off through the broken glass ceiling. The room spun and Evynn experienced a violent onset of vertigo until everything went black.

***

Evynn opened her eyes. She was covered up to her neck in a sticky substance.

Where the hell am I?

It was dark and warm. She could feel and hear everything but had no control of her body. She knew she was upright. She knew she was submerged in a viscous mucus, but that was about it.

The symptoms were similar to sleep paralysis. She felt anxious and wanted to regain full control of herself but couldn't.

She heard five voices—three familiar and two distinct: Judaius, his two girls and what sounded like two older men.

With her other faculties limited, her hearing heightened.

"I told you, she's no longer here," said Judaius.

"False. You were deceitful. You implied she was never here to begin with…" the voice said with agitation.

"Semantics, I suppose. I told you no one named Uriah was ever here!"

"Well, I suppose," the voice said sarcastically. "That's why you're bleeding out. You refuse to speak direct. But pain is an unmatchable truth serum." The man walked past whatever encasement Evynn was in. "Now, where is she?"

"Where is who?"

"The girl!"

"The only girls here are my girls. You want info from me but are not willing to help me help you? Describe this girl…"

"Look, I tracked her here. I see all the animals outside. Even the kid's dog. I know they are here."

"She was slain."

"Unlikely. No man with two girls of his own has the heart."

"I never claimed to be the perpetrator of her slaying, merely commented on the observation she had been slain. Look, I saw animals and I took them. Would you not do the same?"

"Lummis, he fixin' to get on my nerves with all this damn tricknology." The sound of a fist slamming against flesh followed.

Evynn could only assume the second man lost his patience and punched Judaius in the mouth.

"Now look at you. Bleeding with a sore mouth."

"Stop hitting our Daddy!"

"I suppose. Yet, here we are. Me dying and you without the info you're looking for."

The stern-voiced man walked by again. And suddenly his tone shifted from agitation to calm. "If she isn't here the track split off in one other direction. I was hoping it didn't have to come to a confrontation with the Copperheads, but if it must, it shall be well worth the prize. I've hunted many but none with the prowess she possesses."

Judaius grunted. "Hunting for sport. I never get you people."

"Sport? No, for honor and obligation. It's a paladin's birthright. I'm bound by birthright and bonded till death. This is about ethos and blood oath, something you wouldn't understand."

"I suppose…rubbish, and unfortunately I have neither the time nor temperament to sympathize… however, I can assure you… no woman has come here." he paused to catch his breath. "As I stated before, my daughters and I found the animals abandoned and brought them back here. If you must, take them with you as an olive branch."

The man chuckled. "Keep 'em… I'm going to try the Copperheads. If they aren't there, I'll hunt you till the ends of the earth. So, help me, God. So, pray we don't meet again."

Judaius coughed. "Farewell, I suppose."

"Yeah, farewell. You may want to get yourself patched up…"

Judaius groaned as the unfamiliar voices scurried off, coughing and sneezing.

"Girls," he moaned. "Free Evynn. Quickly—she hasn't much time left."

The girls chopped at whatever encasement Evynn was trapped inside. The sound came from near her feet. They chopped for several minutes until a high-pitched squeal resounded.

The walls of the encasement retracted and Evynn, along with the viscous substance, oozed onto the floor.

Evynn was still without control of her body.

Judaius moaned as he inched over to her, clutching his side. "Tilt her head up, girls," he instructed.

The two girls propped Evynn up onto her bottom. She tilted over.

"Lean her forward."

Evynn coughed up the slimy substance until it spilled out of her mouth.

Judaius struggled out of his shirt, exposing a gaping wound across his arm.

The girls gasped and cried. "Daddy! Will you be okay?"

"I suppose," he said, pressing the wound against Evynn's lips. "I suppose being sliced came in handy."

He winced from the pain as Evynn fed. She rapidly regained the function of all her senses. She could recollect everything which led her to believe she hadn't turned, but why was she in a torpor-like state?

She grumbled as she came to, wiping Judaius' blood from her lips.

Judaius fell on his back right into the ooze. "Girls, bring me some water, a t-shirt and a knife. We need to patch the bleeding."

The girls ran off.

Evynn sat for a moment. She looked at the fuchsia-colored ooze she sat in then shifted her sights to the same weird plant she came across earlier. Apparently, she had somehow ended up inside of it.

How?

She didn't know. For how long, she had no idea. She also thought about U-rie. He must be worried sick. Or worse, he could be hurt.

She squeezed her arms and touched her face to make sure she was really present. She took a deep breath.

She then rubbed her belly.

Am I pregnant? Or is the monster pregnant? What's really going on? How much of that was even real?

She felt anxious. She had so many questions. She didn't know what to ask.

She sighed. "Who were the men?"

Judaius tilted his head towards Evynn. "Men looking for you, I suppose."

"I don't know any men that old. What did they look like?"

"One was tall. Silver beard. Rugged demeanor. Peculiar armor. Huge scar along his neck. The other rather short. Rather dumpy. Unpleasant demeanor to match his unfavorable aesthetic."

Evynn had the long-shot idea it may have been U'rie's father but dismissed the notion. The only people who may have been looking for her that she could think of would be Uriah and maybe Fernando. But that description matched neither.

"He sounded aggressive; did he say why he was looking for me?"

"He didn't say but alluded to wanting to kill you. Well, not you per se but you after you have turned…I suppose."

Evynn had heard of the type. Stalkers who get off on hunting turned girls, thinking they'd be the one who could finally kill a turned girl. None ever did.

But how and why did he become aware of me? She scratched her elbow. Great. Even more to add to my plate. Now I have to worry about some psycho-lunatic stalking me for who knows what reason.

Evynn took a deep breath and pursed her lips. "Well, I shouldn't have to worry about him anymore, right? There's no more turning for me, right? We subdued the beast?"

"I suppose. At least for the time being. It is all conjecture at this point. You are the avant-garde."

"And what does that mean, exactly?"

"It means you should be more in tune, more aware, and should be able to mentally keep the beast at bay and in full control of any urges to turn."

Evynn did feel a greater sense of power but wasn't sure what that entailed. And how exactly she was supposed to keep the 'beast at bay.' When the time presented itself, perhaps her control would be intuitive.

But she had bigger fish to fry. She needed to find U-rie. Then she needed to find Adam and explore his solution. If he could eliminate the beast for good, they all could integrate back into the Old World.

"Hey, he mentioned Copperheads? What did he mean?"

"I've only heard rumblings… never confirmed anything about them. But from what I gather, they're a group of um… people of your skin complexion, all men who refuse to cooperate with anyone outside of their race."

Evynn found this to be a remarkable lead. It was plausible. Even if Uriah wasn't with them, maybe they could help locate him. She would just need to conceal the fact she was a woman, of course.

Evynn reached for Judaius' hand to help him to his feet. He grimaced and retracted his arm. "I'm afraid it's worse than it appears."

"How can I help?"

Judaius' face scrunched in discomfort. "It's best you get going. If he comes back snooping around here and spots you, it will not end well for either of us." He rolled on his side. "There are enough plants here to remedy me. My girls will nurse me back."

Alice and Darlene ran back into the conservatory. Alice placed a cup of water to her dad's lips to give drink.

Darlene held a thick paste in her hand. She poured water on his open wound and he winced. She then gently applied the paste.

Judaius face changed from a grimace to an enchanting smile. "Why didn't I think of this. It will both numb the pain and disinfect. Where would I be without my girls?"

Evynn smiled and felt better knowing she was leaving him in managing hands.

She closed her eyes and whispered a quick prayer. "Continue to lead me down the path of righteousness. May You give me the strength to vanquish iniquity. Remove all chaos and confusion."

Judaius stood. He wrapped a torn sleeve around his arm. "EJ, come…" he took her back towards the river, steadying each step. "Down by the end of the river near the bottom of the mountain, there's a gravel road. Follow it until it ends and then head east. Keep going for at least ten miles, and you'll eventually see signs saying "Private Correctional Facility. That's your destination. That's where the Copperheads reside. It's huge; you can't miss it."

CHAPTER 9:
BUFFALO NICKEL

**I CAN'T BELIEVE MY
GIRLFRIEND'S A ZOMBIE**

JACK E. MOHR

URIAH

Uriah was refreshed. He felt soothed. He felt reinvigorated.

Is this heaven?

Who would have thought dying felt so good? Lying on his back, he opened his eyes.

No, he wasn't in heaven. He was in a dimly lit room, the sole source of light coming from a window on the far side.

Thank goodness it was merely a dream. He hadn't been able to recall many of those due to the piyel. *What a surreal nightmare. I can't believe Lummis is even haunting my dreams.*

The voices in his head were teeming. He reached for a pocket to see if he had any piyel left.

He felt nothing but flesh.

Uriah was covered in nothing but a thin sheet. He panicked.

Where are my clothes? Who took my clothes? Where am I?

He looked around. *Where's Evynn?*

The room was eerily silent. He imagined hearing the pitter-patter of mouse steps. Even the sounds of his imagination were bouncing off the walls.

Uriah just wanted piyel to make it all go away. He raised himself, resting on his elbows groaning.

"I am Baba Essau Johnson, Brother. Welcome." The voice was soothing, filled with bass and seemingly coming out of nowhere.

Uriah searched for its source. "Huh?"

Baba sat with his legs crossed, breathing heavily. He ran his fingers through his small afro.

Uriah instinctively reached for his dagger but remembered he had nothing but his loins. No clothing and no fanny pack equals no dagger.

Essau unfolded his legs and approached Uriah's bedside. "Do not be alarmed. You are safe."

Uriah raised. "Alarmed? Hmpf…" he rotated his shoulder in a circular motion. "I'm in a strange place, butt naked, with a stranger hovering over me." He patted his shoulder. "To my recollection I was shot in the shoulder, but as you can see it's practically brand new. My head's spinning and on top of that, I've still yet to see Evynn."

Essau placed his hand on Uriah's shoulder. "I understand, Brother. You've been through much."

Uriah grew angrier with every realization. "You understand? Where's Evynn?"

Essau looked befuddled. "Evynn? Our scouts only brought you in."

"Impossible," said Uriah.

"I can bring them here and you can question them yourself if it will help."

Uriah huffed. His frustration mounted. He was so close to Evynn, and he let her get away. It was all his fault. Who knows

I CAN'T BELIEVE MY GIRLFRIEND'S A ZOMBIE   201

how long he had been asleep…? How could she have survived her torpor? He had to find her!

He whimpered. He tried to hold back tears but he couldn't. They flowed. He wiped his face, but they continued to fall.

Essau retreated a few steps. "Brother, I will send a few scouts back out to find Evan. What's his description?"

Uriah wiped his face. "I'll go myself."

Essau shook his head. "Brother, you are in no condition to go anywhere. You're in the midst of being healed."

Uriah rubbed his shoulder. His mind was so entrenched with Evynn, he didn't stop to think how his shoulder was free of pain. "I feel fine. Where are my clothes?"

Essau folded his arms. "Brother, you are in no condition. You must first be healed. And you cannot be healed until you release your fears."

Uriah didn't know what type of antics Essau was up to but wasn't going to be a passive participant. He got to his feet with the sheet wrapped around him. "With all due respect, thank you for your help. I'm sorry, But I'm going to have to respectfully ask you to piss off," he walked towards the door.

Essau chuckled. "No, I'm sorry." He struck Uriah in the back of the head and his body fell limp, collapsing on the cold linoleum floor.

***

Uriah opened his eyes, feeling refreshed and reinvigorated again. He rubbed the back of his head and felt no pain. Not even a headache.

"Where am I now?" He whispered as he fidgeted in the darkness. "Where's Baba?"

I owe him one for that sneak shot.

A cold, dank dark pervaded. Indiscernible voices and distinct clanging echoed in the distance.

Uriah was again lying down, this time on a single mattress. He sat up, accidentally hitting his head on the metal bunk above him. "Ouch!"

Uriah heard a rustling on the opposite side of the room. He could only make out a large outline through the darkness.

He grunted.

"It awakes," the outline said.

With a candle in hand the outline turned, revealing a mountainous man. He dwarfed any man Uriah had ever seen—ever!

The man held the candle to his face, revealing a smushed broad nose and a crooked smile surrounded by an assortment of facial scars and cauliflower ears. "Good, maybe now it can answer the question," he said.

Uriah heard two distinct voices and scanned the room searching for the other source.

"What is it looking for?" one grunted.

"I don't know, ask him," the other said.

I CAN'T BELIEVE MY GIRLFRIEND'S A ZOMBIE   203

Uriah realized the man was speaking to himself in two distinct voices—the actions of a madman. He also had a unique pungent smell. It was strong and abrasive, powerful like a skunk blast.

Uriah peered around. He was in some type of cell. Why was this man in the cell? Who had the power to confine such a large man to a cell and how long had he been in there?

Uriah deduced potential answers, and none appeared favorable. He must have been a threat to others and had been locked up so long, he developed dual personalities.

Uriah's heartbeat quickened and his throat constricted, making it difficult to swallow. On top of that, he still had no clothes. This man wasn't going to have his way with him—not as long as he had breath in his lungs.

The man grunted. "Ask it, Biggums."

Biggums stood from his crouched position and practically filled the entire cell.   "Why you got my chain around yo neck?"

Uriah looked side to side as though Biggums couldn't be speaking to him. He patted his chest and felt cold metal flopping against it.

How did this get here? If this is all he wants... A simple misunderstanding.

Uriah stood, one hand on his genitalia to hide his shame.

Biggums grunted. "You see that. It thinks it's the big dog. He flaunting yo chain and flashing his meat at you. You gone let him disrespect you?"

Biggums grunted. "Uh-uh, that's my chain!"

Uriah lowered his chin. "Hey um, Biggums. This chain isn't even mine. I don't know how it got here. If you can help get it off. I'll be happy to—"

Biggums grunted several times interrupting Uriah. "Roof Roof," barked Biggums emphatically with a deep growl.

"Yeah! Tell 'im, Biggs!" he grunted. "Let 'im know you the biggest dog."

Uriah fidgeted with the chain, searching for the latch.

Biggums took a powerful step towards Uriah. "Tell it how you gone get yo chain back."

"But I can show him better than I can tell him."

Uriah waved his hands. "Wait! Wait, wait… hold on." Uriah unlatched the chain, offering it to Biggums.

Biggums snorted and grunted. "It thinks it's your daddy. You gone let it tell you what you can or can't have?"

Biggums stomped as if throwing a tantrum. "No, I's the Big Daddy!"

Uriah crossed his legs as his nerves caused him to chuckle. "Here. Take it," Uriah exclaimed, extending his hand and presenting the chain to Biggums.

Biggums pounded his chest. "It really thinks it's your daddy."

Biggums grunted. "You don't feed me! I takes what's mines."

"Oh, no need for hostility, big guy. Here. I insist."

"Uh-uh," Biggums shook his head. "I want to earn what's mine like a man!"

He rushed Uriah.

Uriah ducked and parried his attacker. "Whoa. I said you can have the chain!"

He flinched as his back rolled along the cold concrete floor.

Biggums charged him again. Uriah jumped out of the way and as Biggums lunged by, Uriah kicked his ribs.

Biggums smiled. "Biggums like!" Without winding up, Biggums struck Uriah with the back of his fist.

Uriah was out before his body struck the cell floor.

***

Uriah awakened, feeling groggy. Again, he felt renewed. His head was swimming—like a bunch of voices all yelling at each other—a jumbled white noise.

He opened his eyes and shielded them from an intense light. A huge window filled the room with bright daylight.

He was lying on the floor in some type of office, naked, covered by a sheet. It smelled like lavender-scented candles.

Next to Uriah lay two sets of clothing. One was his actual belongings: his denim jeans, Hyena Man Hoodie, tennis shoes and fanny pack.

Next to it was another set of clothing—striped inmate garb.

Although his head didn't hurt, the voices were causing a migraine.

I know I have some piyel in my fanny pack.

He reached for his fanny pack.

"Uh uh ummm…" Baba cleared his voice, garnering Uriah's attention.

Baba had been seated behind him the entire time just waiting and watching.

Uriah moaned. "You again? I thought you were just a bad dream."

Baba smiled. "On the contrary. I'm here to help you help yourself realize your dream." Baba stopped as though he were carefully selecting his next set of words. "Do you know what you are, young brotha?"

Uriah had never been posed that question. *I'm a human of course. What does he mean by that?*

"I'm Uriah. And I spend each day fighting to live."

Baba took a deep breath. "You think too shallow, and we will help you with that. I didn't ask who you were but what you were. Who—is a matter of function and circumstance. It's fleeting and can change from one lifetime to the next. But what you are is substantive and remaining. It's in your soul and carries with you for eternity. What you are is the substance that defines you." Baba stood to his feet. "Brotha, we are at a crossroads where who we are and what we are must finally and firmly intersect." He interlocked his fingers.

Uriah didn't know how to ingest Baba's banter. He couldn't tell if the man sincerely believed his own rhetoric or if it was just another means of disingenuous manipulation. A part of Baba Essau reminded him of his father, which led Uriah to believe

Baba really did believe himself. That was dangerous. Uriah had already witnessed the destruction caused by one person's unchecked convictions.

He rose to his bottom, tucking his knees under his arms. "I'm a human... what else am I supposed to be?"

Baba smiled. "You still hold onto fear. I see it in your eyes." He walked over to the window, turning his back on Uriah. "Let me show you something."

He has his back to me. If I time it correctly, I could strike and escape.

Uriah reached for his pants.

Baba looked back. "Hold off on those. You need to remain unencumbered and without prejudice. Take a look out this window."

With great reservation, Uriah stood, tightly wrapping the sheet around his waist. He shuffled over to the window adjacent to Baba.

"Take a look." Baba pointed out the window. "We are in the warden's office. It overlooks the entire prison yard."

Outside were dozens of men tending a field of vegetables and fruit. There were various farm animals down there as well. A few men sat in buckets bathing themselves, while men held rubber bags attached to sticks above their heads. The bags had small holes punctured in them, so the water cascaded out like a makeshift shower. *Neat.*

"Look over there." Down there were a bunch of men, some in stripes others in casual clothing, playing handball, lifting weights among other things.

Are those women down there too? No, can't be!

"Ironically this place was built to rehabilitate men, but in its original state, would only sharpen men's ability to survive within a violent, toxic environment." He smiled. "Fortunately, it is now serving it's true intent."

He glanced at Uriah. "What do you see out there?"

Uriah scratched the back of his head. Somehow the man drew him in, suspended his mind from all worry concerning Evynn, escaping, and receiving bodily harm. This strange man managed to engross him completely in the conversation. His grandiose projections managed to supersede Uriah's concerns.

Uriah tightened his grip on the sheet. "A bunch of men working together."

"Very good. But that merely scratches the surface, brother. You aren't looking past the leaves; you must examine the roots."

Uriah hid his bemusement by maintaining a neutral face.

Baba walked to the other side of the room. "This is a one-way mirror. It gives me access to ensure all things are in order." He tapped the glass, motioning for Uriah to look out.

More men and *(women?)* inside. Some were in stripes and others in casual attire. They were segregated into various groups. Some sat around tables reading. Others were playing various games including some type of cards as well as chess and checkers. The women were practicing a choreographed dance routine. It seemed like a lighthearted mood.

"What you see is a social hierarchy. A hierarchy established by a spiritual order," said Baba.

Uriah had no idea what he was babbling on about. He only wanted a way to escape. From the looks of it, there were far too many men to fight his way out. So, he was at this man's mercy until he could discover an opening.

Baba folded his arms. "Now, do you want to discern what you are, young brother?"

Uriah paused, feigning contemplation. Which ironically enough led to actual contemplation. Maybe Baba was onto something. From his experience, men like this didn't get others to follow by accident. Aside from a captivating charisma there was typically something more to him—like his father's ability to 'communicate with the most-high.'

Uriah recalled being shot in the shoulder but now he felt no pain. What ability did this man possess that kept these men beneath him?

He cleared his throat, "I would like to know."

Baba nodded. "You will learn the Copperhead way. Go on. Get dressed."

Uriah looked down at the two piles of clothes. The voices in his head continued to echo. He wanted so much to chew some piyel. He shuffled over to the clothing and reached for his jeans.

Baba shook his head and sighed. "You cannot know what you are until you heal. You cannot heal until you eliminate all fear. What is it that you are hangin' on to?"

Evynn. That's what I'm hanging on to.

He missed his friend and needed her. But of course, he couldn't let Baba know that. No telling what intentions they would have with her.

Uriah relinquished his jeans and grabbed the stripes.

Baba nodded. "You are making a wise decision. Your destiny will repay you tenfold."

Uriah half smiled. He turned away from Baba, released the sheet and changed into the striped prison suit.

On one knee with his back to Baba, Uriah laced up his boots. He heard Baba making his way towards him. Before he could turn, Baba struck him on the back of his head.

CHAPTER 10:
RAISON D'ÊTRE

**I CAN'T BELIEVE MY
GIRLFRIEND'S A ZOMBIE**

JACK E. MOHR

URIAH

Uriah woke and rubbed the back of his neck. He inhaled deeply and forcefully blew the breath out. Astonishingly, he felt renewed again. He sat, leaning against a wall. Before moving or even opening his eyes, he listened, trying to figure out if he was in any immediate danger.

All he could hear was the murmur of white noise. Wherever he was had to be crowded. It was teeming with energy.

He slowly cracked an eye.

Then the other.

Several men shot dice on the other side of the room. Others were playing cards. The sound of fast-beating drums resonated— women danced with rapid footwork to the rhythm. Uriah was fascinated by the scene; he had never heard drums in his life and really had no reason to dance.

Wow! This looks fun. How do they move their bodies like that?

He quickly figured out he was in the main hall below the warden's office.

Uriah rubbed the back of his head: no lump, no pain, not a trace.

But how?

Uriah studied his surroundings, trying not to draw any attention to himself. The room buzzed with energy like the people were enjoying themselves. Most of the men had skin like his—a first. The last man he saw who shared his skin was his dad.

Uriah didn't know a place like this with so many men with his complexion existed. They seemed to be of one accord and jovial.

Uriah didn't feel fear. As he stood, he felt a sense of belonging—like he fit in. A pride set in.

Maybe I was meant to be a Copperhead all along.

Maybe this is why the men follow Baba's leadership. Maybe they just enjoy being here.

Uriah didn't know where to go. So, he headed towards a table where two guys played chess. He watched from a distance with his hands behind his back. He didn't want to disturb them.

A heavy hand slapped his back.

He turned to see an older man with thick salt-and-peppered hair and beard. He was greeted with a warm smile. "Hey brotha, you're up!"

Uriah looked at the man inquisitively. *Were you expecting me?*

The man extended his hand. "Where are my manners? I'm Niko."

Uriah hesitantly shook the man's hand. His palm and fingers were meaty and tough as though he had two cinder blocks for hands.

Something seemed unctuous about his greeting as though he was attempting to sell himself as something he wasn't. Reading people meant survival, and Uriah immediately sensed a duplicitous aura.

"Uriah…"

"That's a sound name. Enjoy it while it lasts. Everyone earns their name in here. You'll get your Copperhead name soon enough. But I'm gettin' ahead of myself," he smiled, "Let me show you around."

He took Uriah towards where the guys were throwing dice. There were six other men—three older guys around Niko's age and three younger men around Uriah's age. "Everyone in here pretty much has a clique. These are my guys. We call ourselves the four horsemen." Niko slapped fives with one of the older men.

"This here's Reggie." Niko motioned toward a taller man with male-pattern baldness.

Reggie laughed. "You finally got you one, huh, Big Neck?"

Niko bashfully smiled. "You know a brotha gone eventually get his one way or another."

Uriah surveyed the group. A few things stuck out as odd. The older men seemed to be having all the fun while the four younger men seemed quiet and anxious—almost feeble. The older men wore everyday attire while the younger men wore prison garb like Uriah.

Why would they call themselves the four horsemen if there were clearly more than four of them?

Niko slapped fives with the other horsemen, introducing Uriah to the group.

The two didn't stay long. Niko seemed eager to show him more of the place. "Those are a solid group of guys. If anything pops off in here, they always have my back. And if you stick by my side, they will have your back too." Niko smiled, looking Uriah in his eyes.

Uriah knew the golden rule. Nothing was free. He wondered what the price was for all this kindness. Even in a place that seemed to function like an altruistic community.

Niko grabbed Uriah by the wrist and led him towards a hallway. "The washroom's down there, but we don't need to head that way for now. This place operates like a well-built machine. There's a team dedicated to bringing in fresh water routinely."

Niko stopped abruptly as though he was flooding Uriah with info. "I know this is a lot, young brotha. Do you have any questions?"

Uriah took a look around and noticed a few sets of eyes on him. One in particular had been watching them since they were near the dice game. Maybe that guy was just curious who the new kid was. He had lighter, almost pale skin and stringy black hair.

Uriah withdrew his wrist from Niko's grasp. Niko frowned albeit only for a moment; it quickly contorted to a smile as though he were attempting to hide his dismay from Uriah.

Uriah took notice. "How does any of this help me discover what I am?"

Niko laughed. "Ahh…. raison d'être," he smiled. "You have no idea of its meaning, do you? Follow me."

Niko accelerated diagonally towards the far side of the yard.

Uriah kept pace, all the while wondering where they were going and why Niko bypassed answering the question.

He noticed the same pale figure was following him, trying to be discreet.

The two men walked down a cinder-block corridor for a few minutes before they approached a small staircase leading up into double doors.

Niko pulled open a door. "It's our library."

The room was much bigger on the inside than it appeared to be on the outside, spanning several floors.   It possessed more books than Uriah had ever seen.

Niko took a few steps in. "We have an extensive, robust collection that is constantly being added to."

Uriah was in awe.

"Follow me." Niko walked past several aisles to the second floor, past a few more aisles until he reached the section entitled "existentialism.' "Raison d'être—your meaning of existence…"

Uriah rummaged through a few of the titles, pulling a book down and flipping through the pages. "Yeah, I was told I needed to discover what I am."

Niko smiled. He snatched the book from Uriah and placed it on the shelf.

Uriah noticed the hostility and tried to locate an escape route. However, Niko had lured him into confined quarters. In fact, he was fairly cornered, surrounded by bookshelves and a half wall.

Niko grabbed Uriah by the collar of his stripes and balled it up into his fist, tugging on the shirt, pulling Uriah closer. "You have plenty of time for that after you pay your dues. But right now, your only reason for existence is whatever I say it is. Hold my pocket."

Uriah's heartrate spiked. His fight-or-flight reflexes kicked in. With an overhead hammer fist, he beat Niko's arm trying to break free. But he didn't budge. His grip didn't loosen a bit.

Uriah swung again, striking Niko in the face.

Niko shook his head side to side and chuckled. He flung Uriah to the ground. "Do we have an understanding? If not, I can make myself clear."

Uriah winced from the landing, but immediately scrambled to his feet.

Uriah had no place to run and had no intention of being beholden to this man in any fashion. He had to fight. No matter the repercussions he had to try something.

Uriah charged Niko.

Niko didn't flinch; he crouched making himself small and when Uriah was within reach, exploded out of the position with a fierce uppercut, knocking Uriah off his feet.

Uriah curled up in a ball, wheezing and gasping for air.

What the hell is going on? Why was he everyone's punching bag? *Why 'rescue' me if you just wanted to squash me like a bug? How would any of this help me discover who I am?*

A rage swelled inside of Uriah. *Forget this!* He was frustrated with his circumstances. Disappointed he was so close to reuniting with Evynn but unable to do so.

He continued to squirm, writhing in pain. All the air had been knocked out of his lungs. Uriah pounded his fist on the ground. *Ain't no way!*

"Have you had enough?" Asked Niko. "I admit you're quite spirited and pack a wallop, but we're hardened warriors down here."

Niko lumbered towards Uriah. "I don't want to hurt you no more than I have to. You're no good to any of us damaged. Get on up and grab a hold of my pocket like a good mentee."

Uriah slowed his breathing by taking deep breaths. He shut his eyes and concentrated on the pain.

"Hey, what the hell going on back there!" A stern voice called.

Niko turned to face the man. It was the same one who had been discreetly observing and following Uriah.

Niko brushed the man off. "This is first floor business. Be gone." He turned back to Uriah.

The man rapidly approached Niko and pulled his shoulder. "Brother, this man doesn't belong down here. Allow me to acquaint him with his proper place."

Niko paused before turning towards the man. Niko then hooted like a howler monkey. He barked several loud hoots in the man's face before stopping. "Do you lay siege to that which has been claimed?"

The man shook his head. "Look, brother, I mean no disrespect. I'm Cottontail from the second floor. It's just a simple misunderstanding."

Niko boisterously hooted several times before several men piled into the library—the four horsemen being among the lot.

The men balled their hands into fists and hooted. The woofs filled the library.

Niko lifted stone hands and released a loud guttural roar. He smiled at Cottontail. "House rules. Thou cannot challenge another man for what he lay claim to without due process."

Cottontail attempted to beat him to the punch by cutting him off. "Look, brother, it ain't got to be all that. We are a civilized people."

"Indeed, we are, brotha. But the purest form of civility is communication without error—in other words—combat." He hooted. "So that we don't mince words— let's allow our bodies to freely express our intent."

Niko brushed past Cottontail, bumping his shoulder. He addressed the surrounding inmates, raising his voice. "This man has challenged my manhood by laying siege to that which I claim. House rules dictate when two are in dispute over such matters, to the victor shall go the spoils. May the best man prosper. To the grass!"

Everyone within the library erupted in an outcry of whooping and hollering. They chanted, "To the grass!" over and over while rhythmically stomping their feet. Everyone filed out of the library, down the steps to the ground floor.

Cottontail reached down to help Uriah to his feet. Uriah still clutched his stomach despite having regained his breath. "Thanks, but I can help myself up."

Cottontail withdrew his hand. "Suit yourself. From the looks of it, you're in no position to refuse any help. It would behoove you to humble yourself, good brother."

Uriah was affronted by the comment. He'd been nothing but abused and beaten down since he came to this bloody place. What did this guy mean by humble?

Uriah staggered to his feet and wiped his mouth.

Cottontail looked at Uriah for a few moments, as though studying him—almost as if he were trying to solve a puzzle and Uriah was the missing piece.

Then he sighed. "Let's go!"

This man was much different than the other inmates. For starters, his skin wasn't copper brown like the rest. It was fairer and he had a prominent nose with sunken cheeks. Secondly, he had a calmness to him, a certain stillness that Uriah felt and absorbed. Uriah couldn't tell why but he seemed to have good intentions, and if not, he didn't appear to be a threat.

Uriah considered exploring escape possibilities, but it appeared he was at the center of the conflict at this point and had to see this thing to its conclusion.

Whatever that entailed.

He followed close behind Cottontail, both of them tailing a fog of testosterone and musty chaos. The men continued to hoot, bark and stomp as they navigated through hallways until they emerged out into the yard.

Uriah's eyes constricted as they encountered sunlight. He hadn't experienced sunlight in this fashion since he was a small boy, and it took some adjusting. He was accustomed to the dingy burnt skies and wondered how the sun seemed to shine so bright out here.

Wherever out here was.

This was the same area he had seen through the window when he was in the warden's office.

The vegetables and fruit were a few plots over. This field was all grass—luscious, freshly trimmed grass—and he wondered what they used to mow the lawn.

The group formed a half circle, which Niko and Cottontail entered. The men beat on their thighs and chests, creating a rhythmic tempo.

Niko entered with a haughty arrogance as though nothing could stop him. He cracked his meaty knuckles then twisted his neck and cracked it as well.

Cottontail entered with a quiet resolve as though nothing could rattle him.

Niko pointed at the crowd and then at Cottontail. "This personage challenges my manhood and my stake in the social hierarchy among the Copperheads." He pointed at Cottontail. "What say you?"

Cottontail shrugged. "It doesn't have to be this way, brother."

Niko shook his head. "What say you!"

Cottontail glanced at Uriah, then pounded his chest. "Ahhhggrrrrroooot!"

The gathering cheered.

I CAN'T BELIEVE MY GIRLFRIEND'S A ZOMBIE

Niko lightly hopped up and down on his toes, displaying his nimbleness. "And when you are defeated. Do you offer up your second-floor privilege as collateral by witness and testimony of all here present?"

Cottontail nodded.

Niko smiled. He extended his hand and Cottontail shook it.

The two men pounced into a fighting stance. Niko leaned forward in a more aggressive stance. Cottontail sat back flexing on the balls of his feet in a defensive posture.

Niko charged ahead, lunging with an overhand right.

Cottontail shifted to his left, deflected the blow and struck Niko with a body shot.

Niko doubled over grabbing his side, but quickly accelerated into an uppercut, connecting with Cottontail's chin.

Uriah grimaced from the impact. It sounded like a hammer striking a side of beef.

Cottontail spat out a trickle of blood.

Niko hooted, tore off his shirt and tossed it aside. Sweat beaded on his skin, refracting the sun. He charged forward and tackled Cottontail.

Cottontail locked his arms around Niko, falling onto his back. As he hit the ground, he tucked his knees underneath Niko and used the momentum generated to toss the other man through the air.

Niko landed face first on the ground. He scrambled to his feet and shook his head. He mouthed the words, "Not bad." As though the older man surprised him.

Cottontail closed his eyes and drew in a deep breath.

Niko howled, charging towards the man, this time being mindful to stop directly in front of Cottontail by chopping his steps.

Cottontail kept his eyes shut.

Niko hooted and cocked back his fist, striking Cottontail with a debilitating body blow. He then cocked his right hand back and repeated the process. He whaled on Cottontail with blow after blow until he tired himself out.

Niko gasped for air. "What the F—?" he mouthed, rapidly inhaling.

Cottontail remained still with his eyes closed in a state of serenity. It was as though his spirit was in another place, a place where pain didn't exist.

Uriah's lips parted.

What am I seeing right now? What power does he possess?

Cottontail opened his eyes and stared into Niko's eyes.

Niko trembled. Not out of an obvious fear, because his face didn't display fear—more so respect and fatigue. But his body cowered. "What's going on with me, brotha?"

Cottontail spoke in a stoic tone. "Your body has recognized a power far greater than itself and is submitting. It's waiting for your mind to catch up."

"Hell nah!" Niko tried to fight the revelation. His knees quivered. In denial, he cocked his fist back and swung but his arm went limp prior to making any contact.

He attempted once more with the other arm but, same result. He fell to a knee. "You a tough summamabitch, you know that?" He coughed. "I give."

Cottontail frowned and crossed his arms. "Show. Don't tell."

Niko sighed and went down on all fours. He assumed a posture of submission, turning away from Cottontail. He lowered his head and bowed.

Cottontail turned to the men gathered around and made eye contact as he scanned them.

After locking eyes with Uriah, he signaled. "Let's go."

What the hell did I just see?

Uriah stepped out of the crowd and hesitantly approached Cottontail. His apprehension wasn't so much caused by fear but due to all the eyes zoning in on him. Uriah didn't know what to do. He halfway expected cheers or more tribal hooting from the men, but they collectively seemed defeated. A bunch of relaxed fists, defeated faces and slumped shoulders—as though Niko's loss was indicative of everyone's loss.

Cottontail patted Uriah on the back. "How are your ribs doing?"

Uriah was so entrenched in the hoopla, he had forgotten about his ribs. He rubbed them. "They're fine."

Cottontail turned towards the penitentiary. "Good." As he proceeded to the prison entrance, his steps were graceful and deliberate but not rushed.

Uriah instinctively followed. "You fought for stewardship of me back there? Does that mean, I'm like, yours?"

If so, you might as well get ready for round two now.

Cottontail shrugged his brow as though juggling the question in his mind. "Technically, but hold your questions until we get back to the cell. I'll answer anything you like."

Uriah had plenty of questions, but he held them for now.

They didn't take the same route into the building. They walked around the corner near a loading dock.

Uriah noticed a slender man in a rifleman's tower, which compelled him to search out more. In total there were seven of the towers—all occupied, as though they were preparing for an invasion.

Cottontail climbed through the loading dock and Uriah followed. To the left was a service elevator, next to it a stairwell. They went up the stairs to the second floor.

The atmosphere and energy felt different. Whereas on the first floor the energy was frenetic and jovial, the energy on the second floor felt reserved and laid back with only a hint of tension.

Even the hallways were painted differently. While the first floor was a drab gray, the second floor had various murals. The one they just walked by had a picture of the sun with a smiley face. Another one had a large painting of a penny, except its face held a man with negro features and above it the phrase 'one percenter.'

A soothing sound permeated the hallways, a sound unlike anything Uriah had ever heard. It was loud and pure, resonating throughout the passage.

Is this what music sounds like?

He had always imagined what it would sound like after hearing descriptions. It felt pleasing to his spirit. The vibrations shifted something in him—practically replacing all of the head noise.

The more they walked the louder it grew. They'd soon come across the source and Uriah found himself giddy in anticipation of seeing who had the magic to produce such a unique golden sound.

Unlike the first floor, all the cell doors were open, although most were empty. They walked past one occupied cell. Inside, incense burned and a slender man with an Afro held a trumpet to his mouth. He lowered the instrument and the sound stopped.

Uriah held back his excitement.

Leaning back against the cell wall with his trumpet at his side he spoke in a rich raspy drawl. "Free the land, beloved."

Cottontail raised his fist, "Tis already free!"

"Right on! Selah!" The man retorted with a chuckle.

The man had a large Afro, and several posters of other men with Afros and their fists in the air were taped to the wall behind him. In the back of the cell was the mural of a huge eye with red veins, and it stared back at Uriah.

228   JACK E. MOHR

The man caught Uriah observing the eye and laughed. "Be careful. The eye sees things you don't always want it to…"

Uriah averted his glance. Something about the man reminded him of his own father. Not the nefarious peculiarity—something else. Maybe it was because they had similar builds—slender, high-cut waist, long legs—or maybe it was the assurance in their eyes—something Uriah strove for.

Uriah continued to follow Cottontail down the hallway, the lush sound of the horn following them.

Cottontail peeked back at Uriah and coughed. "Not much further." He strained to say.

Cottontail's face had turned red and was turning redder as if he had been holding his breath.

"Hey, uh, do you need some help?" Asked Uriah.

Cottontail's stern demeanor cracked, and a sense of urgency appeared as he increased his pace.

He turned a corner and his cell was the first one on the right. It was large, as if the wall dividing two cells was demolished to combine them. The cell was darkened. He had a thick blanket shielding the window from the outside light and another blanket across the bars.

He entered the cell and collapsed on a black fur rug.

Uriah wasn't sure what was going on. "Hey man, you okay? Do you need help?"

Cottontail curled up on the floor in the fetal position. He grimaced as though he was in excruciating pain. Uriah had only seen men cry like this during an attack with a turned.

Cottontail gingerly raised his hand and whispered. "Shut the cell."

After Uriah did so, Cottontail pointed to a candle and instructed Uriah to light it.

Cottontail flipped to his back and closed his eyes. "Have a seat. Let me regain myself."

Uriah sat in a wooden chair near the corner of the cell and watched.

Cottontail exhaled rapidly and he wept. He slammed his fist on the floor and cried out. Uriah wanted to help. Maybe get the man some water, something. But he remained in his seat. It seemed like this wasn't Cottontail's first experience.

After Cottontail hit his peak of pain, he slowly regained his calm demeanor. After a few minutes, his flushed face replenished its color.

Uriah had his own pain to mitigate. His ribs were still sore so he could only imagine how Cottontail felt. And he still had a lingering migraine. The dark-quiet space wasn't helping, only enhancing the loudness already bombarding his mind. At least when he was getting beat up, it provided somewhat of an escape. But without piyel the silence was left to torment him, and he had no way of escaping the chaos.

Uriah hung his head and rubbed his temples.

"Are you okay?" asked Cottontail.

"Huh?" Uriah looked up.

Cottontail was sitting cross-legged in a Zen pose on the carpet.

"Are you okay?" asked Uriah. "What was all that about?"

Cottontail uncrossed his legs and tucked his knees underneath his armpits. "What's your name, Young Blood?"

"Uriah."

"You've seen some things in your day… but you've probably never witnessed anything like this."

Uriah leaned back into his seat. "Can't say I have."

"You undoubtedly have all sorts of questions and don't know where to begin?"

"I know where to begin. What is this place and how do I get out?"

Cottontail chuckled. "Relax, Young Blood. The more you stress the less likely you'll find what you're looking for."

Oh no. Not another one of these mind thieves. He said he would answer my questions. So, he is going to answer my questions!

"What is this place?"

"Safe haven. Home of the Copperheads and you're free to go at any time."

"But?"

He shook his head. "There's no but. You're always free to go but what happens to you once you step out of this compound is an entirely different issue."

"Who are the Copperheads and what's the deal with Baba Essau?"

Cottontail snickered. "Young Blood, those are such basic questions." He grabbed a jug from the corner of his room and filled a basin. He withdrew a burner from underneath the bed and lit it. He placed the basin on top and handed Uriah an empty teacup, also from beneath the bed. "Your questions are primitive. As to our designation of Copperheads. It's an arcane reference to skin color. As you can see not all of us fall under such demarcation," he pointed to his fair complexion. "It once referenced to us being the one-percenters, but that was when we were much larger. A group defected and went south."

Suddenly the cell opened and the man with the Afro entered. "Yeah, Jack. The brothers went one way and the white boys another. Give it to him straight." He picked out his 'fro. "You see this?" He grabbed Uriah's arm and flicked his skin. "You see this? We the original man. Our birthright is in our flesh, you see." He pointed to his forehead. "We the first ones here and will be the last ones to go, Jack!"

Uriah looked at the new man and then at Cottontail, and back at the man. "But his skin is pale?"

"He's smart enough to be on the right side of history, Jack. Ya dig?" Said the man. "Elijah! Brother Elijah!"

"Huh?" Said Uriah.

"You looked confused. That's my name."

Cottontail poured hot water into Uriah's cup and handed him a teabag. "Made this myself; tell me how you like it."

Cottontail offered Elijah a cup but he refused.

"Thanks, but no thanks. I best get goin'. I'm on water duty this week, and it looks like yawl fixin' to get far out. You brothers keep it funky, ya dig?" Elijah extended his fist.

Uriah looked inquisitively.

'Don't just look at it. Dap me up, man."

Uriah stuck out his fist and Elijah bumped it.

Uriah felt an energy pulsate.

Elijah squinted his eyes and tilted his head. "Hmph...Right on." He smirked and left the cell.

Odd. Thought Uriah, as he took a sip.

Cottontail grinned. "Gotta love brother Elijah. He keeps everything light-hearted and upbeat around here."

"So, all that stuff about skin isn't true, he was just pulling my leg?"

"Oh no, that's very much the foundation of this place. But you gotta take it for what it's worth. Everyone has their own beliefs. You just can't take yourself or your beliefs too seriously or else you become a slave to them and can never grow." He sipped. "How's the tea?"

Uriah took another sip. "Good, actually."

"Did you expect something different?"

Uriah nodded. "Hey Cottontail, why'd you do all that for me back there."

Cottontail inhaled. "It's part of what I am."

Uriah took a sip and thought. More of the same weird rhetoric Baba used.

"I'm a seer," said Cottontail. "And so are you. I saw your energy from a mile away. You didn't belong down there... you belong up here with the gifted."

Gifted? Gifted at what? Seeing? Seeing what? 'Cause I didn't see any of this coming.

"Brother Elijah's a seer too…. Of another nature though."

Uriah's migraine ebbed and flowed. The voices in his head were distracting. They were more like a cacophony of gurgles.

"Ahh fuck!" Uriah yelled. "I can't take this head noise anymore!"

Cottontail gave him a cross look. He rinsed out the teacups and jug in the toilet and placed them under the bed. "The Susurrus can be quieted…"

Susurrus?

Cottontail walked over to Uriah and placed both of his palms under Uriah's hands. His calm demeanor was reassuring and soothing. It felt like he was absorbing some of Uriah's tension, alleviating him of his anxiety.

Cottontail chanted in a deep melodic voice over and over. "Sharia—da-da-duh-dun—malakai—sai—ari-ahh" he repeated the chant over and over. "No two gifts are exactly alike. Yours has been with you for quite some time. Denying it can drive one insane."

Uriah's palms perspired, and his mind drifted, focusing on Cottontail's sing-song voice.

Cottontail chanted. "Close your eyes." Cottontail released his hands and rubbed the caps of Uriah's shoulders. "The stress and anxiety is your gift fighting to free itself from your mental oppression—your mind has imprisoned yourself."

The thoughts inside of Uriah's mind stopped yelling. They quieted to a murmur and a constant babble.

"Follow me through a guided journey amongst your thoughts." Cottontail continued to chant. "Find your gift and free it."

CHAPTER 11:
DRAPETOMANIA

**I CAN'T BELIEVE MY
GIRLFRIEND'S A ZOMBIE**

JACK E. MOHR

URIAH

Uriah inserted himself into his own mind, paralleling the physical prison he found himself in.

In an empty cell, he was naked, cold but not afraid. The room was bare and quiet. Uriah wrapped his hands around the chilled metal bars.

Murmurs broke the silence. Uriah listened closely and the murmurs were discernible. It sounded like pleas for help.

Curiosity provoked Uriah to explore his mind.

He stepped outside of his cell into darkness. Boundless shadows. The floor was damp, and Uriah felt a certain eeriness in the ambiance. His eyes somewhat adjusted to the darkness. He couldn't see more than a few feet in front of him and he began following the chants.

He took several steps along the damp, sticky floor. He flinched as rapid steps approached from the adjacent cell as he walked by.

He couldn't make out anything until a body slammed against the cell. "Help me… it's after me again," she whispered.

It was a woman in her torpor state. Her skin was slack as though it were melting off her flesh. She was discolored, her eyes sunken and white with no pupil. She looked like she had been dead for decades.

Uriah shuddered. "Who's after you?"

She rubbed her head back and forth against the bars. "The monster. And it'll get you too," she whispered.

Uriah felt a bad energy and wanted to leave. "I'm sorry. I can't help."

She yanked at the bars. "Where are you going!" she squealed. "Help me!"

Uriah turned and ran down the hall. "Sorry!" He yelled back.

She screamed like a banshee. "You will be sorry! You can't run! You can't escape!"

As Uriah ran down the corridor another zombie-like woman slammed against the cell on the opposite side. It screamed. "The monster will devour you! Coward!"

Startled, Uriah stumbled back against the cell across from it and zombie hands grabbed him. "Help me," it whispered. Cold, clammy hands dug into his naked flesh.

Uriah ripped himself away. "Sorry! I can't. I don't know what you want from me!" He jetted down the hall.

As he passed each cell, zombie after zombie slammed against the bars, screaming indiscernible high-pitched sounds—reaching and grabbing at him.

Uriah covered his ears, stomping through the sticky hallway as fast as he could. The hallway seemed to have no end. He just ran and ran, lungs burning.

A yellow light appeared towards the end of the hallway. Freedom.

Uriah didn't stop running until he reached the light. There, he placed his hands on his knees sucking up wind until he caught his breath.

He peered back down the dark hallway. He couldn't see anything, but the screams continued to pervade.

At the end of the hallway was an elevator, a closet door and a stairwell.

The floor no longer felt sticky, and he looked down at his feet. He gagged. A brownish-crimson substance had dried on his skin, covering his shins and feet.

Uriah swallowed, doing his best to tame his panic. "It's okay. It's okay. It's just a little blood," he reassured himself. "It's not the first time and won't be the last time you've touched a little blood."

Uriah opened the utility closet almost halfway expecting a zombie to pop out. He let out a deep breath when he found a janitor's coverall, mop, rag and bucket.

He used the rag to wipe some of the blood off but most of it had dried, so he left it. He put on the overalls, and they fit perfectly.

The screams persisted.

He stepped out of the closet, debating between the elevator and stairwell.

Uriah had never used an elevator before. He pressed the button and heard a beep. Before the elevator doors opened, Uriah jogged towards the stairwell.

Up or down? Uriah didn't know if there was truly a correct answer. After all, this was his mind, and he was supposed to be unlocking his gift. Were the zombies in the cells his gifts? This was all so confusing.

"Down it is," he muttered.

Uriah descended several flights of stairs at a snail's pace, each step echoing off the cinderblock walls.

At the base of the steps were metallic double doors with a yellow light beaming from the crack beneath. He cautiously pressed his ear against the doors attempting to hear what might be on the other side.

"Nothing... here goes," he said, pushing the doors open.

Uriah exhaled a sigh of relief as a row of candles illuminated the basement.

"At least I can see," he whispered.

He took a step, and the sound ricocheted throughout the hollow hallway.

"Who goes there!" A soft, frightened voice cried. "Baba, is that you?"

240   JACK E. MOHR

The voice didn't sound decrepit as the others, but alive. Uriah thought of his own mother and wondered if that's what she would have sounded like.

Uriah swiftly proceeded down the hall which opened to a large chamber. He scanned the room but only saw several large stone pillars.

The clinks of metal garnered his attention, and he approached a pillar in the far corner of the room. A toilet was fastened to one side.

Uriah circled the pillar and restrained himself from gasping.

A gaunt woman sat with her arms chained to the pillar.

She cried out. "Oh Baba, if you won't allow me my child at least give me back my sight."

Uriah retreated a step.

The woman climbed to her knees and then to her feet. "You aren't Baba, are you?" She asked.

Uriah swallowed, hesitant to respond.

"Your silence says enough." She opened her eyes. Her pupils blended with the white of her eyes, contrasting her bronzed skin. "Come near, so I can see you."

Uriah looked around the chamber and slowly approached the woman. He took arduous steps as though his feet were drudging through quicksand.

"How can you see—"

"Shh," she interrupted, reaching out for his face. She rummaged along his face then felt his shoulders then ran her hands back along his face.

She gasped. "You're him!"

"Who? I'm who?"

***

Uriah rolled his eyes. *I would awaken at the most pivotal point.*

"Figures," he said.

Cottontail smiled. "How was your first experience?"

Uriah rubbed his head. "Different."

Cottontail tilted his head. "It becomes easier the more you do it."

'You're him. You're him.' Who was that lady?

Uriah was puzzled. It was enough waking up in this prison. Now he was finally able to listen to the voices in his head and it was some woman. Saying he was him.

Cottontail put his socks and shoes on. "You look like you're a size 13?"

Uriah hadn't owned many pairs of shoes. Just those he could salvage from dead bodies. There were the few times Evynn and he were brazen enough to venture into metropolitan areas and explore shoe stores. That was so dangerous. They ran into a turned. And if it wasn't for her being a contagion, sparking Evynn to turn—they would have been toast.

"Yeah, how did you guess?"

"From experience, 13s are scarce. Hopefully we'll be able to find some on the forage."

"Forage?"

"Yeah, you didn't think you were staying with me, did you?"

"Honestly… I was hoping not to stay at all… but…"

"I see. But this place grows on you. Your cell will be at the end of the hall. You'll need to make it your own."

Cottontail exited the cell and shut the door behind them.

Uriah followed him to the end of the hall to cell E44.

Cottontail took the key out of the lock and handed it to Uriah. "We typically leave everything unlocked on the second floor. But to make you feel comfortable…"

Uriah grabbed the key and ran his fingers along the metal. He had never had his own space. He had never had to be confined. He always lived on the lay of the land or with his dad and Evynn. But it did feel good not having to sleep in fear despite the infringement of freedoms.

He didn't plan on staying any longer than he had to. Who knew where Evynn was?

If I found her once, I can find her again.

The cell was about as empty as Uriah felt. And that wasn't necessarily a bad thing. Granted, he had no plan of action but for the first time he could remember, the voices in his head were quiet. They weren't completely silenced but quiet enough as to not feel distracting.

"How long do you plan on just standing there?"

"Oh." Uriah shut the cell.

"We'll get you a mattress and blanket on the way back. Everything else we'll need to forage for."

Uriah followed Cottontail to the end of the hallway until they reached an elevator, closet and stairwell that appeared exactly as it did within his dream.

Uriah squinted as he examined the elevator. "Hmm…" he opened the closet. "Wow!" The same jumpsuit, mop and rag.

"What are you looking for?" Cottontail stopped at the top of the stairwell.

"Nothing. It's just, I've seen this before. in the meditation."

"Deja vu—"

"Huh?" Uriah furrowed his brow.

"It means to experience time twice." Cottontail paused. "Could be coincidence or could be part of your gift." Cottontail continued down the stairwell. Uriah pressed the button on the elevator. Not functional as he presumed. In his dream, it was powered.

When the two ventured through the first-floor yard on their way to the mess hall, murmurs across the yard silenced and eyes stared daggers into them.

Cottontail found it to be hilarious, chuckling the entire way to the mess hall. Uriah, on the other hand, didn't understand their fear, if physical exhibitions happened as often as they made it seem.

The array of food was astounding. They had plenty of meats, vegetables and fruits and more. *How did they acquire such abundance?* Uriah hadn't had a decent meal since he left his father's compound. Cottontail had no intention of staying, but Uriah asked if he didn't mind stopping to eat. Cottontail acquiesced and Uriah scarfed down a plate of food in less than ten minutes.

After Uriah finished eating, Cottontail put some meats, fruits and peanuts in a sack for the road and prompted Uriah to do the same. While exiting the mess hall they ran into Elijah.

For some reason, Elijah appeared much taller. Uriah was a fairly tall person himself, but Elijah made him feel small. He had to be at least six foot seven inches.

Elijah's lengthy, gangly limbs and rounded back moved fluidly, which was counterintuitive. His movement took little to no effort at all, like he was more floating than walking.

Elijah fist-bumped Cottontail and greeted him.

He then turned to Uriah. "Whaddup, Young Blood?"

Uriah smiled. "Sup, brother Elijah?" He extended his fist.

Elijah slapped Uriah's fist away. "Ace!"

Uriah frowned. *Ace?*

"Call me Ace. I'm a Gemini."

"Okay."

"Now, if you address me properly, we can proceed." Elijah snarled.

"Ace?"

"Right on!" Elijah smiled and fist bumped Uriah. "Where you brothas headed?"

Uriah looked at Cottontail. It was pathetic he didn't know where he was even going—blindly putting his trust in Cottontail. But he hadn't misguided him so far.

"We're headed down to the train station to forage."

"Ain't that place been ransacked enough? Can't hardly be anything left."

I CAN'T BELIEVE MY GIRLFRIEND'S A ZOMBIE

"Train station is pretty bare but there's a haberdashery and gas station a few miles west that not many know about."

"I can dig it. I can use a few supplies myself and there's always strength in numbers."

"The indirect self-invite: nice."

"I knew you'd dig." Elijah chuckled. "We better use the donkeys, 'cause we have to be back before the Oblation."

Oblation?

"Speaking of which, who's among the selected?"

Elijah looked down at Uriah. "Who knows. Could be Young Blood." He laughed.

The three proceeded to the outer yard. It was but a few minutes before beads of perspiration gathered on Uriah's forehead.

They walked past the stalks of corn to a stable full of animals. Several men pulled huge barrels on horseback. They unfastened the barrels and poured water into troughs for the cows and repeated the process for the pigs, donkeys and hens.

The three headed to a stable filled with several horses, a few donkeys and some mules. There were a few shelves with riding boots, Above them hung winter coats and a couple cowboy hats.

"Young Blood, I see you eyein' the black cowboy hat."

"Huh? Oh."

"That hat's for real hombres—you don't wear a hat like that—you earn it. You gotta really be ready to fuck stuff up and get it real messy if you want to wear that."

Uriah rubbed the rim of the hat to get a feel of the texture.

"Uriah! Over here." Cottontail was further down the stable.

Uriah put the hat back on its hook and sought out Cottontail. He stood next to a large jenny with a thick grey and white coat.

"This here's Betsy. She's partial to new riders," Cottontail handed Uriah the reins.

Elijah snickered as he grabbed a mule. "Hey, John-Albert!" He rubbed the mule's belly. "Be careful with that one, she's antsy at times."

Uriah reached to pet Betsy's head and she spat on him.

Elijah laughed. "See what I mean?"

Cottontail chuckled. "Now that wasn't nice, Betsy." He grabbed the reins of another mule. "Hey Big Bo. How you doing, boy?"

The mule brayed and reared in place. Elijah and Cottontail mounted their respective mules.

Uriah wiped his face. *Great. I get the donkey with uh attitude.* "Easy girl, I know you didn't mean it."

Betsy spat on him again and reared back.

Uriah took a deep breath. "Are you sure I couldn't ride any of these others?"

Cottontail pulled the reins of Big Bo. "She's the only one that takes to new riders. Try humbling yourself."

She just spit on me twice. How much humbler can I get? Uriah took a step back and closed his eyes. *Most High imbue me with patience.*

He opened his eyes and smiled. Without hesitation, he approached Betsy as though he had known her for years, petting between her ears and rubbing her neck.

Betsy brayed, bouncing her head up and down.

"Good girl!" he said. "Do you mind if I mount you?" Uriah rubbed the side of her head. "Thank you!" He climbed on top of Betsy and turned to Cottontail and Elijah. "Let's boogie, Ace!"

Elijah smirked. "Right on, Young Blood. I like your flava."

The trio headed around the front of the prison, bypassing the yard, heading towards the west of the building near the basketball courts.

The heat bounced off the blacktop and Uriah wiped his brow. He was thirsty but thought it better to conserve the water supply he had.

As they approached the exit, Elijah raised a fist and Cottontail saluted the rifle tower.

Cottontail led the way with Elijah slightly to his rear and Uriah to the right of him. It wasn't long before they approached an odd structure. Not even a quarter mile from the entrance, near the rear of the prison, a cross sat on top of a grassy mound.

As they drew closer, ravaged clothing and bones lay sprawled along the base of the mound.

Hmm. I've seen Evynn pick meat from bones in the same way. Not a pleasant way to go…

Uriah pointed to the scattered bones. "Over there. Woman's work?"

Cottontail turned. He hadn't even acknowledged the mound initially, as though he had gone by it hundreds of times and it was just routine. "Perceptive."

"When you're been out here on your own as long as me, you learn to steer clear of any signs of danger."

"Right on. I, personally, have never seen the Oblation but I've heard the screams from the cell. Used to give me nightmares." Elijah shuttered.

"That's the second time you mentioned Oblation. What exactly is it?"

"Baba Es—," Elijah chuckled. "He got me calling him 'baba' now. Brother Essau came up with the concept a few years back." He placed his finger on his chin. Looked towards the sky as though he were pulling the memory from the heavens. "The idea, we should offer up a sacrifice to the creator for imbuing us with these talents." He snapped his fingers. "Yo, Cotton, how did he put it? You're better at keeping up with his nonsense than me."

"Oh," said Cottontail, chuckling. "We are the one-percenters." He withdrew a dream catcher from his backpack. A penny dangled from it. "The chosen, elected by God to prolong and protect humanity. We offer up a piece of our humanity to live another day."

"And you guys really believe that?"

Cottontail and Elijah broke out in laughter.

Elijah laughed the hardest. "You can't take yourself too serious, let alone another. I've seen a lot in my day. Nothing like these past few decades, but what always holds true is no one man ever has all the answers." He looked at Uriah. "No matter how convincing they are."

"Well, why do you do it? Why do you follow him?"

Cottontail pulled on the reins. "Let's pick up the pace, gents. We don't want to lose all our daylight before we have to set up camp."

Elijah slapped his reins on the mule's neck. "The man has some good points. Don't get me wrong… let me tell you a story…"

Uriah slacked his reins to keep pace. The animal's hoofs slapping the ground made it difficult to hear.

"Okay."

"Essau really turned this place around. Cottontail is second generation but I was here before the plague."

"What do you mean?"

"Prison, Youngblood." He gazed down at Uriah. He scoffed and laughed at the same time. "I forget, you don't even have a concept of what prison is, do you?"

"I've heard stories."

"Stories, huh? It's a place where society, 'the state,' leaves its undesirables to fester. You can imagine what type of savages it produces…"

"What were you there for?"

Cottontail looked back with an air of curiosity, as though this part of the conversation intrigued him.

Elijah's face lost expression and a somber glint flickered in his eyes. "I've never told anyone this since the plague. Not that it matters much now. But a frat boy," he paused, "trespassed against my sister." He turned his eyes to the horizon and took a few moments. He brushed off his shoulder and softly chuckled to himself. "And I introduced him to the wrath of God, ya dig?"

Uriah chuckled.

Elijah cut his eyes at him.

"You mean they punished you for defending your sister's honor?" Uriah couldn't wrap his head around the thought. *The idea seems obscene. Men kill each other every day. The idea that you could be punished for such is preposterous.* "Could the state not see the justification?"

"It was premeditated… allegedly." He laughed. "I lived during a time where if it wasn't state approved, you couldn't do it. Sure, I felt I was in the right, but…" Elijah shook his head. "Never mind all that. Before Brother Johnson arrived, we were still living in that prison mindset. Hopeless. He gave us structure and purpose. Something to strive for. Without purpose a man wastes away."

Uriah thought back on the different compounds he encountered. And had often wondered why men would gather and follow the rule of another. This one actually made sense.

"What really did it in. Before Brother Johnson came. A doctor told me I had stage 3 pancreatic cancer and had less than a year to live." Elijah inhaled and choked up a bit. "That was over a decade ago."

Uriah put the pieces together. His arm. The getting knocked out and waking up feeling refreshed. Baba could heal. That was his gift. *That's his strongarm!*

"Well, if healing is Brother Essau's gift. What's yours?"

Elijah smiled. "I'm a seer."

"Oh, like me?"

"I doubt it. I see what's already happened."

"What do you mean?"

"For instance, I know you're in love. And you'll do anything to protect that love."

Uriah was skeptical. Seemed pretty vague and not specific.

"Does the name Evynn ring a bell?" Elijah raised his eyebrow, anticipating Uriah's response. "Thought it might."

Uriah was amazed but creeped out in the same breath. *How did he know?* He felt violated. *How did he have entitlement to my thoughts and memories? Those are mine!*

Elijah nodded. "Relax Youngblood. I can't see everything. Just what Jah allows."

Uriah didn't like the explanation and withdrew from the conversation. Elijah didn't add anything to reassure him either.

There wasn't much talking the remainder of the excursion. Cottontail wanted to pick up the pace. He insisted on arriving at the train station before sundown. Safety was always a concern. Aside from that, it was nearly impossible to salvage at night.

The train station had several large doorways, opening to a lobby. One of the doors barely hung on the hinges. The walls on both the interior and exterior had huge dents and holes.

It's obvious quite a few turnings have gone down here.

No one had figured out the rhyme or reason that certain areas drew more turned women than others.

Elijah opened up one of the lockers. "You know, in all my years, I've never been out to these parts."

"Not many have…"

"Tend to steer clear where women have been sighted." He shut the locker.

"With rewards always comes risk," Cottontail looked around as though searching for something.

Uriah grabbed his head and moaned.

"Has the susurrus returned?" Cottontail jumped down onto a train track, startling a murder of crows. They cawed and disbursed in several directions.

Elijah hopped down after him. "That ain't the best sign. Scavengers tend to gather near their meals."

Cottontail climbed an empty railroad car. "Agreed. Sun's down now. Better we find shelter for the night than head back and risk ambush." He slid open the door of the first car and quickly shut it. He kept opening and shutting doors until he reached a car that met his satisfaction. "This will do." He smiled.

"I'll scope it out while you and Youngblood bring the animals around." Elijah opened the car door and took off his backpack.

Cottontail and Uriah went around the front of the station where the animals were tied up.

Cottontail untied Big Bo. "Is the susurrus back?" He rubbed Big Bo's head. "Once we're settled in, try meditation again."

Uriah reached for Betsy. "No… well yes. but not like before. There's just one voice and she's babbling. It's not loud, just a foreign tongue."

A crow cawed loudly, startling Uriah. The murder gathered and squawked. Uriah knew exactly what that meant. It was one of the signs that helped him find Evynn after she turned. *The bunnies that gathered around her while she was in torpor were some of the tastiest.*

Uriah united Betsy. "We better get back to Ace. That ain't a good sign. We should stick together for safety." He rubbed Betsy. He tugged her rein and she yanked back with a hint of panic in her eye. He rubbed her side. "It's okay girl."

Cottontail untied John-Albert, climbed atop Big Bo and pulled John Albert along.

As Uriah rode atop Betsy, the carrion hovered above. "It's like they are following us."

I don't like this one bit.

The susurrus intensified, sounding like splashes of incoherent babble—as though whoever was speaking was attempting to convey a message, but a message Uriah failed to comprehend.

Uriah reached the train cart first. "Yo Ace! I think there's more than an ambush we need to worry about!"

Uriah awaited, anticipating that deep, raspy calming voice. But received no rebuttal.

"That's odd, huh, Cottontail?"

"He could be searching other cars…"

Uriah placed his face against the window but the curtains were drawn. "Wait here, Betsy." He whispered before dismounting.

Uriah climbed into the car while Cottontail kept an eye on the animals.

"Ace! You in here!" Uriah walked down the aisle of the train, past empty seating. Uriah slid open the cart door leading to the individual pods.

A rustling of feet captured Uriah's attention. "Hey Ace, is that you?"

A few metal taps behind a curtain on the left side of the train drew Uriah—the second room on the left.

"Ace, you couldn't hear me?" Uriah said, pulling back the curtain. "I said I think we have more to worry—"

"Well look-uh here! Jack pot! Intuition be uh whore! And the good lord knows, I love me some whores!"

Uriah mouthed, "Jimbo!"

Jimbo had a revolver pressed against Elijah's back. He pushed him in Uriah's direction. "Stand next to your fella, there." Jimbo smiled. "See, I knews it. When I first scent ya." He pointed the revolver at Elijah. "I told myself. Dis boy a coppa-head. Them fancy words, that colored skin." He tapped his foot. "Lummis swears you's different. I said nahs. I just couldn't figure your end game 'til you brought them damn freedom fighters. You wanted us to kills each other off and yawl was gone take the spoils—our water! Y'all been eyein' it for years."

Jimbo wasn't the brightest. Dispelling his silly conspiracy would add more fuel to his blazing fire. Elijah just didn't want Jimbo to make any rash decisions.

He bent his wrist, jiggling the gun. "Admit you uh coppa-head."

Uriah wanted to tell him whatever would appease him. But...

"You fixin to lie ain't cha? This tall fella done already told me the troof." He smiled. "Just need you to say it."

Uriah's breathing was shallow. He sensed Jimbo's animosity towards him. It was like Jimbo blamed all the world's ills on Uriah. Uriah put his arms up in a sign of surrender.

Jimbo chuckled. "What yawl up there doin—drugs and hunchin' all day?" He yanked Uriah's arm, pulling him close. examining his arm. "What happened to the tracks on your arm, druggie?" He vigorously shook his head. "Get on over there... next to ya lil boyfriend." He hit Uriah with the butt of his gun.

Uriah rubbed the back of his head and groaned.

Elijah flinched. "A man, no need to get physical!"

Jimbo looked at his gun in confusion. "Do I got the big dick or do you?" He stroked the gun. "You coloreds think you really takin over, huh?"

A snarl fastened across Elijah's face. "This ain't about color man. It's about survival."

Jimbo mimicked him in a sing-song high-pitched voice. "You know what you people's problem is? You ain't got love. You can't have true progress without real love!"

He yanked Elijah and Uriah out into the hall. "Gone out to that other fella."

He pushed Elijah.

"Watch it, Jack!"

Jimbo bopped Elijah on the back of his neck. "Or else what?" He paused. "That's what I thought."

Jimbo hummed to himself. "Like I was saying. I lost love. A lover and a friend. And I wasn't the only one! All 'cause you pricks thought you could set us up. Oh, you gone pay. And pay in front of everyone you will!"

"Like I said before, Brother, I'm sympathetic for your loss. We've all suffered a great deal. But I don't have any idea what you're referring to."

"Refereeing to... there go dem big fancy words, yawl love usin'—of course you don't know what I refereeing to! You ain't ever been in love, yawl up in the big house hunchin' without connection!"

"Brother, I let it slide the first time. Prior to the plague I hadn't been with a woman in over a decade. Through self-discipline my orientation never wavered. Now what people do in their leisure is their business." He sniffed. "I don't judge. I just ask that you please leave me out of your fantasies..."

Jimbo pistol-whipped him across his back.

"Muthafucka!"

"Don't sound so fancy now?"

When they reached the end of the car, Jimbo pushed Elijah and he stumbled into Uriah and both crashed to the ground.

Cottontail helped the two up. "What's going on?"

Crows cawed rapidly.

"What we got here? You musta been a prisoner of war?"

"I beg your pardon?"

"Which one of these is not like the other?" Said Jimbo. "Ding ding—the injun!"

Uriah dusted himself off. "You know you wouldn't be so bad without that gun!"

"What you say to me, boy?"

"I bet that gun don't even work. Probably all out of bullets."

Jimbo chuckled. "You bet huh?" He shot Elijah in the leg.

"You muthafucka!"

The crows squawked and scattered.

"I don't know what you want from us. Take what you want and go. We mean no harm." Cottontail kept his hands in the air, showing he wasn't a threat. "Our friend needs medical attention. We need to go now!"

"Don't get fresh wit' me boy. You gone sit right here 'til Lummis get back. If he bleeds out, he bleeds."

Elijah reached for his thigh and applied pressure. Oddly enough he didn't express any outward sign of pain but more so frustration and disappointment as he shook his head and muttered. "Look, Jack, we're sorry for your loss, but you got the wrong cats."

"You ain't sorry but you will be." He pointed the gun at Uriah and motioned him to come over. "This one knows, and when Lummis gets here, he gone admit to it all!"

Elijah walked towards Jimbo as though he were wearing cement boots.

"Oouuu, I wish that was you I shot. But Lummis says—" he cut himself off mid-sentence.

"Look man, I know what's it's like to lose someone you love. The one person you look forward to seeing every morning. The one person you would do anything for. The person who gives you reason to keep going when you…" Uriah paused. "When you wanna give up on everything. I get it. Lee was your purpose."

Jimbo sniffed and wiped his face as though we were attempting to hide a potential tear. He gave Uriah a hard look over, cutting his eyes back and forth—as though strongly considering the possibility Uriah could relate. "Don't you dare say Lee Lee's name. You can fool Lummis with that bull. But you ain't foolin' me." He clenched his teeth.

Uriah shook his head.

Jimbo snickered, "For a moment there. You had me goin'."

Crows cawed loudly.

Betsy reared back on her hind legs and tugged free from her tie. The other two mules spooked and brayed emphatically.

Jimbo was distracted by the uproar.

Uriah seized the moment and used the palm of his hand to strike Jimbo on the bridge of his nose. It staggered him, and he doubled over writhing in pain. But he maintained possession of the gun.

Uriah sprinted towards Betsy and jumped on her back. With sporadic movements, she took off in the same direction as the train tracks.

The susurrus increased as though Betsy were heading directly towards it.

Betsy ran erratically, bucked and tumbled, but Uriah held the reins tight. Any direction away from Jimbo was the right way to go and she would get him there the fastest.

Uriah rubbed Betsy's side, whispering, "It's okay, girl."

It dawned on Uriah he was free. Despite him warming up to Cottaintail and Elijah, he had no obligation to them. His plan the whole time was to seize an opportunity to escape. And this was it. He should be smiling. Now he could focus on finding Evynn.

He hung his head. He didn't want Elijah to bleed out. He liked Elijah. But he needed to save himself. He needed to save Evynn. That was it. It has always been the two of them versus the world.

He considered how he would retrace his steps. How he would go back to where they last separated and use that as his starting point.

He squeezed his thighs as tight as he could as Betsy's erratic running increased as did the susurrus. It wasn't becoming louder but clearer. Despite not being able to understand the dialect, it was clear.

Betsy ran along the train tracks, galloping at a rapid rate.

A few hundred meters ahead a wooden gate came into view with bright yellow tape and an 'under construction' sign.

"Easy girl, slow down… I know you see that sign." He said in a wavering tone.

Betsy only increased her pace. Uriah debated leaping from the animal but wasn't sure if that would fare much better—maybe a collapsed collar bone or a dislocated shoulder.

If he could just steer Betsy, veering her path. They'd be fine.

He tugged on her reins.

Nothing.

He tugged harder, the leather straps digging into his palms as he yanked. Betsy was too powerful, too focused and too recalcitrant.

Gritting his teeth while grunting, he pulled with all his might. But she wouldn't budge.

He stiffened and closed his eyes, anticipating impact.

Wham!

Betsy toppled over the gate. Uriah, still holding tight onto the reins, catapulted off her, crashing into the dirt.

Betsy careened over the fence, landing on Uriah's ankle with an audible crunch.

"Awww!" He screamed in agony.

He made a bad situation worse. Betsy wasn't moving. She was stuck on top of his ankle. He hadn't created much space between Jimbo and him—not even half a mile if he had to guess. And even if he could move, he wouldn't get much of anywhere with his ankle how it was.

He did about the only thing he could do. He prayed.

Most High, I know I haven't made the best decisions up until this point. But you have continually shown favor and have always provided a way. I am appreciative of this. Thank you.

He sighed. The whistling of the wind provided his only company.

He used his free leg to push Betsy off him, but she didn't budge. He yanked at his leg but couldn't pull it out.

He still had the concealment of the night sky which would hopefully buy him some time. Maybe Betsy would wake up by morning. He only had to worry about snakes and other little critters.

He reached into Betsy's saddle bag and pulled out water and took a drink.

He thought of Evynn as he looked into the night sky and traced two half-moons in the dirt. He closed his eyes and tried to make the pain go away.

The pain ebbed. As long as he didn't move it, he couldn't feel much but an ache. But as soon as he moved, the blood rushed to his ankle.

Uriah's head rested on the dirt. The starlit sky provided his only means of escaping his feelings of anxiousness. So many stars in the night sky. Combustions zipping and whizzing as a bolide illuminated the heavens like fireworks.

The susurrus continued at a constant pace and he spent several minutes trying to decipher what was being said but it just sounded like foreign babble.

"Pitiful…"

Uriah combed the darkness towards the sound of the voice.

Jimbo had caught up to him. "To think you can escape a master tracker? If my pa ain't teached me anything. he taught me to hunt…" he walked over and kicked Uriah in the head.

"Ahh…"

"Shhh." Jimbo kneeled next to Uriah, his rank breaths hitting Uriah in wave after wave. "Does the little Copperhead have a booboo?"

Uriah grunted. *If only I had my knife. What I wouldn't give…*

Jimbo sauntered over to Betsy. "Here, let me help ya out." He sat down with his back to Betsy, dug his heels in the dirt and used his leverage to push against the donkey until Uriah's leg was free.

"Ahh!" Uriah winced. All the blood rushed to his ankle at once.

Jimbo tapped his lip and looked down at Uriah's leg. "That won't be working anytime soon. Poor fella."

"What do you want from me, man?"

Jimbo's smirk turned into a frown. "What do I want from you? Can you give me back Lee Lee? You can't give me nothin!" He spat on Uriah. "That's what you could give me!"

Uriah tried to raise himself but his legs had no sensation.

"I told you. Once Lummis gets here. You gone admit your wrongdoing and you gone atone for yer sins."

Uriah considered debating the man. He considered pleading. But it was evident his mind was made up. Whether justified or not, he was going to blame Uriah for all his shortcomings and tribulations.

"I didn't mean for any of this to happen. I just wanted Evynn back…"

Jimbo shook his head and sucked his teeth. He dug his finger into Uriah's ankle. "You still don't get it, do you? You ain't the only one with loss. Just cause you suffering, don't give you no right to disturb another man's peace." He dug his thumb deeper. "Oh, but you gone learn," he said with a snarl, jamming his thumb harder into Uriah's swollen ankle.

Uriah yelped in agony. He tried his best to hold it back, but the pain pulsated vehemently.

The susurrus loudened and Uriah shifted his focus to the murmur, escaping the pain.

Jimbo leaned against Uriah's torso and slapped his forehead and mocked him. "I just wanted Evynn back," he said in a whiny tone. "It's always about you innit? Well, Jimbo just wants Lee Lee back!"

Betsy regained consciousness and lay on her side, kicking her legs and braying.

"Hells gotten into her?" Jimbo scrambled, moving several feet, putting distance between him and the raging beast.

Betsy rolled to her feet and trampled in a circular motion, altering between clockwise and counterclockwise.

In the darkness a huge outline appeared several meters behind Jimbo. Uriah's eyes bulged. He crawled backwards through the dirt, pushing off on his healthy leg.

"Where you think you goin?"

The ruckus amply distracted Jimbo. He had no clue a gargantuan beast was right behind him. The color was difficult to discern in the dark but it wasn't much taller than Betsy. It stood on all fours as well but had twice the girth. And its red eyes locked onto Uriah.

Uriah didn't feel fear. However, he stammered. "B-b-b behind y-y-"

"Spit it out, boy."

The beast tilted its head and examined Jimbo. It looked as though it was analyzing more so than sizing him up.

Betsy brayed uproariously.

The creature squealed in unison.

Startled, Jimbo spun to find the source. "Oh God!" He drew out his revolver. "This is how it ends, huh?"

The creature bounded towards Jimbo.

"Damn that!" He placed the revolver in his mouth and smashed the trigger.

The beast caught the body before it could crash onto the desert surface.

"Please, please… no!" Uriah pleaded.

The beast slurped up Jimbo's blood. Lapping his face like an excited puppy.

Uriah felt remorse. But hoped Jimbo would be enough to quell the monster's appetite.

Uriah trembled. He had never been this close to a monster without it being devoured by Evynn or it being Evynn herself.

This monster was strikingly calm. It wasn't frenetic and bestial like every other beast—it reminded him of Evynn in that way.

It took a large chunk out the side of Jimbo's head and separated the remainder of his skull from his spine, effortlessly.

Uriah fainted.

CHAPTER 12:
OPPOSITES DETRACT

**I CAN'T BELIEVE MY
GIRLFRIEND'S A ZOMBIE**

JACK E. MOHR

URIAH

A cold wall of water slapped Uriah's face. He woke up in a panic and attempted to wipe his face, but his arms were restrained, hanging in the same manner his head hung. They were connected together by a wooden device, preventing any movement as he kneeled across a chopping block.

Okay, where am I now? He wrenched his neck from left to right but couldn't turn his head more than a fraction in either direction.

A meaty palm wiped the water out of his eyes. He recognized his father's rough, callous-filled hand.

"Dad," Uriah whispered.

Another dream. Cool. I can do this.

"Hmm hmm…" Lummis cleared his throat. "State your final words before you meet your fate—execution by axe!"

Albert kneeled beside him, rubbing the top of Uriah's head. "Son, I warned you. Stay ye away from that Jezebel spirit of deceit, but you had to be hardheaded." He wrangled the back of Uriah's head. "I told you—pain, chaos and destruction will follow her all days of her life until she's vanquished." He shook his head and drooped his eyebrows in pity. "Now look at you… paying for her sins."

Uriah's upper lip trembled in anger.

Albert took a deep breath and looked out towards the gathering and back at Uriah. He teared up, looking down at Uriah. "All you had to do was be a man… but didn't have the guts…You couldn't make the hard decisions." He took his open palm and struck Uriah across the face.

Uriah absorbed the blow without flinching. But it did hurt his pride.

"You deserve whatever's coming to you," Albert whispered.

Uriah fidgeted, trying to grab a hold of him. When he couldn't do that, he tried to bite him. Then he spit towards his father.

Albert gathered his composure and turned his back to Uriah. His slumped shoulders and hung head were something Uriah wasn't accustomed to seeing from such a proud man. "I loved you, son."

I know this is a dream, but it hurts. He raised me but never showed any sympathy for my feelings. How could he ask me to harm a friend? A girl I knew my entire life. A girl he even claimed to have loved as his own. How could he be so cold about it? Just acknowledge she is important.

Lummis stepped forward, adorned in an opal white robe, a purple stole and an ornamented Biretta. His metallic boots made the wood squeal as he walked across the stage.

He stopped directly in front of Uriah and looked down at him.

The piercing sun struck Uriah directly in the eye and didn't allow him to look up too long at the authoritative figure.

Lummis faced the gathering. "Hear ye, hear ye, do you, Albert Young Blood, take accountability for your trespasses by fair witness of the greater public? And by such admission do ye seek pardon?"

He looked down at Uriah, awaiting a response.

"Yes."

"To the former or latter or both?"

"Both."

"Very well. It is by the power vested in this high court. We find thee guilty. Acts against the betterment of humanity. Reckless endangerment of the innocent. Possessing weapons of mass destruction. And disturbance of *peace. Pardon waived. Suitable punishment—Death by Axe!" he rang out. He adjusted his robe and yelled at an even louder audible. "Axe man!"*

The axe man trudged up the steps, dragging an axe as long as his body. He couldn't possibly move any slower. Despite the hood, Uriah could tell it was Jimbo by his short pudgy frame and peculiar gate.

Jimbo reached back with his left hand and grabbed the axe, its blade refracting the sun's beams. He stroked the handle as though reveling in the moment.

He took his time strolling towards Uriah, each step methodical and exaggerated.

After he reached the wooden contraption securing Uriah, Lummis raised his palm motioning for Jimbo to stop.

"Before we commence, are there any last words?"

"I object!" someone shouted from the crowd.

Uriah couldn't peer out into the audience but recognized the smooth, raspy laid-back drawl. "Young Blood was merely in love!"

"Enough! Is there another?" Lummis paused. "No?" He looked down at Elijah to ensure he wouldn't utter another word. "Very well. Axe man, you may commence!"

Jimbo squeezed the axe's handle in his left hand and used his right to remove his hood. He smirked. "I told ya, I was gone get ya boy! This one's for Lee Lee"

***

"My brother, you are back. I hope now you have greater understanding of what the Buffalo represents."

Uriah rubbed his eyes. He reached for his ankle. It was healed—no pain, completely brand new.

Was it all just a dream? He was back in the warden's office.

"My brother, you will find yourself in one piece and in working order." Baba Johnson chuckled as he squeezed Uriah's shoulder. He looked Uriah in the eye—the look was peculiar as though he had hidden knowledge. He then stood and took a seat behind the warden's desk.

Uriah raised himself to a seated position and slowly placed his feet on the ground. He took several deep breaths before he mustered the courage to stand.

"By now I presume you have an understanding of what I am?"

Uriah rubbed the back of his head. The susurrus returned but at a low manageable rumble. "You heal."

"A bit of low-hanging fruit. And you are welcome, by the way."

"Thank you…"

He tossed Uriah a coin. "It's the rare buffalo nickel. The buffalo were once a staple of our people. They provided everything we needed in a time ago—food, clothing, shelter. Even their bones could be used for protection."

Uriah examined the coin.

"We are the embodiment of the buffalo. Each of us serves a purpose." He slammed his palm on the desk, jarring Uriah. He smiled. "That's what we are about, here. Using our talents for the benefit of the greater whole."

Uriah rubbed the coin. "I see."

"I apologize for what you may or may not have endured. But gifts aren't created, they are revealed and emerge through trials and tribulations. I'm certain by now, you at least tasted a semblance of your gift? After all, that's what this is all about— discerning what you are."

Uriah rubbed his neck as the susurrus dissipated. Instead in its place was a woman's voice. A voice clear as day—a familiar voice he struggled to place. *"Baba my daughter needs me!"*

—The woman from the guided meditation. She's real? She must be...

Uriah sniffled. "I think I have. It's hard for me to explain but I think I can communicate with things that aren't there—if that makes sense."

Baba scratched his chin. "A telepath or empath. I've only come across one other with a comparable ability." Baba stroked his chin as though reminiscing. "He didn't use his gift for the greater good. Only to go on wild witch hunts, trying to slaughter the turned. In many ways, some perceived that as good. But those were our mothers, sisters and wives he was desecrating—drawing energy from depraved destruction." Baba shook his head. "But this isn't about harping on past negativities but relishing your breakthrough."

Baba's demeanor was night and day from their prior meeting. He was upbeat and jovial.

Cottontail and Elijah? Are they okay? Of course they are; how else would I have gotten back here? I just need to see their faces and be sure. "Is Elijah okay?"

Baba cut his eyes in suspicion. "What reason would he have not to be?"

Uriah thought for a moment. *Elijah had been shot right? Maybe Cottontail only could save one of us and he left Elijah out there and would come back for him. Or worst maybe Lummis got the ups on 'im and someone entirely different brought me here.* So, many scenarios. Somehow, he didn't feel comfortable presenting Baba with the truth of what he witnessed.

"I don't know, I had told him, I'd see 'im when I got back and didn't want him concerned."

Baba tapped his finger on the desk after giving Uriah's statement consideration. He let out a singular chuckle, then snapped his finger. "Oh, where were we? Your gift!"

Uriah was relieved the brief bout of tension dissipated. It felt like it was some sort of test but somehow: *I passed.*

"Let's see what it's all about!" Baba heartily stepped toward the exit. "Oh, and leave the nickel on the desk."

Uriah looked out toward the courtyard, still teeming with men, although they were noticeably less frenetic. Men weren't playing cards, or dice or other games at the tables. They were gathered around, some had their heads in their palms, others just stared off.

Uriah tapped the glass… "They seem different…"

"Don't mind them. They're always like this before the selection for the Oblation."

Oblation? Oh, the guy who goes on the cross. Wait, he chooses who goes on that cross, but how?

I CAN'T BELIEVE MY GIRLFRIEND'S A ZOMBIE   273

Baba's chubby cheeks widened "When you give to nature, she will give back tenfold. Commit that to memory."

Uriah nodded, stuck the nickel in his pocket and followed Baba out of the office and down a flight of stairs.

In the distance, the pure sound of a horn pervaded. It soaked up the somber energy and gave it expression. *Elijah! He's okay! Maybe Ace could teach me how to play one day. Well, if Baba was the only healer why was he questioning the veracity of Elijah being harmed?* Something didn't sit right.

The voice in Uriah's head spoke, interrupting his thoughts, *"The prophecy has spoken. You cannot argue with fate."*

"What?" asked Uriah.

"Excuse me?" asked Baba.

Uriah cut his eyes away. "Oh, I thought I heard you say— never mind."

Baba continued down the flight of stairs, past the first floor.

The familiarity of the stairwell sparked Uriah's mind. He found himself in an awe-inspired disbelief. *If part of my meditation was real, does that mean all of it was?*

Baba continued down the stairs until reaching the bottom. There was a certain grimness to the environment that gave Uriah goosebumps. It seemed to be the dankest, darkest place in the prison.

Only an amber-colored light emitted from underneath a double door.

Baba withdrew something from his pocket and fidgeted with the knob.

The lady from the meditation must be down here. The déjà vu created a giddiness within Uriah. Like he was solving the last piece of a puzzle.

Baba opened the door. Several candles were lined along the pathway.

A shiny, hanging object reflected some of the light but Uriah couldn't make out much of what it was.

Baba walked with his shoulders back and his chin held high toward the end of the hallway. His stride carried a haughty arrogance.

The two walked past the shiny object towards the end of the hallway into an opening.

Heavy thuds approached them in the pattern of footsteps. But the stride was too long to be a man.

Maybe she wasn't down here at all. Maybe she turned?

Several grunts jolted Uriah's memory.

"Biggums!" He let the name escape from his lips.

The shiny object dangling now made sense. *The chain… Not this again…*

A deep voice grunted. "What Baba got for Biggums?"

A massive figure turned the corner, his shoulders filling the entire hallway. So much so, he had to turn sideways to get through as he tucked his head to avoid hitting a hanging pipe.

"Why Baba bring little doggie? Lil doggie want my chain back?"

He grunted. "Lil pup ain't learn the first time." Biggums slammed his fist into his palm.

Uriah took a few steps back.

Baba chuckled. "Lindfield, stand down. This is a brother and that's no way to greet a brother."

"He lil dog, though?"

"No, Lindfield, he's a brother." He slapped Biggums on the shoulder.

Biggums frowned as though someone took a toy away from a child.

"Out of the way Lindfield, we've come to visit LaShaun."

"But you say nobody but Baba can visit."

"Who makes the rules, Lindfield?"

Biggums pointed at Baba.

He smiled haughtily. "Thank you." He brushed past Biggums. "Pardon us." He motioned towards Uriah. "Come on."

Uriah tip-toed past Biggums, maintaining eye contact but stepping as softly as possible. He wasn't sure why, but he didn't want to provoke the colossal man.

The two turned the corner and were greeted by darkness. The only light came from the hallway behind them.

In the distance two shiny ovals materialized. They hovered and provided an additional source of light.

"Baba, is that you?" A voice emerged from the shadowy, dank confinement and warmed the entire room, a voice as pure as the horn Ace played.

It's her. It's the woman from the guided meditation. But her voice wasn't weak and broken. It possessed the same unique twang but was full and robust.

"Bonjour, mademoiselle," Baba said in a soft tone. He kissed her extended hand softly. "Profuse apologies for your arrangements… or lack thereof. I'd never treat the love of my—"

She interrupted as though she had heard the excuse a thousand times. Perhaps he wasn't so much apologizing to her but to Uriah for having to witness his mistreatment of her. This must have been his idea of minimizing her chances of turning.

"I know. It's okay. It's for our best interest." Her silver eyes brightened as she peered at Uriah.

Baba noticed. "Oh, this is—"

"An introduction is unnecessary. I've seen this young man many times." Her cheeks widened. "Come Uriah." Her moonlight eyes illuminated the sneer on Baba's face.

Baba's spine tightened and his shoulders stiffened. "But mademoiselle, he has yet to be named."

"His name was birthed to him." She extended her hands. "Please stop stalling, you brought him down here for a reading, no?"

"You are my milk of magnesia, and I trust your wisdom and guidance. I only seek confirmation that Jah would find this a suitable hecatomb."

Hecatomb? What does he mean by that?

She smiled. "I understand."

Uriah was enamored by the woman's eyes alone. Her soothing tone was enchanting. *How could she maintain such grace and regal bearing in such a dire situation?* If his mind wasn't clouded with Evynn, he may have thought he was in love with the older woman. Even her streaks of gray were modestly peppered into her curly hair.

He found himself unconscious drawn towards her, like a honeybee mesmerized by a blossom's sweet nectar allure. He placed his hands into her palms.

"Those are Mississippi Bayou hands, boy. The cradle of civilization… Feel honored."

Uriah ignored Baba's jab and closed his eyes. A gentle bolt of energy surged between the two.

A silence ensued.

Uriah wasn't sure what to think. He wasn't sure if he was supposed to be an active participant. Part of him thought he would be able to communicate with her on a psychic level. After all, he did see her in his guided meditation.

He tried to put his mind in a meditative state but couldn't.

He just patiently waited for her to finish. He knew somehow this was tied to fate. Ironically enough, this was the only time his mind was completely silenced and at peace.

Uriah's legs grew tired after a while, and he tried not to rock back and forth but that was the only way he could alleviate some of the pain and fatigue.

How much longer?

Uriah inhaled deeply as a stronger jolt of energy shot between the two.

LaShaun squeezed his palms and then withdrew her hands. She tilted her head and smiled at Uriah. She pulled him closer and kissed him on the forehead and whispered. "Thank you."

Baba cleared his throat. "Pardon my interjection but what are you thanking him for?"

"You would like to know what Jah revealed?"

"And what took you so long? A simple yes, he is an adequate sacrifice would suffice."

Uriah had a look of confusion plastered across his face. *Sacrifice? Wait a minute now? What? Me, sacrifice?*

LaShaun took a few steps back and sat against the stone-brick basement walls. "I envisioned him harvesting the seed of nations. And I saw my daughter happy, flourishing."

Baba adjusted his blouse. "Now, LaShaun, be careful what you speak. You always told me you couldn't picture the one who would bring forth a new nation…"

"I couldn't, but now it's clear."

Baba's voice quivered and his hand trembled. He bit his lower lip, fighting to hold back his disappointment, "Wha-what are you implying?" He said, composing himself. A neutral expression crossed his face and he clenched his left fist. "I'm sure this is a simple miscommunication."

This guy is seething. What's the big deal? He can find someone else to sacrifice. Why does he have it in for me so bad?

"Biggums!"

Grunts and heavy steps resounded throughout the basement. Biggums moved swiftly for such a large man.

Biggums grunted. "Baba called. See what him wants."

"Yes, Baba?"

Baba rocked on his heels. "Biggums, I need an objective ear. My lovely queen here is having difficulty communicating. Now, I thought I heard her say something but I'm unclear. Do you mind assisting?"

Biggums grunted. "Baba need help. Of course, me help him."

"Biggums you're a good brotha and the Almighty will bless you for many years to come."

"Selah!" replied Biggums.

"Mon cheri, would you mind repeating the prophecy you so eloquently divulged but a moment ago, so our dear brother, Linfield, may discern."

What is going on here? It was clear what she said.

"Baba don't do this," she pleaded.

"No, no. It's okay. It's okay," he placated.

The light of her eyes dimmed. And she bowed her head.

"It's okay."

"Essau, I don't like when you get like this."

"Get like what?" He placed his hand on his chest. "It's okay. I only request you repeat yourself."

She swallowed and closed her eyes. "I saw him as the sower of the seed that would bring forth nations. I saw my daughter elated."

"Thank you, love. That wasn't so bad." He slapped Biggums on the chest. "What did you hear, Leinfield?"

Biggums appeared giddy, rubbing his legs together like a child attempting to hold in his urine. "Uhh…"

"—speechless, I know." Baba exaggerated an insincere frown. "I can't believe she wants this good brother to be this retrograde's Oblation…"

"Me can't believe, Baba."

"But that's not what she—"

Baba quickly turned to Uriah, staring daggers through him. "That's not what she what?"

Uriah's breathing was heavier due to the mounting tension. *Baba isn't happy with whatever he heard for whatever reason. And now, somehow, he wants me to voluntarily offer myself as a ritual sacrifice to spare his arrogance?*

Baba wiped off his beard like he had crumbs in it. "Well, upon further thought it doesn't make sense. This boy was given opportunity after opportunity. Let's see. He was brought in specifically for Oblation but second floor claimed to see something special in him. So, I sacrificed a part of myself—healed the kid and offered him a chance to live here. He rejects the offer. So, I give him another chance. Tell the second floor to groom the kid. Let's see what he does with a little freedom. He tries to escape. Not only does he spit in the face of our generosity time after time. He now tries to seduce my tree of life and convince her to have his seeds."

Wait. wait. no. that's not how any of this happened.

Uriah held his tongue. Anything he would say would only further fuel Baba's delusions and give him more material to feed from. He was drunk with rage and was only seeking confirmation bias.

Baba's lip slowly curled into a snarl and his nostrils flared.

LaShaun rubbed her elbow. "Baba, you're being emotional and unreasonable. We all have been asked to sacrifice in order to make this thing work. It's about the future of humanity…"

Baba smiled and directed his attention towards LaShaun. "And some must sacrifice more than others. The young brother must do his part. Now, there is always one way out of his duty of Oblation."

Biggums grunted and poked out his lips. "Biggums born ready!"

LaShaun stomped her feet. "You're not even considering our daughter! And her future!"

"But mi amor… that's where you're mistaken." Baba snapped his fingers. "Linfield, kindly escort our young brother upstairs." He stormed past Biggums.

Biggums grabbed Uriah with both hands. Uriah didn't bother fighting. He didn't want his last breath to be in some dungeon in the middle of nowhere.

Biggums slung Uriah over his shoulder and followed after Baba.

As Uriah hung over his shoulder, he locked eyes with LaShaun.

Her eyes brightened. *"Please, look after my lil' girl…"*

A sincerity in her tone struck Uriah. *What little girl?* What did she expect from him? How was he to care for anyone when he didn't know his own place in the world? But her earnestness empowered Uriah—if she believed, perhaps, he could. *But who is her daughter? Where is her daughter?* He needed to find Evynn. That was his obligation. Besides, whatever Baba had planned for him seemed to have a finality to it.

Baba walked with deliberate weighty steps as though on a mission. "Brother Uriah, we are pleased by your act of humility. This evening the ceremony will commence."

As they neared the exit, Biggums grabbed the gold chain and placed it around his neck and Baba locked the door to the dungeon behind Biggums.

Uriah adjusted himself. "At least leave me some dignity."

Baba looked Biggums up and down, and then smoothed out his dashiki. "My brother…" he tapped Biggums on the shoulder. "Drop 'im."

Biggums lowered Uriah.

Uriah scowled at him.

"Uriah, it's imperative that you understand this isn't about power but about order."

Great. Here comes the justification. They always have a justification for their nonsense.

"I'm the most important person in this facility. I heal the sick, the infirm, the injured, the broken. I mend men." He looked Uriah in his eyes. "Do you get what I am?"

"I see what you are. No different than the rest of them. Power is convenient as long as you wield it. Any threat to that is an enemy. Save me your BS. I never asked to be here." Uriah's tone grew in its defiance. "If you're going to kill me. Just do it. I don't need your silly rationale. It helps you sleep at night—not me."

Baba toyed with his beard as they continued up the stairs. He didn't utter another word as they entered the Warden's office. He dismissed Biggums, sat at his desk and glanced out the one-way mirror. Uriah sat on the bed across from the desk.

Baba and Uriah remained in their silence for hours. Uriah considered breaking the stillness but had no idea what to say. He wanted to keep his dignity, and pleading to a man who already had his mind made up was unproductive. Baba seemed to be in heavy cogitation. He never bothered to even look at Uriah, merely continued to gaze out of the window.

Uriah couldn't discern if Baba was having reservations. But the silence spoke volumes. Uriah was something special. He wasn't sure why, but he now knew he was special. And that feeling alone inspired a confidence within him.

Just as he knew Evynn was special that day his own father perceived her as a threat. He knew the Most High would help him find a way out. He knew the Most High would provide the way.

After hours of silence, Baba turned to Uriah and scoffed. He walked over to him and pulled him up by his collar. "You're no threat. You're a lie!"

CHAPTER 13:
U OF HARD KNOCKS:
INSTITUTIONALIZATION 101

**I CAN'T BELIEVE MY
GIRLFRIEND'S A ZOMBIE**

JACK E. MOHR

EVYNN

"What's your name, boy?" Evynn leaned down and whispered into the horse's ear while rubbing the side of its belly.

She didn't expect a response but needed to take her mind off things.

Anxiety swelled and she wanted simple banter to relieve the stress.

I have a good feeling about Uriah, but I'm worried for him. How will these men perceive me? Could I pass as a boy?

She was always able to retain size even during periods of drought and men generally never even considered her as being a girl from her girthy build. But lately she had filled out, gotten a little hippy and added a few curves, which might prove more difficult to disguise.

Add to that, some maniac was hunting either her or Uriah, it was unclear which. Oh, and the fact she potentially could be pregnant and Adam or some mysterious Algorithm god needed her baby to preserve the human race.

Too much to wrap my mind around. First things first, I need to find U-rie.

"Larry… yeah… I like the name Larry. Do you mind if I call you Larry?"

She waited for a response.

"You don't mind?" She clapped her hands. "Splendid! Larry it is!"

Larry took smooth strides, traveling at a steady lope. Evynn felt guilty about leaving Bliss behind, but didn't want to put her in harm's way. It was guaranteed there was going to be plenty of harm along the way.

After a few hours of traveling, Evynn grew anxious. "I wonder how much longer?"

It couldn't be too much further.

A small fire blazed several hundred meters ahead. She could barely make it out in the bright daylight. *If a fire is still burning, whoever started it must be close.* Something seemed suspicious about the fire. This was why she and Uriah always stuck to obscure routes. No telling who one would encounter on a frequented passageway.

Evynn ducked off the highway and scoped the place out for about twenty minutes until she was satisfied no one was coming back to that fire.

Maybe they just left and hadn't put the fire out or they were leaving it as a marker to come back to. Either way it seemed peculiar, but time wasn't on her side. Who knows how many days she was unconscious and the more time elapsed, the less likely she would be able to find Uriah?

She studied the horizon one final time. She couldn't see into any of the brush ahead but hadn't seen any movement.

"Okay, Larry, when I say 'yah!' I want you to take off as fast as you can down that road and don't stop till I pull back your reins. Deal?"

Larry neighed.

Evynn smiled. "Good boy!" She rubbed his side. "Ready!"

Three... Two...one...

"Yah!" She squeezed the reins and flapped them hard as she could and Larry rocketed forward. "Whoa!" Larry sprinted faster than she anticipated. He veered to the left of the fire and kept going. Evynn felt some relief, having overreacted to the fire. She squeezed Larry with her legs and eased on the reins to slow the stallion.

As he slowed, Evynn sighed, still studying her surroundings.

Ahead of her to the right an odd movement rattled the leaves of the brush, spooking Larry.

Larry veered towards the opposite side and bucked. "It's okay, big fella." She yanked the reins sideways.

Larry neighed and increased his pace.

"Bingo!" A loud voice echoed from the brush.

Evynn looked back to see an object hurtling in their direction. It entangled Larry's legs, hurling the animal forward and launching Evynn.

As she flew through the air, she tucked her shoulder and rolled upon impact, minimizing the damage.

"Oof!"

The fall knocked the wind out of her and she coughed, then sprang to her feet.

She turned back towards the direction the bolo was thrown.

Two men approached, walking carefree and methodically as though they had read this book a thousand times.

Damn it!

Evynn turned the opposite direction and two more men approached, walking with the same arrogance.

"No bother running. No bother fighting. We can make it as easy for you as you make it for us."

The men were a good twenty-five meters away and closing in.

Damn it. Damn it. Damn it. "Damn it!" Evynn stomped her foot in the dirt. "Look. I'll make it even easier. Take what you want and I'll be on my way. No one has to get hurt."

The shorter of the men laughed. He had a mangy orange beard and tattered clothes and ratty hair. Didn't look like he had bathed in months. And he wasn't the worst of the lot. "One out of three ain't half bad. Is it boys?"

A lanky man with stringy, gray hair chuckled. He wore all black like a Western outlaw. He approached from the opposite side. "Lep, I'd certainly say so! We definitely will be taking what we want. It's just the nobody has to get 'hurt part', and the, 'I'll be on my way part' he got wrong!" He said with air quotations.

"You fell for the eldest trick in dee book."

"The ol 'fire in the middle of the road' trick." He tsked, and shook his head, feigning empathy.

The four sauntered towards Evynn, leisurely boxing in their prey.

Nothing left to do but fight her way out, but she wouldn't show her hand immediately.

The four stopped when they were about ten meters away.

"Incredulous. I would at least thought you would have a gun. What idiot would be out here by themselves with what? Let me guess: a knife?"

"What makes you think I don't have a gun?"

The four uproariously laughed in unison. "Cause you would have pulled it by now?"

They continued chuckling as though this was the funniest joke they had heard.

"This boy's a character! I gotta know his name!"

Evynn always went by initials when meeting strangers. She wasn't the best at lying so it helped.

"EJ…"

"Well, EJ, I must say, you one funny summabitch. If I was half the man I used to be, I'd almost feel bad for what's 'bout to happen to you."

"One could say the same," replied Evynn.

The group erupted in more laughter. "Since we're exchanging pleasantries. And of course, we're in no hurry. Allow us to introduce ourselves. I'm Lep, short for—"

"Let me guess… Leprechaun."

"Well, you ain't dumb as you look!"

"I'm Brett," said the thin, stringy-haired one.

As the adrenaline settled in, she became more cognizant of their wretched smell. If she hadn't wanted to expose her vulnerability, she would have covered her nose.

"Short for…" he waited for a response. "No, fooling you. Brett ain't short for shit."

"The other two gents don't speak. On the account they got their vocal boxes mangled." Lep shook his head. "Terrible accidents. On back-to-back weeks. Hence why we never run up on anyone anymore. We like to take our time. Utilize a little brains, you know?"

"Glad you were able to learn from your mistakes. Now, if you allow me to go free, I can learn from mine and you'll be giving back to the universe."

They erupted in laughter again.

"You know who we are, boy?"

"Foul-smelling bandits?"

"Close…I mean, yes…But—"

"Shut up Brett. We are the infamous Bohica Bandits."

Evynn exchanged glances among the men. "Infamous? I ain't never heard of…Bohica… is that tropical?"

The group laughed.

"You're golden! But no. Bend. Over. Here. It. Comes. Again. It's French for when you see us… you done really messed up…"

In unison their smiles turned to frowns as though they had rehearsed this very moment time and time again.

"I'm starving. Can we get this over with?"

Hold up… starving?

"I prefer dark meat, it's always extra tender." Lep chuckled.

Evynn reached for her dagger. "Get back! You guys aren't laying a finger on me!"

"How 'bout a tooth?" The group laughed.

"Boy, you don't think we seen plenty of those little salad cutters." Lep raised his shirt to display a chest full of scars like an abstract tick-tack-toe board.

"You miscreants keep back!"

"Miscreants? That takes me back. Ain't heard a word like that since my undergrad lit 2 class… back at State," said Brett.

"State! You went to college?" asked Lep.

"Yeah…"

"Prove it. What's miscreant mean?"

"Even if I didn't know the word, I could use context clues. It means bad guys, wrongdoers."

"Contet clues! By golly, you did go." He looked bewildered. "Then what the hell you doin runnin' with the lots of us. You institutionalized maggot!"

"What's that 'posed to mean?" asked Brett.

"Mean you was supposed to evacuate wit the rest of them city-slickers," Lep said with a lingering disdain in his tone.

"I'm a free thinker!"

"Not if you went to college you ain't!"

One of the mutes crossed his arms and huffed.

"Un-freakin' believable. Is this really the time to be having this discussion?" His voice cracked to a higher pitch like he was in the midst of breaking character. "Guys it's me, Brett! We been doing undesirable things together for damn near a decade!"

"Guess you never really know a man…"

"Really? Guys… really? We can talk about this later."

"Ain't no later. You're a deceiver and a city slicker, and you can't be trusted."

Brett chuckled in disbelief. "You guys are serious?"

Lep cracked his knuckles then pointed at Brett. "After we finish him, you's next."

The heavier mute grabbed Brett and they tussled.

"Go, help Timmy! I can handle this chubby lil boy on my own!" ordered Lep.

Lep took off his shirt and looked down on Evynn. His heavy breathing and slumped eye appeared more menacing the closer he approached. His worn, leathery skin was full of scars from years of combat.

It was intimidating, but Evynn had come face to face with monsters no man could survive—even if she hadn't been conscious of it, she knew it had happened. She was a monster herself and that knowledge in itself was powerful. Although, in this circumstance it wouldn't help much. She never decided when she turned, it usually just sort of happened and when it did, she had no control.

Even so, she had rumbled with men twice his size and none of them lived to tell the story. She removed the hood of her cloak. She holstered her knife and balled up her fist and nicked her thumb across her nose.

Lep cracked his knuckles. "This is gonna be fun." He opened his mouth wide, displaying several jagged and rotten teeth. He swung a wide left hook, aiming at Evynn's head.

In reflex she lifted her right forearm to block, then jumped back to gather her footing.

Whoa! He's quick, for an old man.

Lep looked impressed. "This will be funner than I thought." He shot out a quick left jab.

As Evynn dodged, he followed it up with a sweeping right hook toward her head.

She placed her left fist to her ear to protect her head and stepped towards Lep. His hook glanced off her fist and she countered with an uppercut to his gut and a cross jab to his face, knocking snot from his nose.

He stumbled back. He chuckled as he wiped a trickle of blood from his mouth. "Ok."

He took two quick steps towards her leading with his left foot. He feigned another sweeping hook. When Evynn went to block, he kicked the side of her leg. The blow caused her to drop her guard and he followed with a right hook to her ribs.

Evynn doubled over, holding her ribs. Without hesitation, Lep grabbed her head and pulled her into his body, placing her in a headlock, wrenching her neck as she bent over. She grasped at Lep's arms, trying to free herself as his forearms were squeezing on her neck, cutting off her oxygen. He only squeezed harder, pulling her closer to his body.

Lep's breathing was heavy. "I must admit. You ain't half bad. I almost feel bad having to choke out such a worth adversary." He cranked on her neck. "From just lookin' at you. I wouldn't of thought you would have put up much of a fight."

Evynn gasped. It felt like the vertebrae in her spine were being pulled apart. His grip was like a vise and he cut off her breath. She flailed her arms.

"Them soft hands and extra layer fat you have— it's like you been living good." He chuckled as he yanked harder.

Evynn stopped flailing and reached for her knife.

"If I didn't know no better, I likeded to thought you was a woman." He scoffed.

Evynn finally reached her knife. She quickly drew it and stabbed Lep in his side.

"What the—"

Before he could finish his statement. She stabbed him several more times, then dropped to the ground. She rolled back and forth, catching her breath.

Lep groaned and grimaced, struggling to his feet.

Evynn swooped up and sliced the blade across his jugular before he could regroup.

She turned towards Brett. He was struggling to hold on. She couldn't let those two mutes finish him off, and two on two was much better odds than two against one.

The three were entangled. One was lying on his back with legs and arms locked around Brett, restraining him. The other one was pounding on his face.

She sprinted towards the one knocking the teeth out of Brett's face. She pulled him off Brett, slicing his throat in one motion. She strained, trying to discard his mammoth body.

While Brett was still restrained, she drove her dagger through his heart.

The tall mute beneath Brett tried to toss Brett, but before he could, Evynn stabbed him three times in the neck. He placed his hands around his neck to curtail the bleeding.

Evynn watched his panic-filled eyes. She shook her head. "Nobody had to get hurt." She wiped her knife on the mute's pants to remove the excess blood and then wiped her hands as well.

Evynn walked away, panting, ignoring the man's gurgling.

She scanned the area looking for Larry. She stopped mid-stride. "Most High, thank you for imbuing me with the courage to survive. Show pity on the souls of the ignorant. But vanquish the iniquitous." She lifted her cloak until her scar was exposed. She pinched the skin on her collarbone and added four additional ticks. She grimaced with each cut but when she finished, she smiled.

She walked over to Larry and leaned over him. "I'm sorry you had to witness that side of me, Larry. But I'm sure you understand." She rubbed his side. "You took a hard fall back there. You okay?"

Evynn reached for her ribs. As the adrenaline wore off, a sharp pain emerged. With each breath, the pain surged.

Evynn climbed atop Larry, took a swig from her canteen and continued along her path.

As Larry galloped by the Bohica Bandits or what was left of them, she didn't even bother to look down—like they were discarded debris on the side of the road.

Evynn gradually cheered up. She no longer felt nauseous or queasy. She felt relief. Killing those men provided some satisfaction. It gave her a release for her anxiety without any hint of guilt. She relished 'them or me' situations. They made her feel most alive. The subjectivity was always eliminated from the circumstance and reduced survival to a business decision. Especially when it was unprovoked.

"Most High, I give you thanks for guiding my path and surrounding me with your protection. I trust and love you."

Evynn continued along her journey, hoping her baby wasn't harmed in the scuffle.

After a few miles, she rode by a sign displaying 'Proctor State Correctional Facility in ten miles.' Her heart fluttered with nerves.

Is Uriah really there?

Larry trotted along the trail. Evynn still felt uneasy traveling down such a common path by herself. She didn't want to try her luck any more than she had to. She was beating herself up for forgetting to loot the Bohica Bandits. Despite their raggedy presentation, one could never downplay any treasures they could have possessed.

She passed by an abandoned federal prison bus and heard something bump against it. She pulled Larry's rein, but he yanked back.

"What's wrong boy?"

He bucked, lifting his hind legs off the ground, neighing.

"Hey, hey, boy. Relax!" She couldn't calm him, so she hopped off his back.

What has him spooked? If I didn't know any better, I would have thought a turned was out here, but Larry's male.

Larry snorted and stood still.

But something behind that bus kept rattling. *Could this be another ambush?* Evynn leaned back against the bus, then ducked to a knee. She looked as far ahead as she could, but couldn't spot anything obvious. She looked back from whence she came: still nothing. She slowly inched her way around the bus until she reached the back. She peeked around the corner.

Brush had grown high, but a canopy stuck out of the brush.

The rustling continued.

She drew her knife and tip-toed toward the canopy. This time she would be the one doing the surprising.

She pulled back the canopy.

She gasped and stood still.

Not much was outside of her realm of possibilities, but this was something she didn't anticipate. She wanted to turn and run but her muscles were petrified.

"—A turned." She uttered.

The monster was chewing on a bone, like a hungry dog. Only this bone was attached to a man's leg.

She had never been this close to a turned without turning, herself, and of course she couldn't recall those instances. The only time she had seen a turned was from afar, and that was when she and Uriah would sneak into the city as kids. Those monsters were always belligerent, chaotic, full of rage. This one was calmly dining.

No…this was something she had never expected to see.

Why haven't I turned? Part of her hoped she would have turned, so she wouldn't have had to ever come face to face with such a hideous creature.

Was this the fear all her victims felt?

The chewing stopped as though it heard something out of the ordinary. It quickly looked over its shoulder and locked eyes with Evynn.

Its large bulbous eyes stared without blinking. It dropped the leg and tilted its head as though it was equally surprised to see Evynn.

Where was her aggression? Why wasn't she attacking?

Evynn sensed the creature's calm and it eased her. This one wasn't like the others she had seen as a child. They were raging, rampaging with non-stop aggression. This one seemed inquisitive, like it wanted understanding—it possessed an adolescent curiosity.

"Hello," Evynn didn't know what else to say.

The creature flinched.

"Sorry, sorry. It's okay."

The creature drew back.

That's fear. It's actually scared of me! She's turned but has control of her own mind. Remarkable. When I turned, sometimes Uriah swore he could see glimpses of me but it was usually surrounded by a whirlwind of fury and bestial impulse. But she's different.

Evynn slowed her breathing, calming herself. "Okay, let's see…" She slowly stuck out her hand, presenting the back of her palm to the creature.

The creature uncurled, displaying its massive frame. It vigorously shook its head like a puppy, slinging saliva and flesh from its jaws.

Evynn wiped a flung chunk of meat from her cheek. *Why would you possess any fear of me? It looks like it could eat me in two maybe three bites, tops.*

The creature sniffed as though it was analyzing the air. It took a few steps toward Evynn and sniffed again.

A stream of sweat trickled from Evynn's armpits. *This creature could use my arms as toothpicks.*

It placed its snout against the back of Evynn's hand and smelled.

So far, so good.

It then turned and rubbed its head against Evynn's hand, nestling against it.

Evynn drew in a deep breath and slowly exhaled. *This is a really good sign.*

"Hey girly, what's your name?"

The creature released a high-pitched shrill.

Evynn rubbed her temples. "We're excited, aren't we?"

The creature shrilled louder and jumped in place, salivating from the mouth. In its excitement it excreted a tart odor.

Evynn wrinkled her nose. "Okay, this is different. How bout I call you Gurly for now. Until we think of another name for you."

The creature's excitement increased. It spun in a circle, dislodging the bus several meters.

She can understand me. Or at least understand my intention isn't harmful.

She pounced on Evynn, pinning her to the ground and licking her face.

Evynn giggled. "Okay Gurly, calm down. You'll have to let me up." She laughed as she pushed Gurly's face away.

"Hold still… I don't want to hit you in error." A man spoke with a deep, calm voice.

Evynn tried to locate the voice but Gurly's mass prevented any clear line of sight. It sounded like the voice was coming from on top of the bus. Interestingly enough, it sounded familiar.

"Ugh!" the man grunted, as though he were heaving an object.

Gurly squealed as something tore through her shoulder.

Evynn spat as blood trickled onto her face.

Gurly rolled off Evynn and licked her wound. She looked up towards the bus and whimpered.

She's never been hurt before. Wait a minute. She's supposed to be indestructible. Everyone who turned was, that's what made them such a threat. They were only destructible to each other. *But she's hurt?*

Evynn flipped over, allowing the hood of her cloak to conceal her face. "Wait!" She cried out.

"Uriah, don't move. You can't protect her now. She's caused enough destruction. I'm going to jam my sword into the back of her neck, and end this reign of terror."

That's it. This is the voice from Judaius's place. The one looking for Uriah. He thinks I'm Uriah. Which would mean he thinks she is me.

The man adjusted his shoulder pads and snuggled his head into the helmet. He gripped his sword as he measured the jump, leaping through the air.

Evynn lowered her shoulder and knocked the man off course, mid-air.

Gurly took off in a blurring dash.

The force knocked Evynn to the ground and she grimaced, reaching for her shoulder. It hung limp. *I think it's dislocated.*

The impact dislodged the man's helmet and sent his sword soaring through the air. He stumbled to his feet and released a guttural bellow. "You made me lose her! You fool!"

Evynn stood; her right shoulder hung. She grimaced. "My shoulder!"

The man grabbed his helmet, sword and tossing knife and approached Evynn. "It's not wise to come between a man and his affairs!" He pointed his sword at Evynn. "Uriah, you've caused enough problems." He flicked Evynn's hood with the tip of his sword.

"You're not Uriah?"

"No shit. Can you help me with my shoulder?"

He examined Evynn and then stared back at where Gurly had been. He tapped his leg rapidly as though in a conundrum.

"It was an accident. I didn't mean to interrupt your affairs. Now can you help with my shoulder?" She grunted.

He inhaled deeply. "I was so close." He muttered. "I can't lose her." The man jogged back around the bus. And within a few moments, he galloped off on a white horse.

Evynn was in part relieved that the man hadn't discovered her gender. Yet, she remained frustrated that she put the life of that docile creature at risk. It wasn't like the others. And now she had to figure out how to put her shoulder back in the socket.

Evynn walked towards the front of the bus, grabbing her limp arm. She pulled it up until she was able to grip the bar connecting the side view mirror. She dropped her weight and hung, then kicked and contorted her body so that it swung. She gave it a huge yank and the shoulder popped back in.

She gasped in agony and released her grip.

She finally had a face with the voice. She had two options. Either get to that man before he reached Uriah or get to Uriah first. In either scenario that man was a threat… and that threat had to be eliminated.

CHAPTER 14:
REIN MAN, GIVE US REIN!

**I CAN'T BELIEVE MY
GIRLFRIEND'S A ZOMBIE**

JACK E. MOHR

URIAH

Uriah breathed through his mouth to avoid the vomitous odor of putrid flesh. The rank smell was the least of his worries.

I knew I should have left when I had the chance. Stupid!

He hung from a wooden cross. He was just glad it had a footrest to support his body weight.

Aside from him being a sacrifice, it seemed a rather joyous occasion. The sun was descending so it was beginning to cool off a bit.

Heavy percussion permeated the atmosphere, fueling the gathering's energy with rhythmic drumbeats. Ace played an up-tempo melody with his trumpet while other instruments Uriah couldn't recognize accompanied him.

The same group of women who were practicing the choreographed dance in the yard were putting on a dazzling display. They were "cutting up," as someone from the assembly yelled out. They had bright neon-colored hair, to match neon-colored tutus, black thigh-high socks and halter tops. They stomped their feet and whipped their hair back and forth in unison to rhythmic drums. Each one wore a different color of face paint.

An updraft of roasted pork, beef and chicken passed by every so often, masking the rotten smell emanating from the pile of bones below the cross.

Part of Uriah was envious he wasn't allowed to partake in the festivity. Minus the whole human sacrifice element, it would have been a splendid occasion—something he had never experienced.

Baba Johnson stood near the base of the knoll, cheesing and two-stepping as though he was having the time of his life. He wiped sweat from his brow with a handkerchief but didn't miss a beat.

With heavy steps he walked to the top of the mound and stood next to Uriah. He struck a triangle instrument to summon the mob's attention.

The crowd was huge and impressive. It seemed like everyone was there including Biggums, the only exception being LaShaun.

Baba struck the triangle until the crowd quieted.

"We are!" He exclaimed to the congregation.

"Because I am!" The crowd retorted in unison.

"We are!"

"Because I am!"

Baba paused, adjusting his dashiki. "And I am!"

"Because we are!"

"Louder!" Baba held up a fist. "I am!"

"Because we are!"

Baba spoke with thunderous bass and inspirational enthusiasm as his voice carried, propelling across the entire gathering. The natural acoustics transmitted his voice all the way to the prison. His charisma and vigor were undeniable, and it was easy to see why men gravitated to him.

His conviction was infectious. Uriah found himself involuntarily participating in the sing-song back and forth. If the circumstance was different, he wouldn't necessarily mind being a member of this community.

Baba wiped his brow. "Men, Brothers and fellow leaders of the Free Land, we come in celebration. We come in celebration. I said we come… in celebration. Give it up for fellowship one time!" He clapped.

The crowd roared.

"That ain't enough. Copperheads, give it up for fellowship!"

The decibel of the cheering increased.

"This evening, we not only come in fellowship and adulation of fraternity and new beginnings, but we come as survivors." Baba paused to take a drink of water. "Let me hear a big root for survivorship!"

The gathering released bass-packed woofs.

"As survivors we understand man alone controls not his destiny but God alone elects the fate of men. I said the Most High elects the fate of men!"

"Speak on it, Baba!" someone shouted from the crowd.

"We may not know the workings of the creator, but we do know we were chosen by Jah!"

"I know that's right!" the same voice yelled out.

"Tonight, we offer sacrifice to the Creator. Not as a means of exacting our subservience. Not out of fear. But out of appreciation. Out of peace!"

"Selah, brother Essau!"

"Although we are among the chosen elite, God is still teaching man a lesson. Since we did not appreciate being the top of the food chain. Since we weren't righteous rulers. Let me hear you say righteous rulers!"

"Righteous rulers!"

"God dropped us down a peg. The Most High, in real time, is enacting lessons of humility. A lesson we must learn before we can regain prominence."

Baba paused theatrically.

"We understand this is more than a sacrifice. This is a treaty. A covenant bond made to quail the tension between Mama Earth and all her seedlings. A show of meekness to demonstrate. I said to demonstrate. I said to demonstrate! To Mama Earth that we give graciously and with an open heart. So, that which has naturally become predator of man, may not view us as prey or adversaries but as allies and cohabitators. Until Jah shows us a greater way, healing Mama Earth of her infirmity!"

Baba smiled proudly. "Selah!"

The crowd erupted with a "Selah" of their own.

"Free the land!" cried Baba.

"It's already so!"

"Free the land!"

"It's already so!"

"I said free the land god damn it!" Baba stomped his feet and danced in a circle.

The crowd cheered and trombones played "When the Saints Come Marching In."

As the song played, Uriah's legs weakened. He felt anxious, wanting them to hurry along with their ritual or let him down. If he could get down, he'd punch Baba square in the face. He regretted not having the courage to do it before, but hope had restrained him. Hope of finding an amicable way out. But now all hope was gone, he wanted to act on impulse.

The song finished and Baba struck the triangle. "As is customary. We function as a brotherhood and must act in accordance. With that being said, any brother may come forth now and offer objection to said sacrifice and offer adequate replacement."

The murmur of the crowd descended to a silence. A lingering silence— the kind that made it feel awkward.

"I offer intercedence!" someone yelled.

Baba's shoulders slumped, and his smile dimmed. "Uh… Humph… Well, come forth!"

It took several minutes but Cottontail emerged from the sea of people. Adorned in brown leather pants, shirtless, with a headdress full of violet as well as black and white feathers.

His expressionless face exemplified the seriousness of his demeanor. He stared Baba in the face without breaking gaze.

He climbed the mound with forceful steps of determination. "I offer myself in his place."

Baba folded his arms across his chest and swayed from side to side, searching for a response. He anxiously scratched the back of his neck. "You may want to reconsider this. You are integral to the function of our community. Your leadership is irreplaceable."

Cottontail took another step—chin held high, unwavering. "Which would make the sacrifice all the more meaningful."

Baba smirked as though he were playing chess and had just been placed in check.

Uriah gulped. *Wow! Cottontail would do this for me? Even after I abandoned him and Ace. But why?* "Cottontail, you don't owe me anything? I can't let you suffer for me—"

"Silence! This is bigger than you," Cottontail said.

"The kid raises a good point, Cottontail. He accepts his fate. It's okay."

"It isn't what we are about. If we are to stand on principalities then we must consistently stand tall on those principles."

Baba looked towards the crowd as though he were searching for something or someone. "Fine. You must prove yourself a worthy sacrifice."

"What?"

"You heard me. Prove you're worthy. If you are as worthy as you say you are. It shouldn't pose an issue."

Cottontail's demeanor broke as a look of confusion surfaced.

Baba's bravado increased. He rearranged his dashiki. "Biggums!" he yelled out.

The mob must have been completely silent, because Biggums' footsteps rattled the earth as he stomped through the crowd.

He chewed on a roasted turkey leg and tossed it towards the base of Uriah's cross as he reached the knoll.

He grunted. "Did Biggums enjoy the gobble-gobble?"

"Very much so! He like, he like." He smiled and rubbed his belly.

"Who let this guy out! You know he's a menace to us all!" a voice yelled from the crowd.

He grunted. "Why no like Biggums?"

"They just hate because they want to be Big Dog, like Biggums."

If Cottontail possessed a hint of fear, no one could tell. He remained stoic, staring a hole into Baba.

"Oh, do avert your eyes, Emory. It would fair far better, if you eyed your adversary." Baba said, rubbing his beard.

"Baba, you have truly lost sight of who you are, but I see you clearly."

"Finally putting that seer ability to good use, huh," Baba muttered. He postured toward the crowd projecting his voice. "Great nation of One-percenters. We are because I am. There is one among us who believes he has a greater sacrifice to offer. As is the custom, God hears the voice of us all. As nature is the language of God, we must allow God to answer in kind. A test of survival."

He raised his right palm to the audience and a deep, bass-filled drumbeat began.

He struck the triangle and it stopped.

"We have before us mighty men who will joust for the fate of our Oblation. The outcome will determine which sacrifice is appropriate for the Most High." He cleared his throat. "On the one hand, we have Emory, offering himself. On the other we have Linfield, representing Uriah."

Baba raised both hands and the drums sounded.

Baba struck the triangle. "If Emory proves the victor, he earns the right to be deemed a worthy gift. However, if Linfield is victorious, we continue the Oblation as presumed."

Baba raised his hands, and the drums resumed.

"Emory! Linfield! Let the jousting commence!!"

The crowd roared.

Cottontail was unshaken throughout the commotion, not taking his eyes off the taller, stronger foe.

Biggums smiled and bounced around jovially, circling his opponent. He hopped on his toes, displaying his agility. "Him scared!"

He grumbled. "Him should quit before him get punished."

Cottontail sank into a stance, putting both fists in front of his face. His breathing was slow and steady.

Biggums spontaneously lunged at Cottontail. Cottontail stepped to the right, dodging Biggums and as he flew by, Cottontail pelted him with a back fist, striking the rear of Biggums' skull.

The crowd erupted.

Uriah smiled. Although he didn't want Cottontail to take his place, he still wanted him to whoop Biggums' ass.

Biggums shook his head and grunted. "He think he slick!"

"Him no slick, him a tricky coward."

Biggums spun around to face Cottontail. He cautiously approached, throwing out a few jabs.

Cottontail slapped the jabs away, remaining in a defensive stance.

Biggums feigned a left jab and struck Cottontail with a left sweeping kick, buckling his leg. Then he lunged.

Despite Cottontail's leg buckling, he jumped out of the way, dodging Biggum's attempt. When Cottontail landed, he grimaced, reaching for his knee.

"Him hurt."

"Yeah, he hurt. Him no deserve me chain?"

Cottontail limped away from Biggums, buying himself some time to regroup.

"You want my chain too?"

Cottontail took a deep breath. "I do not desire you chain, brother. This is about principalities."

Biggums stomped his feet. "He uses reverse piecology."

He grunted. "Him try to psychologize you. Show him who the boss!"

Cottontail relaxed, closed his eyes and controlled his breathing.

Uriah shifted his weight to his other leg. He smiled. "He's doing that thing he did from the first fight."

Biggums pounded his chest. "Him scared. Him don't wanna see. But him can't be saved."

Biggums charged Cottontail, leaping with a large hammer fist, striking the crown of Cottontail's head.

Cottontail didn't flinch or budge even a smidge. His eyes remained closed, his breathing steady—oblivious to any force Biggums doled out. And Biggums continued pounding with all of his might—uppercuts, hooks, jabs, kicks, elbows, hammer fist, anything he could think of.

Biggums ran out of steam. With heavy labored breaths, he placed his hands on his knees. His bravado transformed into defeat. He took several steps back and his shoulders slumped forward. "Huh?"

He grunted. "Hit harder!"

Biggums took a deep breath and resumed pouring down hammer fists like a berserk gorilla, hitting Cottontail in every location he could conceive—thunderous blows to the sternum, neck, arms, torso.

Nothing phased Cottontail.

Uriah cringed. He knew Cottontail would have to pay on the tail end for all this punishment he was taking. *How much longer can he withstand this beating? Biggums hits way harder and has more stamina than Niko.*

Biggums relentlessly attacked, his breathing intensified. He continued to swing and dropped his hands to his knees, panting.

"Biggums tired."

He grunted. "He make you quit?"

Biggums looked at Cottontail. Biggums' frown exuded his discouragement. "He no feel no pain."

Cottontail kept his eyes fastened shut, disconnected from the present moment—non-localized.

Biggums held his chest and fell to a knee. "Me heart."

Cottontail opened his eyes and turned towards Baba. "It is finished. He can no longer go on."

A rage within Baba's eyes roared. He stomped over to the fallen Biggums. "This isn't over!" He grabbed Biggums by his head and placed both hands on his temples. He stared into Biggums eyes. "You better get up and compete!"

Uriah fidgeted on the cross. "That's not fair! He's cheating! He's healing him!"

"Get up! Get up, Biggums!"

Biggums stood to his feet and pushed his chin with his thumb, cracking his neck. "Biggums no tired." He bounced side to side, springy and full of renewed energy.

A horror came across Cottontail's face. He had broken his trance. It was only a matter of time before all the pain he displaced came surging back.

Biggums wiped the sweat from his forehead. He slowly approached Cottontail, each step striking the earth like a sledge hammer.

Cottontail regained his composure, but sweat dripped profusely. He tightened his lips as though he were holding back a scream. His facade crumbled and he reached for his ribs.

Biggums spotted the opening and without hesitation lunged with a wide left hook.

Cottontail jumped back, dodging the blow. He yelped as though the blow had hit him.

Biggums followed up the left hook with a straight right jab.

It knocked saliva out of Cottontail's mouth. He groaned.

Cottontail reached for his head, then hunched over grabbing his side. He fell to the ground wailing in agony.

The displaced pain could no longer be restrained and rushed back all at once.

Cottontail convulsed.

Biggums leaped up in down with his hands raised in triumphant victory. He displayed his chain. "I'm the big dog! I got the big chain!"

Baba flapped his arms in an attempt to hype up the crowd. They looked on in silent astonishment.

After a few moments, drums beat and a few gatherers reluctantly clapped until more gradually joined in. Before long sparse barks sounded from the crowd until eventually the majority joined in.

Baba struck the triangle. As the crowd silenced, he looked down on Cottontail in contempt. "Somebody get him out of here."

I CAN'T BELIEVE MY GIRLFRIEND'S A ZOMBIE   319

After several minutes, Ace appeared at the base of the mound with trumpet still in hand. He shook his head. "You know you ain't right for this Essau…"

Baba scoffed. "Be careful whose hand the lil doggie bites."

With a strained voice, Ace released his frustration on the crowd. "Will somebody get up here and help me, damn it!"

Cottontail's convulsions slowed.

Baba didn't bother sparing a glance as Cottontail was carried from the mound back to the prison. "Is there no one else who disputes tonight's Oblation?" He waited several moments. "Very good. And it shall begin!"

***

Uriah didn't know how much time had passed. Hanging on that cross in discomfort and pain distorted any sense of time and some sense of reality. It felt like many hours but it could have been just one.

He had clear sight of the moon and looking at it reminded him of Evynn. *Bonded by the moon's double crescent.*

He felt bad he wouldn't get to see her again but felt worse she wouldn't get any closure for his disappearance.

"Most High, place peace on Evynn's heart. I know she's still alive. Please surround her with an aura of safety and security and look after her. And if is in your will, provide her a safe return to the Old World."

Uriah's arms were numb, and his legs ached, feeling like lead. His breathing grew faint, becoming increasingly difficult with each breath. Whatever Baba had planned, he wished he would get it over with.

The entire gathering had retreated to the prison some time ago. Only he and Baba remained. Wind whistled by as the temperature dropped.

For the last thirty minutes, Baba had been sitting at the base of the mound with his eyes closed, muttering. He was in heavy concentration, directing all of his energy towards whatever he was uttering.

Uriah couldn't decipher what was being recited but if it was any other man, he would have believed it to be a prayer or some kind of sacred pleading. But Baba's arrogance didn't lend to him being the type to sincerely acknowledge any greater power.

What was his real purpose for doing all of this? Liars are only motivated by one thing and that's self-interest.

Baba stood and raised his arms towards the moon, vividly ornamented with stars in the clear night sky.

Baba placed seven candles on each side of the cross, creating a path leading to the symbol of sacrifice. He lit each candle all the while not paying Uriah any mind.

"Hey!" Uriah said. "Hey, what do you get from all this?" Uriah possessed an added jolt of energy, twisting his torso on the cross. "Hey! I know you hear me."

Baba continued ignoring him.

"Is it fear? Keeping the inmates in fear so they stay under your thumb! Cause I ain't scared of you!"

Baba paused and calmly looked up. "My people need not fear me. I'm a man of virtue, a man of the people—appointed by the people."

Uriah scoffed and spat. "How 'bout you get me down from here and you offer me that same deal you offered Cottontail? How 'bout it? Me and you... one on one. Nobody's out here!"

Baba continued to lite the candles, ignoring him.

"What's the matter? You scared of someone half your size, fat man?"

Baba chuckled. "Since you haven't much longer on this earth, I'll entertain you." Baba stood to his feet and wiped off his knees. "You know your problem?"

Uriah grunted as he adjusted himself. "I'm sure you'll tell me."

"You don't realize how insignificant you are. I've tried time after time in so many ways to enlighten you, but you're too dense. This isn't about you or me, brotha. This is about progress."

"Progress? You mean the green-eyed lady's dreams?"

Baba chuckled and whispered to himself. "The green-eyed lady's dreams..." He scratched his neck. "That 'green-eyed lady' is a bayou prophetess who foresaw everything leading to this point from before the cataclysm!" His volume increased. "Those aren't dreams but realities needing to be achieved!"

"You lie!"

"I lie?"

"She saw me in that future! That's what this is about!"

Baba shook his head. "There's endless possibilities, young brotha. That's what you fail to comprehend."

Uriah gasped for air. His breathing became gargled and laborious. "You still lie. Even though I'm facing death. You ain't lying to me, you're lying to yourself."

"Young brotha. This is for the people. Nothing is bigger than the people, truth or lie." He lit the last candle and approached Uriah. He muttered a prayer to himself and drew a dagger.

A ringing sound pulsated in Uriah's head followed by a voice. *"She's near."* It was LaShaun, but how could she communicate so clearly? Was this message even for Uriah?

Uriah involuntarily repeated the phrase.

Baba held steady the sleek blade, lifted Uriah's shirt and sliced it across his torso.

Uriah squirmed.

Baba smiled. "As the prophecy goes. My seed shall repopulate the earth. I just need to keep her alive long enough to heal her…"

It finally clicked for Uriah. Somehow whatever was coming to feed on him was related to Baba. *Maybe his daughter had turned? But why not keep her below the prison like LaShaun?*

It still didn't make sense.

More ringing resounded in Uriah's head. LaShaun sobbed *"Baba, allow me my child!"*

***

Baba lit large torches on both sides of Uriah. After doing so, he sat with legs crossed facing him.

Uriah's breathing was faint and weakened almost to the point of nonexistence. He wiggled his toes and fingers but everything else was numb.

Baba leaned forward and touched his leg. "Uh-uh un... not yet. We need your vitality intact, young brotha."

A surge pulsed through Uriah, and a tingly sensation spread throughout his body as he regained sensation.

He's healing me just enough to keep me alive, sick bastard.

"It shouldn't be much longer," Baba chuckled. "Speak of an angel and she shall adorn you."

Baba stood up and took a few steps backward. The crackling of the torches' flames taunted in compliment with Baba's doting demeanor.

A large, indistinct creature stumbled towards Uriah. He had seen a good amount of these behemoths and despite the wide variety, his imagination was able to fill in the blanks. The light from the burning torches only allowed him to see so far.

The rumbling steps clumsily approached and the outline of the creature slowly materialized.

Baba's grin couldn't grow any wider. The look of anticipation was of a famished man salivating over his first bite of warm roast.

It's the same thing that ended Jimbo. That's Baba's daughter?!?

The creature stumbled towards Uriah, extended its green proboscis and sniffed Uriah up and down. A viscous dark liquid trickled from its hairy shoulder.

It's bleeding?

Uriah felt an odd peace, in contrast to how he thought he would feel. Perhaps, this being his second encounter with the bestial creature helped.

The creature was massive, menacing and mutated, but it possessed no aggression. In fact, the way it wobbled its head back and forth reminded him of Bliss when she was a puppy.

Uriah halfway grinned.

"Come here, sweetie!" Baba spoke in a high-pitched puerile voice.

The beast wobbled towards Baba and nestled into his arms.

Baba hugged the creature's head, then rubbed his hands along the creature's shoulder. "Uh oh! What's this?" Baba inspected its shoulder. "Did somebody hurt you? Let Baba heal you." He kissed her shoulder, and the creature made a strange, guttural squeal.

The buzzing resumed, resonating in Uriah's head. *"She's hurt! I need to see her."* Cried LaShaun.

"Hey Baba!"

Baba sneered. "What!"

"Why don't you let her see her? You know that's what she wants more than anything. She only wants to see her daughter."

Baba sighed. "To be frank, it doesn't concern you. But if you must know." He rubbed his daughter's head. "She emanates a must that could turn LaShaun immediately, depending on the proximity."

Uriah felt sad for LaShaun. She only desired to see her daughter. And he could physically feel her melancholy. And to some extent, he felt bad for Baba. For obvious reasons he couldn't allow the creature around the facility, but he had a bond with her. It was apparent, despite her grotesqueness, he loved her. Uriah wondered what she looked like when she wasn't turned.

"How old is she?"

"Huh?" Baba placed his hand on his chest and tilted his head. He was taken aback by the question.

"Your daughter, how old is she?"

"Evy is going on 15 months."

"Evy, huh… so close to Evynn."

From the corner of his eye, he caught a shining blade vault out of nowhere, striking Evy in the shoulder, ripping out a huge chunk of flesh.

Uriah gulped. These monsters were impenetrable. He had only seen one man with the ability to damage them. And that was…

"Lummis! What the hell are you doing here! An act of War! This is hallowed ground!" yelled Baba. He reached for Evy, healing her.

She howled in pain.

The buzzing sound resonated in the cortex of Uriah's head. *"My baby!"* LaShaun was distraught and her voice exuded urgency.

Baba stepped in front of Evy as a protective shield. "How dare you break our truce!"

Lummis was adorned in full armor—the makeshift, discarded body parts of once-turned women. He removed his helmet and picked up his sword. "Me? I broke the truce?" He smirked and pointed the sword towards Uriah. "You and your abomination are responsible for the death of good men. Good men of dignity."

Baba's eyes narrowed. "I don't know what you're talking about. She's a child. She's not aggressive."

"Of course, you don't." Lummis methodically approached Baba. "Is it true what they say? A man can heal the world but still can't heal himself?" He said, lunging at Baba with his sword.

Baba jumped to the side but couldn't avoid the sword slicing his arm. "Ahh!" He grimaced.

Lummis pointed his sword towards Uriah. "I'll deal with you later!"

Evy growled at Lummis.

Baba held his shoulder in agony. "No, Evy, stay back!"

Lummis twirled the sword from one hand to the other with a broad grin. "That's right. Purr for Poppa. Make me earn it!"

Evy stomped, jumping up and down. The impact rumbled the mound, shaking Uriah's cross.

Uriah's head buzzed. *"She's scared. She needs me!"* exclaimed LaShaun.

The monsters were indestructible beasts that destroyed everything in their path, but recent events turned this notion on its head. Uriah had seen Lummis' trophies and had witnessed him take down a freshly turned beast as no one else had; not even the bombs the US government had dropped phased the creatures.

But how? How was he able to achieve what no other has been able to?

And before today, Evynn had been the only monster he had witnessed with any semblance of consciousness, but this creature was shifting the paradigm. She was not only conscious, she was thoughtful, loving and protective.

Uriah attempted to work his hands free from his bondage but had no luck. He needed to get down. He had to do something. This was all his fault—a trail of bad events leading back to him.

I'm the only common denominator of all of this. Maybe it is my fault...

Evy snarled exposing jagged teeth and leaped at Lummis.

With preternatural reflex, he spun to the side slicing her hind leg as she leapt by.

"No!" Screamed Baba. "You won't make it out here alive. You better kill me too. If you allow me to leave, every single Copperhead will be at your doorstep and we won't stop until blood flows like the Mississippi!"

Evy limped, turning to face Lummis. She whimpered. An oily must pooled near her temple and spilled down the side of her head, sticking to her fur.

The buzzing sound intensified within Uriah's head causing it to throb. He groaned in agony. The susurrus returned as a raging babble.

CHAPTER 15:
WATER FOR THE ROOTS, NOT JUST THE LEAVES

I CAN'T BELIEVE MY GIRLFRIEND'S A ZOMBIE

JACK E. MOHR

EVYNN

Although the intangibles weighed on Evynn's spirit, the elements were much more forgiving. A clear blue sky and a warm crisp night eased her travels. She was tired, hungry but determined.

The crescent-shaped moon reminded her of Uriah. She'd hoped to come across twin crescents in the dirt or anywhere for that matter—just an added glimpse of hope indicating he was close or at least had been nearby.

Even so, she remained resolute, allowing intuition and faith to guide her and keep her purpose validated.

Evynn rubbed her belly as Larry trotted. This was the first time she contemplated what could potentially be growing inside of her.

Am I really pregnant? Is it truly possible? Wow, this could really be true. What kind of mother would I be? Will I have another little Evynn or U-rie Jr.? She smiled. *Or Twins! Uriah's going to be so shocked.*

Her smile dissipated.

More hopeful thinking. She didn't want to get her hopes up too high only to have them crash and burn.

On the horizon several large structures appeared.

That must be the prison.

She tugged on Larry's reins. "Easy big boy. We're here. Now, I'm going to leave you. I'll need to case out the place first."

Evynn tied Larry to a street sign a half mile from the facility and covered the remainder of the journey on foot.

As she neared the penitentiary, the two guard towers detoured her from entering through the main entrance. Although there were two more towers near the rear, there was less open space and the shadows gave her cover to hide in.

Concealing herself amongst the shadows, she made her way to the rear. The commotion of men yelling captured her attention.

Two pillars of fire burned in the direction of the voices.

Best to explore all potential threats.

She withdrew her blade and gripped it firmly in her left hand. Her chest rhythmically rose and fell as she steadied her breathing.

She spun around as the sound of a rubber tire rubbing against asphalt caught her attention. She couldn't make out what was coming her direction, but it was large and traveling with immense velocity.

In the dark, Evynn could make out two silver orbs zooming towards her. She ducked behind an abandoned SUV.

A large beast ferociously slithered by, hell-bent on getting to where it was going. This was a unique monster in its own right. The two silver lights were glowing diamond-like eyes.

The creature was as long as a bus and almost as girthy. It slithered like a snake despite having arms and legs—they flailed like they were there just for show.

Fascinating. The monster was full of chaos but its wrath wasn't taken out on any and everyone. It possessed a tremendous focus.

This is the second turned that possessed socially developed traits. Were they changing? Are they evolving?

I CAN'T BELIEVE MY GIRLFRIEND'S A ZOMBIE   331

Evynn tucked in right behind the serpent. It would create enough of a distraction for her to snoop around and find a viable entrance to the facility if all else failed.

Evynn jogged until she caught up to the creature. The serpent didn't stop until it reached the area with the two burning fires.

By the time Evynn caught up, the uproar had escalated. The serpent cried out and to Evynn's surprise, it wrapped itself around Gurly.

The serpent appeared to be shielding Gurly, who was shrieking in pain.

The man from the bus was there—fully covered in his crudely constructed armor.

Evynn's heart fluttered. "Oh no! Uriah, what have they done to you?" She held her blade to her chest.

She looped widely around the mound, being sure to conceal her presence. She crawled up the back of the mound. "U," she whispered.

Uriah searched both sides of the cross. "Huh? Ev, is that you?"

"Shh… I'm going to get you down." She cut through the rope securing Uriah's arms and legs.

He fell from the cross, landing on the pile of bones. He tried to stand, but his legs didn't work, and it took him a few moments to regain the feeling in them.

Evynn hurried over to him and embraced him, holding his head in her lap and kissing his forehead.

Uriah only had enough strength to hold on to her forearm. He nestled into her arms as though she absolved him from any care in the world. He looked into her eyes then glanced at the moon behind her and smiled. "How did you find me?"

"We'll have plenty of time for that later. Let's get out of here."

"Wait…"

"Wait?"

Uriah's legs tingled and he pulled away from Evynn's clasp. "We have to stop Lummis. He won't stop till he hunts down both you and me. We can run forever or end it here."

"Lummis. Let me guess. The one with the armor?"

"Yeah."

"Ran into him earlier. From the looks of it, his hands are full already."

Uriah grabbed a femur bone and held it like a weapon. "I've seen him take down two of these beasts singlehandedly."

Evynn's eyebrows furled. "Then what do you expect to do with that?"

Uriah clutched the bone and crept to the backside of the mound. "You got your knife, right?"

"Uriah, I think we should regroup and approach this some other way with clear minds and a thought-out plan."

Uriah paused. He was thinking. Evynn loved when he stopped to think.

"Okay."

Lummis slid his sword along the ground, tracing a snake in the grass. "Well, the gods have truly sought favor on me in this most auspicious of nights!" He retreated several steps away from the creatures. "Praise be to the round table and all her knights. I prayed for one beast but I've been blessed with two!"

Baba's arm hung. He clenched his jaws, masking his obvious pain as he approached Lummis. "Brother, it's not too late. We can undo this. This isn't anything I can't heal. It's not too late. We can still honor the truce and pretend this never happened."

Lummis gripped his sword with both hands and smiled. "Pretend this never happened..." his grin possessed an ambitious greed. "Pretend half my men haven't lost their lives? Pretend I haven't traveled without food or water for days to reach this very fortuitous point in time?" Lummis nodded at Baba with a sardonic smile.

"I know it's a lot. We have both suffered loss. But—"

Lummis wielded his sword and before Baba could finish his statement, it sliced through Baba's arm.

The arm hit the ground and rolled towards the creatures.

It took Baba a moment or two to register the fact he was missing an arm. He dropped to a knee. In a panic, he grabbed his arm and tried to reattach it.

"Now we have all suffered loss. Now let me ask you, Baba. Do you still want to pretend like none of this happened?"

Baba cried as he continued to attach his arm. There was so much blood.

"Fuck you, man!"

Lummis chuckled. "Thought so." He widened his stance and changed his focus to the beasts. "Guess what they say is true. The man can heal everyone but himself!"

Lummis circled the serpent.

The serpent's only concern was the protection of Gurly. Under any other circumstance it would be going berserk—frenzied in an all-out assault. But this creature was different. There was a method to its madness.

Did she not understand she needed to protect herself? She must attack. If she doesn't who will be here to protect Gurly?

LaShaun's head swayed like a pendulum. The glow of her silver eyes brightened as she hissed at Lummis.

Uriah squeezed Evynn's hand. "Ev, I don't know. Sometimes it's bigger than just us."

Evynn understood Uriah's hesitation. Despite her deep desire for self-preservation, she felt a level of guilt too. Gurly was innocent.

Lummis was a madman consumed by vengeance and couldn't be reasoned with. He wouldn't stop until he was physically forced to.

She squeezed Uriah's hand. "You're right. We gotta do something."

Lummis gripped his sword, stalking in a circle as though he were plotting for the perfect time to strike.

A loud blaring horn, filling the atmosphere, captured everyone's attention.

Evynn and Uriah ducked behind the mound.

A large convoy approached with tons of lights, illuminating the night. Leading the caravan was a large RV, mounted with an immense searchlight that shot straight into the sky. From the looks of it, the light was powerful enough to touch the moon.

"Adam!" Evynn whispered.

"But where did all of this technology come from? And why haven't you turned yet?"

Evynn grabbed Uriah's hand. "I'm not sure, but we need to leave now."

Uriah gently pulled away. "Now hold on. We do need to leave but let's hear what they have to say first."

Two SUVs pulled up beside the RV with men hanging out the windows with rifles in hand. The men wore all-black protective armor. Helmets with clear face shields covered their heads.

The gear appeared to serve a dual purpose, protection from combat as well as limiting contact exposure as though the men were aware they were within a 'contaminated' environment and didn't want to risk exposure.

The convoy bombarded LaShaun for two straight minutes with a hail of bullets.

Lummis hopped out of the way, rolling out of the line of fire. "Don't bother." He said, waving his sword. "This blade alone has the power to slay these majestic bestial deities!"

The RV slowly approached, stopping several meters in front of the mound. The commotion drew everyone outside from the penitentiary.

Evynn and Uriah retreated further into the shadows, ensuring they wouldn't be detected by either party.

Fernando emerged from the SUV and an enlarged hologram of him projected several feet above the RV on display, allowing everyone to see. His voice was projected through amplifiers.

He waved a miniature flag of the US. "Mi amigos! I come bearing salvation and restoration. The state has come back to rescue her abandoned babies."

Uriah covered his mouth in disbelief. "Ain't no way!" He nudged Evynn. "I literally saw you rip him in half!"

Lummis rested the tip of his sword on the ground. "Something isn't right. I saw you perish. You're dead."

Fernando chuckled. "Si, no, you saw but an image of me expire. The algorithm has the power to both reproduce and resurrect!"

Another powerful light blasted from the RV, illuminating the entire penitentiary.

"I come as the bearer of light and opportunity."

Lummis sighed. "Well, it appears you certainly have life all figured out. Why bother us lonesome, primitive creatures of the night?"

Fernando chuckled. "That is sarcasm I detect."

"Nothing gets past you, Fernando."

"I come as a representative of the States that are United of America's government."

"Pardon? You mean United States of America?"

"Yes, and we have a proposition."

"And if we say no?"

"Please. Allow me to profess the proposition before you oppose."

Lummis huffed, more than agitated that his epic showdown was rudely interrupted with a nonsensical pipedream.

"We can reintegrate everyone back into society."

"We've heard that before. And it almost wiped out half my men."

"Please, turn yourself around, Señor Lummis."

Lummis turned and his jaw dropped. LaShaun stood naked, in a cooled-down zombie state, in front of a whimpering beast.

Lummis slammed his sword on the ground. "No. No. No! You idiot! You took her from me. She was my birthright! "

"Si, as you can discover, we have the science to thwart any turned creature. But this is only temporary. And this is where we require your assistance."

An engine revved up and a projection of Evynn hovered next to Fernando's.

"Ev's you're famous!"

"Not funny, U's"

"She is the missing link—our Rosetta stone. We ask, if you find her, bring her to us. Within her body lies the cure to permanent termination of the turning and any future turning."

Those gathered in the yard from the penitentiary murmured. Someone yelled out. "And what if we don't wanna integrate back into the US? We're felons, lowlifes, outlaws, renegades, degenerates and undesirables. We made a decent way for ourselves out here where we don't have to be treated like dregs of your society!"

Fernando's projection smiled as the crowd became rowdy. He waited a few moments for the rumbling to die down. "Thank you for expressing your concerns. We have it covered. Please take a look above you."

A thin red beam of light shot across the crowd and scanned everyone's face. In the sky above the RV, an enormous projection displayed replicas of everyone, simulating life as though they were integrated back into a thriving metropolitan city. "As you can see. You will have access to the finest cars, luxurious homes, unlimited resources—the world will be your oyster. The States that are United of America's government will make sure of that."

A voice from the crowd yelled out. "Hey! Why you keep calling it that, yo?"

"Yeah, you tryna pull a fast one?"

"We can tell you now! Take your fancy technology. Take your funky government. And eat it!"

A plethora of bullets discharged towards the RV.

By the time the shots fired, Evynn and Uriah had reached Larry. They had all the answers they were looking for and no desire to become casualties of the crossfire. As they mounted the horse and rode towards safety, thunderous weapons roared back and forth between the brigade and the prisoners.

An all-out assault ensued.

Evynn dug her heels into Larry's side. Uriah wrapped his arms around her waist and squeezed tightly as they rode as fast and as far as they could until they suspected the horse would give out.

They stopped in an open field and dismounted from Larry, who was breathing heavily. Uriah rubbed his mane. "It's okay, boy. Try to catch your breath and relax."

Evynn surveyed the landscape, looking for someplace that was inconspicuous and would provide a level of protection from potential looters and assailants. "Let's dig in for the night. I know a place we can hide out at in the morning."

"Just like ole times, huh, Ev?" Uriah hugged Evynn. He gripped her like she was vaporous and if he let go, she would disappear.

She smiled. "You're being dramatic... but I feel the exact same way." She squeezed Uriah just as tightly and was just as unwilling to let go.

They kissed.

"You know. I've been thinking," said Uriah.

"Don't hurt yourself."

"No, really. I'm a changed man."

"So, you're a man now?" Evynn smiled and kissed him on his cheek. "I have something to tell you as well but I'm eager to know what's on your mind first."

"Ev, I'm a changed man. You go first."

"Uriah… please."

"Okay, okay," he nudged her playfully. Uriah stepped away from Evynn and interlocked his fingers behind his head. He took a deep breath and looked up at the moon.

A gentle breeze caused a layer of goosebumps to surface on Evynn's neck.

Uriah exhaled. "You know, I've been thinking. Despite how much I want it to be about me. None of it is." He laughed. "Whatever 'it' is. It's bigger than me and my fears. If intuition is compelling you towards the Old World, I say, let's give it a chance."

Uriah's newly inspired revelation was bittersweet. The words she always wanted to hear were satiating like a sip of cool water on a parching desert day. But not now. Evynn had something inside of her that could jeopardize her dream. She knew that's what Fernando and Adam needed as a sacrifice to reintegrate into the Old World.

If she kept it to herself, perhaps she could spare Uriah and she would only bear the pain of loss. They could live happily ever after in that downtown flat like she always dreamed of and he'd be none the wiser. But was that the right thing to do? *Would I be exhibiting the same selfishness I always criticized U for having?*

Uriah's eyes widened. "I no longer fear death. I don't fear nothin'. Whatever happens, happens, and I know it'll be for the best." He reached for her hand. "What do you say?"

Evynn had never seen Uriah with so much conviction, determination and enthusiasm. He wasn't wayward. He seemed rooted in his purpose. It was persuasive and reassuring.

Evynn took a deep breath. She smiled ever so faintly. "Let's do it!"

It wasn't so much she was eager to fulfill her wishes, but she liked this version of Uriah and didn't want to do anything to discourage him from staying in this light. He had turned a corner. And it felt good.

"Great! One thing. If we take up this Fernando guy's offer. We do it on our own terms." He bowed his head. "That means we'll have to split up once more."

"Uriah, no!"

"Trust me. I'm going to scope these guys out and put a plan in place. Once that's done, I'll come back for you. I need to ensure you will not be in any danger whatsoever."

"Where should I go in the meantime?"

"Anywhere. And fast. Can't risk anyone finding you before I do."

"And how do you plan on finding me?"

Uriah grabbed Evynn's face and pressed his forehead against hers. "Remember those voices in my head that I always complained about? Turns out they can be used to my benefit. Within the rivers of noise, sometimes I'm able to reach in and elevate a single voice above the rest."

Evynn scrunched her face.

"Trust me. That which is within you will cry out."

"Not that I don't believe you. But if that doesn't work. I'll be at the Old Conservatory, it's 20 miles that way, along the main highway." She pointed. "I'll leave crescents."

Uriah scratched the back of his ear.

She kissed him. "Everything will be okay. Let's pray." She grabbed his hands and pressed her forehead against his. "Most High, thank you for everything. We truly appreciate your blessings and protection. May we honor you with our actions and allow your Will to be done. Lead us onto the path of righteousness."

"Selah!"

"Huh?"

"It's like Amen. Learned it… you know what? Never mind."

"Be safe U-rie… I mean it."

"Let's not prolong this. The quicker I get goin' the quicker we reunite."

CHAPTER 16:
ONLY THE DESPERATE SEE MIRAGES

I CAN'T BELIEVE MY GIRLFRIEND'S A ZOMBIE

JACK E. MOHR

URIAH

Uriah felt anxious. He hadn't had piyel in some time and he could really go for some. Not for the susurrus, but to ease his nerves.

He still had on these stupid prison clothes and that bothered him.

He was bound to come across a dead man sooner rather than later. They were plentiful in these parts. As long as carrion eaters hadn't gotten hold of them, their clothes would be salvageable. Even the attire of a dead man would be better than his prison garb.

Everything had happened so fast. He didn't have an opportunity to digest any of it. He wasn't the greatest planner, but he was literally going on a whim. He hadn't had a chance to collect his thoughts. He was just going, going, going. He didn't stop to ponder Fernando's intentions, nor did he consider the fact that the man seemingly resurrected out of nowhere plus the sudden influx of technology in a technology-forsaken land.

The only conclusion he could draw was somehow Fernando was in cahoots with the Old World. *But how and for how long?*

Uriah found himself on the way to negotiate with a man whose death he had witnessed. If that wasn't bad enough, he had no leverage other than the whereabouts of Evynn—who they wanted to do who-knows-what to.

He felt like he had no control of anything. "Relax Uri, you can do this."

The sun poked through the mist at the horizon. A fresh, early-morning breeze brushed against his flesh. Uriah yawned and stretched his arms.

He hadn't realized how long he had gone without sleep. He rubbed his temples.

He was vulnerable. No weapons. No plan. But doing what he did best: pushing forward, driven by an impetuous will.

His only solace was the fact it would all be over soon—one way or another.

Like clockwork. Uriah came across a flock of vultures. He threw a rock at the wake and they scattered, revealing four freshly slain men.

Uriah sized the men up. One was rather large. One was dumpy-looking with red hair, and the other two were near his size.

"Jackpot!"

He disrobed the lankier of the men, removing his overalls. The man had a bloodstain on his long sleeve, so he took the thermal from the smaller man. The larger man had small feet, so Uriah took his boots. He patted the redhead down and removed a knife from his pants and tucked it into his boot.

"Hmpf... what are the odds? Someone left a perfectly good killing. It's like they knew I was coming. Peace to the Gods!" He chuckled. "By the looks of 'em, bet they had it coming to 'em."

Uriah continued in the direction of the penitentiary. A sign on the side of the road said it was less than five miles ahead.

I CAN'T BELIEVE MY GIRLFRIEND'S A ZOMBIE   347

Uriah wasn't sure how the Copperheads would receive him. If Ace and Cottontail were still alive, he had allies. He hoped. He would need as much help as possible. No way he could pursue Fernando by himself, and if he had to go alone, they could at least let him know where Fernando was headed.

Uriah approached the entrance of the penitentiary not knowing what to expect. He stopped dead in his tracks at the prison's entrance. A hollow silence pervaded. It was eerie. The foreground was littered with bodies, shell casings, blood-stained asphalt and grass.

The stench of death lingered.

There were more dead bodies than the vultures and coyotes could consume.

"Damn…is anyone alive?" Uriah scanned the bodies, hoping he wouldn't see Ace or Cottontail.

He proceeded through the prison's entrance, and it was a ghost town. He traveled from the basement to the warden's office and not a soul was left alive. But there weren't enough bodies outside to account for everyone.

So, what happened to the rest?

Uriah ate, washed up and rummaged for more supplies and weapons.

Once suitably equipped, he went around to the stable. He eyed those cowboy hats hanging on nails. "What did Ace say? You only wear this if you're ready to wreak havoc?" He picked up the tan one, rubbed his finger along the brim and placed it back on the hook. "Nah." He grabbed the black wide-brimmed Stetson and placed it on his head. It matched his black overalls.

He felt badass. The outfit empowered him, spiking his confidence. *Look good. Feel good.*

"Big Bo!" He was surprised to see the mule. "Hey, big fella. You remember me?" He rubbed his side. Big Bo brayed and nodded in affirmation.

Uriah saddled Big Bo and rode him to the front of the prison.

He stopped at the prison's entrance. He tilted the Stetson and gave a final look around. "Bless the souls of the righteous," he whispered.

He was all set. *Now to find Fernando.*

Fortunately, the RV left fresh tracks on the dusty road.

Uriah hadn't followed the tracks for twenty minutes before he saw him. It was Fernando, standing on the side of the road, waving with a wide disingenuous smile.

Were his eyes deceiving him? Why would Fernando be out here by himself on the side of the road, unless he was trying to be found?

Uriah tugged on the reins. "Whoa, boy." He rubbed Big Bo's side as he dismounted. "Fernando! Is that you?"

Fernando continued to wave as though he were flagging Uriah down.

Strange.

Uriah peeped at his surroundings, glancing from side to side, ensuring this wasn't some type of ambush.

As he drew closer to Fernando, he stopped waving and his gesture changed into a large unctuous smile. "Have information on the girl?" Evynn appeared out of thin air right next to him.

Uriah stumbled back.

"That's isn't really Evynn. This isn't really Fernando. What kind of magic is this?" he whispered.

"Mi amigo. Do you have info about this girl? If so, say yes. If not, dismiss yourself."

Uriah was close enough to notice the contraption on the ground projecting their images. He reached for his knife.

"Aye yi yi. Don't do that, my friend. It will not end well for you." A projectile launched from the device, whizzing by Uriah's ear.

"What the hell?"

"Do you have information about the girl. If so, say yes. If not, dismiss yourself."

The rendering of Evynn flashed. It was uncanny how much like Evynn the hologram appeared. He reached out to touch her but his hand went through the image. "Oh." Uriah didn't have a good feeling about this, but he went against his better judgment.

This is what I came here for. "Yes. I have info."

Fernando's smile broadened. "You will be blessed. Please remain where you are. Muchas gracias. A representative will be with you in an hour or less."

The contraption scanned Uriah's body.

Something wasn't right. This technology wasn't supposed to be out here. This is what his dad and everyone fought to escape.

This technology had cast them out. But now he was supposed to trust that it had a change of heart?

I guess it's the only way back into the Old World. And this is what she really wants. If this is what they use, I'll have to get used to it. Uriah had plenty of time to contemplate.

An electric-powered motorcycle pulled up in less than thirty minutes. The rider parked it next to Big Bo, removed his helmet and approached Uriah with a pep in his step.

"My friend. I am—."

"Fernando. I know."

"Pardon me, have we met?"

Uriah wanted to seize control of the conversation and keep the ball in his court.

"Not officially. You wanted information about the girl?"

Fernando smiled and nodded. "Evynn."

The way he said her name was unsettling and caught Uriah off guard.

"Um, yes. We are interested in your offer."

"Ahh… yes… my offer. And what might that be?"

"I'm not sure. But with her, you can integrate us back into the Old World?"

"Ahh… yes…Do you understand the significance of Evynn?"

To me yes. But to you… Uriah shook his head.

"She is the key to the reset of humanity."

"That's a lot of pressure."

"No pressure mi amigo, only opportunity. Do not think your action will go without reward."

"What's the catch? What does it cost us?"

"It cost you nothing. We just need what's inside her and her compliance."

"But why her?"

"She's what we call, miraculous." Fernando picked up the contraption and entered a code. He handed it to Uriah. "The first to be with child after having had turned. It is not her we need but the child within."

Uriah gulped. *Child? I'm a dad?* He accepted the contraption from Fernando. "What is this for?"

"This will lead you to the quarantine complex. There you will find representatives of the States that are United of America. If you are serious about effecting change, you know where to find us." Fernando put his helmet on, mounted the bike and zoomed off.

Uriah stood motionless for some time.

Evynn's pregnant. But how? I'm going to be a father. Is this what LaShaun meant as the fulfillment of the prophecy?

Uriah placed his hand over his face. "Wow! This is nuts."

He felt giddy but saddened. Evynn didn't know. He couldn't let her know. No way he could crush her hopes. If she knew she was pregnant, there's no way she would give up her baby. He wouldn't let her know. But he had to.

CHAPTER 17:
WHY WOULDN'T THE GRASS BE GREENER?

I CAN'T BELIEVE MY GIRLFRIEND'S A ZOMBIE

JACK E. MOHR

EVYNN

"Bliss! I'm so happy to see you, girl."

Bliss dashed towards Evynn, jumped into her arms and lapped her face.

"I see, you're happy to see me as well." Evynn rubbed her side fervently.

Evynn's strides were heavy and trying. Her stomach growled. She hadn't noticed how fatigued she was until now. She just wanted to lie down and rest her bones. She wanted to piece together everything. She felt so relieved Uriah was safe, but now that he was back in harm's way, she was nervous all over again.

She wanted to find Judaius and share the good news, but before she did so, she headed straight to the river.

She cupped her hands and splashed the refreshing water on her face. She scrubbed off all the dried-up blood and picked at the residue caked beneath her fingernails. She cupped her hands again, filled her mouth with water and swallowed.

"Ahhh!"

Part of her felt she should have told Uriah about the baby. But why burden him? He seemed so resolute and confident. Her shoulders slumped. *Why add problems at this point when we already have enough to solve?*

She sighed.

She had no qualms about killing men. Most had it coming. But the life within her was unique. No turned person had ever been pregnant, let alone carried it to term. Maybe she should try and give up on this farfetched dream.

Then again, if she could get pregnant once, who's to say she wouldn't get pregnant again?

I'm sure the Old World has hospitals and all sorts of technology that could help.

"Yeah… it's for the betterment of society."

Alice and Darlene ran towards Evynn and hugged her.

"Evynn! Evynn! Evynn!"

"You made it back!"

Even tapped Alice's nose with the tip of her finger. "I did! And I have good news."

"Really!"

"Yeah… where's Judaius, so I can share it with everyone."

"He resting."

"Come on!"

Evynn followed the girls up the incline towards the glass house until they reached a snug living quarters catacorner to the greenhouse.

Judaius rested with his legs sprawled out on a trim bed, sipping tea, still wearing his golf hat. When he laid eyes on Evynn, he smiled, then sat up, groaning. "A sight for sore eyes. I'm going to be honest—honest enough, I suppose. I gave you a 50/50 chance of making it back."

Evynn halfway smiled. "That's fair," Evynn sat in a straw chair next to the door. "Hey, I have good news."

Bliss lay at Evynn's feet and the girls sat next to their father with wide eyes fixed on Evynn.

"We're going to be reentering the Old World!" Evynn said with a smile.

Judaius adjusted himself. "That's good news, I suppose."

The girls gave each other high-fives. Judaius' demeanor remained unchanged.

"You don't seem as happy as I thought you would be. You'll finally get that Frappuccino you've craved."

Judaius hugged his girls. "At what cost?"

Evynn rubbed her stomach. *Didn't he know?* "Old World found a possible cure… so, no more lawlessness!"

He kissed his girls on the forehead. "Everything has a price. Out here I know the price of all my actions. I know one day my girls may turn. I know I live with the constant threat of danger. But I also have the luxury of not answering to anyone for nothing!" He rubbed his shoulder and took a deep breath. "A cure means an expansion of the Old World." He sighed. "Freedom is the price…I suppose."

***

The night was warm, and Evynn bedded down on the grass near the river, staring into endless heavens. Being this elevated made the sky seem like it was wide open, so close she could reach up and pluck a star out of the firmament.

She hadn't anticipated that response from Judaius. Who would choose this hell hole over the comfort and luxuries of the Old World? Why?

He's mad! Did he not remember his family? His home filled with love and joy? Neighbors you could trust and not fear? The safety of a structured society. The reliable day to day. The convenient food and water. Is absolute freedom worth giving up all that? He acts like you can't have both. If he wants to stay here and wear that stupid hat, let him!

The smell of fresh water from the stream relaxed her. She placed her hands behind her head and wondered why a slice of the moon wasn't visible. "Oh, Mom. Thank you for believing in me. I miss you even though I know you're always here. I just miss having you actually here."

The moon always made her think of Uriah. Hopefully he'd be back sooner rather than later. She had left plenty of half-moons for him to follow.

Bliss licked Evynn's face.

"I missed you too, girl."

Bliss barked and nestled on top of Evynn.

"Bliss, do you think I'm making the right decision? What would you do?"

Bliss couldn't respond, but she was a great listener.

"I know, girl. You'd keep your pups. But just think. I wouldn't have to fight anymore. I wouldn't have to kill. Wouldn't have to be on the run constantly. No more fear of what I can do or may become. I just want it all to stop. I'm tired of fear dictating my every encounter." Evynn huffed and Bliss licked her face.

Bliss jumped off Evynn and faced the darkness in a defensive stance. She barked emphatically.

"What is it, girl?"

Bliss dashed down the decline on the river's embankment.

A figure on a dark horse emerged from the darkness. He had a black cowboy hat pulled over his eye.

Evynn reached for her knife.

"Can I interest you in a trip to the Old World, Missy?"

Evynn chortled. "Uriah!" She eased her shoulders. "You almost got a knife to the chest! You play too much. What took you so long?"

Uriah feigned being stabbed. "Had to clear my mind. But I'm here now and that's all that matters."

"Where'd you find the horse?"

"Back at the prison. And he's a mule." He hopped off and hugged Bliss. "Am I glad to see you girl!" He rubbed her fur fervently.

"Well…"

"Hold your horses, ma'am," Uriah chuckled. "So, I met with Fernando. Weird guy. But he gave me this." He pulled out the device and handed it to Evynn. "A device that will lead us to their location. Once there, they will explain how you can save the world." He nervously laughed.

No sign of changing. Technology isn't so bad after all. "So, what do you think? Should we do it?" Evynn asked the question with minimal expectation. Her voice wavered and didn't possess the vigor to elicit a thoughtful response.

Uriah looked intensely at Evynn, studying her eyes as the moonlight reflected off her coffee-colored complexion. "I honestly don't know. Since we've been apart, I've experienced so much. I thought all compounds were pure evil, run by egotistical maniacs. Granted, that's still the case, but the prison and even Lummis's compound showed me that most men were just good people but afraid and looking to be led. And despite the crummy leadership, they were still prospering." He scratched his elbow. "If the leader in charge was truly righteous, out here wouldn't be so bad. And if there truly is a cure…"

"Uriah, if there's a cure this world disappears. Don't you get it? Without the threat, the Old World will expand and rebuild society. And we'll get to go to college, have jobs…" she rubbed her belly. "And start a family."

Uriah rubbed the back of his neck. "Start a family…Yeah…"

An awkward silence ensued.

Should I tell him?

"I know how much you dreamed of this. Your mom told you to keep hope and you could change the future." He took a deep breath. "Here's our chance."

CHAPTER 18:
NEOTENY

**I CAN'T BELIEVE MY
GIRLFRIEND'S A ZOMBIE**

JACK E. MOHR

URIAH

The two decided to spend one last night in the only world they'd ever known.

Uriah was happy he was finally doing something for the benefit of someone besides himself. With Evynn, he felt whole. He felt at home. He held her in his arms the entire night while Bliss rested at their feet.

Evynn wanted to leave before the sun rose. Something about not wanting to say goodbye.

Uriah hadn't really slept the entire night anyway, so it made no difference to him. His mind was too full of thoughts and possibilities to sleep. He still had no clue what he was getting himself into, and his nerves kept him on edge. His main concern was keeping Evynn safe at all costs.

Evynn held onto Uriah's waist as they rode on Big Bo. Bliss kept pace alongside the mule.

Uriah tried to figure out the contraption. He headed in the direction of the penitentiary. As they drew nearer to the prison, the contraption activated itself and provided instructions.

"Are you looking for your destination? Reply yes. If not, say no."

"Yes," he said.

"Continue along this road for twenty miles and then turn right."

"Well, seems simple enough."

Evynn squeezed him. "Yeah… technology makes things easier. Takes you right to where you need to go."

Uriah couldn't tell if he detected sarcasm, but he didn't respond. He remained silent for the duration of the journey, only speaking to check on Bliss and stopping a few times to make sure she was hydrated.

Despite knowing the cause was worthy, the guilt of not informing Evynn that she was pregnant gnawed at him. He never kept anything from her.

He wondered why Evynn hadn't spoken but figured she was figuring out what she would do first in the Old World. So, he let her dream.

"Turn left and your destination is on the right in 900 feet."

"Well, Evs, you ready?"

She hugged Uriah and laid her head against his back.

A large facility surrounded by sleek metal walls stood out in the middle of nowhere like an intrusion into its natural surroundings.

The building dwarfed the size of the prison and seemed like it couldn't be more than a few weeks old. *Incredible…*

"Wow," Evynn tilted her head back. "I've never seen anything like it."

They dismounted in front of the main gate—a black granite wall with a metallic auto-retracting grid.

Uriah's susurrus screamed. It hadn't been that prominent since LaShaun but as they got closer to the quarantine complex the murmur intensified. "*Bring her to me. Bring her to me. Bring her to me, now.*"

Uriah shook his head. "No."

"Huh?"

"Oh, nothing. Thought I heard something."

Bliss barked at the gate.

"Calm down, girl. We're going in."

Evynn approached the gate searching for a way in. A red laser examined her. Upon its completion, a beeping sound ensued.

"You may now enter."

Evynn patted her pocket, double-checking her knife was there. "U's, are you getting a weird feeling about this?"

Uriah reached for her hand. "I thought it was just me."

"We didn't even pray."

"Close your eyes. Most High, lead us on the path of righteousness. May your will be done above all. You have kept us safe and intact. For that we give thanks. Selah."

"Selah. What's up with you and this Selah?"

"I don't know. I like it. It's something new, and I'm trying it out."

The building was long and wide. There were a few hangars to the right and a separate smaller detached building to the left.

A huge American flag waved in the wind atop the facility.

Fernando appeared out of nowhere at the top of steps leading to the entrance of the main building. "Bienvenidos, mis amigos!" He extended his arms wide. "Come, come!" He smiled.

Uriah and Evynn hesitantly walked up the stairs. Bliss barked.

"Oh, you brought a doggie!" He bent down and rubbed Bliss' head. "What's his name?"

Something isn't right here. Bliss was the reason he died in the first place. No way he could forget that. This couldn't be the same Fernando.

"Her," said Evynn. "And Bliss."

Fernando. "Ahh... like how the rest of your life will be after today." He smiled. "We're going to perform a small procedure that'll be over in a blink, and we'll have you folks back in the Old World in a jiffy."

"Procedure?' asked Evynn.

"Ah sí, titivate like moi." He smiled and posed with his hands on his hips. "A few minor alterations."

Evynn rubbed her chin. "You're different than the last time we met. Something's off."

Fernando frowned. "I can assure you, it's simply nerves. You're taking a huge leap for mankind. Unprecedented strides manifested through the diligent algorithmic perfection."

Evynn squinted and whispered under her breath. "No. that's not it."

They walked towards the entrance of the facility. A sign reading: Welcome to The States that are United of America.

Uriah scratched his face. *Shouldn't it be the United States of America?*

Fernando stopped at the entrance. "Few housekeeping rules before you enter. First, we'll have to get you immunized." He removed two needles from his pocket. "If you don't mind extending your arm."

Evynn looked at Uriah. "No offense, but we don't feel comfortable doing that just yet. Maybe after we get a little more explanation of everything."

Fernando's smile dissipated into subtle agitation. He stared at Evynn and then Uriah. His eyes narrowed. "Fine. No problemo!" He smiled again. "Come on in!"

Uriah's susurrus raged. And kept repeating the phrase *bring her to me!* Over and over.

"Let me show you some of the men who have already undergone titivation and sterilization and will be integrating back into the Old World as well."

Uriah smiled.

This is where they all went. He was relieved. After all that gunfire and all the dead bodies, he was afraid the Copperheads were wiped out clean, but they were all here.

Fernando waved his hand and motioned for someone to come over.

Cottontail approached.

Uriah hardly recognized him with the slicked-back hair and the khaki pants. His face looked off as well—near the mouth area.

Uriah's smile widened. "Free the land!"

Cottontail looked confused. "Oh yes, we will be free in the Old World soon enough."

"Huh…" Uriah shook his head. "So, this is where you guys went. It's like a Copperhead reunion here."

"Copperhead? Ah yes, so this must be the one they call Evynn."

Uriah hadn't noticed until now, but he had the same perfect teeth as Fernando. Something definitely wasn't right.

Uriah whispered to Evynn. "Let's go!"

"Way ahead of you. This is just creepy."

They nervously shuffled towards the exit.

"Hey, where are you going?"

Fernando slipped in front of the door.

Bliss barked emphatically.

Several men wearing all-black armor and toting large weapons appeared from the back of the room and stood beside Fernando. Others stood along the walls of the facility—weapons drawn, pointing at Uriah and Evynn.

Fernando took a deep breath. "You stole the ruby egg once. I won't let it out of my grasp again."

Evynn's eyes squinted and an expression of "eureka" flashed across her face. "Adam!" she said incredulously.

"I beg of you. Please don't make this any harder than it has to be."

Uriah squeezed Evynn's hand.

"Okay," she replied calmly.

Uriah squeezed her hand harder. "But Ev's, you're pregnant."

She squeezed his hand and looked into his eyes coldly. "I know." She bowed her head. "Let's simply get it over with."

She knew all along?

Uriah released her hand and pulled out his knife. "I'm not going down without a fight."

Evynn placed her hand on his forearm and pulled it down so she could kiss him. "Trust me."

Fernando pricked the two with needles. "Don't fight it… you're going to feel a tingling sensation. Then your body will drop. It's all part of the process. Then… titivation."

Fernando motioned two of the armed men. "Titivation for him." He smiled. "Extraction for her."

The room spun. Uriah's legs weakened. *"Excellent!"* The susurrus exclaimed.

Uriah tried to lunge at the men with his knife, but his grip faded and the knife fell to the floor. Soon his legs collapsed, and the two men dragged him through the back of the facility— down a long hallway, through multiple sets of double doors. The bright lights made his head hurt and amplified the susurrus.

"Stop! You're hurting her."

LaShaun! She's still alive.

The men hauled Uriah past a huge hangar. LaShaun was in chains while several men taunted her. Evy lay on her side moaning and crying out. Men were hitting her with whips and she cried in agonizing pain with each lash.

Weren't the turned indestructible?

LaShaun trembled and turned. They stuck her with a needle and she quickly retracted into a zombie. The men laughed in her face as though they were getting a rise out of it.

Who knows how long the men had been at it?

Uriah's entire body felt numb. The men dragged him into a back room, placing him on a cold steel table. Then they exited, leaving him alone. Here he was again, in another precarious situation, completely helpless, but this time he had no one to blame but himself.

He had made a grave mistake, leading Evynn and him into a trap. It wasn't supposed to be like this. It was supposed to be a smooth transition without the eeriness. If this was a taste of the Old World, he wanted no part. It was the same controlling depravity he had always witnessed. Men were men no matter what setting you put them in.

If he could shake his head, he would have. He tried to get up but couldn't move his arms or legs. He then attempted to rock himself off the table but couldn't move a muscle. If this was his fate, he could only imagine Evynn's.

A solitary tear trickled from his eye.

"Ah… don't cry. Let me get that for you." Someone wiped Uriah's face. "Everything is going to be okay. We call this part the rebirth—titivation. Mother's going to make everything perfect once she finishes with Evynn." The man cleaned Uriah's face and smiled.

"Ace?" Uriah mumbled.

"Elijah, actually. Don't try to speak. Save your strength."

It was Ace but he talked just as funny and had the same perfect teeth. Was that a prerequisite to enter the Old World? *What's the deal with the teeth?*

Ace grabbed Uriah's hand. "Everything is going to be perfect. You just wait and see. Momma has it all under control."

Who is Momma? Uriah had no memories of his own mother and the thought of calling someone else Momma was unsettling. If he thought about it long enough, it would probably be infuriating. He had an asshole of a dad. He didn't need some asshole encroaching, calling herself Momma.

Uriah's susurrus erupted. *"I finally have her! With the baby and her in my possession, all further opposition is futile."*

Uriah concentrated, focusing on getting his words out. "Momma," he took several breaths. "Controls." He paused to muster more strength. "You."

'Controls?" Ace laughed and shook his head. "Momma merely suggests and urges. She'll be urging you too as soon as she finishes with Evynn. After all, Momma knows best."

CHAPTER 19:
FREE THE LAND

**I CAN'T BELIEVE MY
GIRLFRIEND'S A ZOMBIE**

JACK E. MOHR

EVYNN

Evynn had a plan. She just wasn't sure it would work. She didn't know if it could work. She had a feeling something sinister was going on as soon as they neared the facility. The moment they walked through that gate, her stomach jumped and kicked.

She hadn't turned in a while and being face to face with Evy had her questioning if she could still turn since the lucid reverie with Judaius.

But being here awakened something within her which enlivened her true power. It wasn't that she couldn't turn anymore; it was the fact she could control when she turned—at least she hoped that to be the case.

She felt herself teetering over the edge a few times, but she pulled in the reins each time.

There was something in this facility provoking her. Something powerful. If she was going to turn, she would wait until she was face to face with it. She wouldn't risk turning any sooner and definitely wouldn't turn any later.

She couldn't feel her body. Two men slung her into a still, dark room. The only sound breaking the darkness was a low buzz.

A reek pervaded. A recognizable stench only Adam could produce. A screen illuminated in front of her, displaying an avatar of her waking up in the Old World and watching television.

The screen turned black, and Adam appeared. "A sight for sore eyes!" He winked. "As I promised, I have brought God's people to the land of milk and honey." He frowned. "Alas, I cannot continue as I am, but the new Adam…er…Fernando will reap my joy and live on."

Evynn felt the urge within her surging. She just needed to lay eyes on him. That was the only catalyst she needed to turn. She knew his fat, smelly, festering, decrepit excuse for a body was nearby.

She could practically taste the rot.

"My final gift before my transition is to unite you with the true redeemer. I have offered myself as a temporary vessel for the one called Momma. Momma is ready and pleased with your selfless act of sacrifice."

Images of Imani cascaded through her thoughts. Imani stood in front of a rising sun, smiling. *Oh, Momma, how I miss you.* Evynn's eyes watered.

"Who are we kidding? This isn't a completely selfless sacrifice, right? Old World's the goal?"

Evynn patiently waited for him to finish his verbose rhetoric. At some point, someone would have to show themselves. Whether it be Adam, this Momma character or even Fernando.

The screen returned to black. And only the buzzing sound and stench remained.

Heavy, slow breathing emanated behind her a distance away. She couldn't move and even if she could, it was too dark to see anything.

The breathing became increasingly laborious as it drew nearer. The source seemed above her.

"Illuminate," a strained voice said.

The room lit up and a decomposed Adam hovered over her. "I'm sorry you have to see me like this." He stared at her with the same hollow eyes. How he was alive was beyond her. There was no possible way for him to come any closer to death.

If Evynn could cringe, she would. If she could scream, she would have done that as well. The rage within her was being held back by a dam of her willpower. Although tempted, she still awaited the perfect moment to allow it to burst through.

"After you thwarted our first attempts. I had to seek a power greater than Adam by going straight to the Source. Adam was a gift that allowed me to be a vessel but he had limitations, I needed more than omniscience—I needed omnipresence, ubiquity— Momma herself. Once I presented her with irrefutable evidence of a cure, she embraced me with open arms."

Evynn didn't know what the hell he was talking about. *Were these real people or abstract concepts?* But if Momma was real, that would explain the new compelling force she felt.

Adam's flesh was barely hanging from his face. He smelled and resembled a living corpse.

"Momma will now perform the extract. Thank you. And goodbye."

Adam breathed a final breath and fell limp on top of her. His massive body crushed her as it pinned her down, suffocating her.

She couldn't breathe. His fat smothered her. She panicked.

A sizzling emerged along with the smell of burnt flesh. Adam's body fell to the ground.

A high pitch shriek sounded.

This is her. This is Momma.

She was inside of Adam living within him like a parasite. Momma tore through Adam's body and clung onto the ceiling and stared into Evynn's eyes.

She had large, bulbous black eyes without pupils. Her flesh was dark grey and leathery. Her build was thin, with frail wings and twig-like limbs.

She shrieked and several men entered the room.

"Okay Momma," said one of the men.

Each grabbed one of Evynn's arms and they propped her up.

"Yes, Momma."

She's somehow communicating with them. It was as though she spoke into their minds.

One of the men placed his fingers into Evynn's mouth and pried her mouth open, ripping apart her jaws.

The time is now! Evynn squirmed. *Okay, any minute now.*

Pain shot straight to her temples. She forced her jaws shut, snapping off the man's fingers. She had turned, *but when?* She hadn't blacked out. She was fully conscious and aware within the moment.

A rage filled her and took control with a primal instinct. She became a witness of herself, tethered to her willpower but not exacting it. Something else was acting, something dark and relenting. Something that thrived off chaotic annihilation.

As Evynn drifted away, she watched herself like a spirit witnessing an out-of-body experience. But at least she was finally able to observe herself.

Her body changed and she observed it for the first time. *Eww, is that me?* Tendons tore. Bones snapped, the skeleton rebuilt itself, skin fell, thick muscle mass accumulated. It was as though the hands of the Most High were crafting her from the clay of the earth right before her eyes. Pure beauty from a divine artisan.

Men scattered as the final product tore through the room and engulfed the entire hanger—a red, leathery-skinned, winged creature reminiscent of the one whose egg she once captured. The creature expanded its wings and roared. The power of the roar slammed Momma and the men through the reinforced hanger walls.

Evynn tugged on the tether like a mountain climber's rope, pulling herself closer and closer to the beast. She kept yanking, hand over hand until she hovered in front of the beast, peering into its eyes.

"Destroy," she whispered.

The beast roared! It blasted into the air, tearing through the facility's ceiling. It turned on a dime and dove back down towards Momma. Momma shrieked and dashed with preternatural agility towards the front of the facility.

Men shot at the beast but everything they fired cascaded off her tank-like flesh.

During the hail of gunfire, Evynn lost track of Momma and lingered in the bright sky. She spotted Uriah.

She hovered down and gently scooped him in her mouth and tucked him into a fold.

Evy yelped.

LaShaun lay motionless. Evy whimpered.

There was nothing Evynn could do but destroy them all. Gill-like appendages on her neck drew in a vast amount of oxygen and a rumbling erupted within her belly. She spewed a streamlined inferno, scorching the facility.

Momma darted in the air, shrieking.

It captured the beast's attention. The beast took after it, with elongated flapping wings. Momma darted quickly with sporadic movements like a hummingbird, changing directions mid-air and darting towards the facility's entrance, landing on the ground in front of it.

She shrieked and all of the men emptied out of the facility surrounding her with weapons drawn.

Evynn soared above them and drew in even more oxygen through her gills.

The men fired in succession. A hailstorm of projectiles struck her. A few penetrated but most ricocheted off.

Evynn felt herself growing sleepy. *Oh no.* She was turning back. She had to hold on.

She pulled on the tether until she felt her spirit enter the body. She assumed complete control but for how long?

She discharged a broad stroke of inferno, making ashes of the men.

Momma shrieked in agony.

Evynn became more and more woozy. She slowly landed in front of Momma, who was writhing in pain.

Fernando ran over to Momma and threw himself on top of her. He wept. "You animals! You're killing her!"

Evynn wobbled. She couldn't hang on much longer. She was fading—going in and out of consciousness with each blink.

"Es okay. Momma is ubiquitous. She shall rise like La Fenix from the ashes."

Evynn dug deep and with all her might, released one last string of fire, engulfing Fernando and Momma.

She could no longer hold onto her consciousness and crashed to the ground.

CHAPTER 20:
NO PLACE LIKE HOME

**I CAN'T BELIEVE MY
GIRLFRIEND'S A ZOMBIE**

JACK E. MOHR

URIAH

Uriah regained agency of his body. He lay, staring in the sun with Bliss fervently licking his face. Evynn lay on top of him, naked, zombified and groaning.

What had he just witnessed? He'd seen her turn before, but never like this. Never to this extent. Never on such a grand scale. She was more powerful than anything he'd ever witnessed.

Uriah gently pushed her off and placed her on her back. He pulled up his sleeve like he had done so often in the past and placed his arm against her mouth.

She fed.

He stroked the side of her head. She needed rest. Heck, he needed rest. They had been through so much in such a short period.

He rubbed her belly and smiled.

Bliss barked.

Evynn came to quicker than he expected. She was disoriented, like someone awakened her out of a dream.

"Evynn, are you okay?"

She groaned. "I will be. Give me a sec."

"You were amazing. You freakin' turned into a dragon!"

"I said give me a sec." She rubbed her temples. Her body ached and she trembled. "Dragon, huh?"

Uriah was full of excitement. "You wouldn't believe it!"

Evynn groaned. "Red skin?"

"You remember? You remembered! I knew it was you this time. It just felt different."

"I'm cold U-rie…" Evynn's legs convulsed. "Help me to my feet."

Uriah helped her up.

She tried to balance but her legs gave out and she collapsed.

Uriah caught her before she hit the ground. "You okay?"

"Yes, thank you."

Uriah was always most cautious when she was most vulnerable. He held her in his arms and looked towards the facility. Some of the structure remained intact. "Maybe there's a blanket or something in there." He knew whatever he was able to find wouldn't be nearly as effective as piyel.

Evynn moaned.

He carried her in his arms up the steps. "They gotta have something to eat and something warm to wrap you in."

He searched the place until he found a black uniform for her and some vacuumed-sealed meals. They sat together and dined.

"Well, what now?"

"I honestly don't know."

"I say we nix the Old World and make our own world, out here."

A banging and crashing sound disrupted the two. Bliss barked.

"What was that noise?"

Ace stumbled through the rubble towards them, bruised and battered with blood trickling from various open wounds. He limped but still managed to maintain his grace like he was walking on clouds. A wide smile displayed those false teeth. "Hey, Jack!"

Uriah looked at him with caution.

Ace put his hands up in a show of capitulation. "It's me, Ace."

Uriah's shoulders relaxed. "You sound like yourself again."

Ace hugged Uriah and kissed Evynn on her forehead. "So, this is what all the fuss was about. The love you risked it all for." He chuckled then re-anchored himself in the reality of the moment. He shook his head. "Not many of us survived."

Uriah grabbed Evynn's hand.

Ace pointed towards his forehead. "She got in us but not through to the third eye. She had to use technology. It's the technology she controlled." His demeanor sobered as he bent down and reached for a piece of debris. He took a deep breath and held it in firmly as he slammed the chunk against his mouth repeatedly, knocking loose his teeth.

Uriah flinched after the second blow.

Ace's eyes watered as he pulled out his incisors. He held up a tooth and displayed the underside. It was a computer chip.

"I knew there was something about those teeth."

Ace wiped his mouth and touched Uriah's head. "We're true Seers. And I done seen a lot." He spat out a wad of blood, saliva and mucus. "While she was a part of me, I was a part of her."

"What do you mean?"

"Do you remember when we first met, and I asked if the name Evynn rang a bell? And it spooked you."

"How could I forget?"

He pulled out a pack of smokes. "The Momma that was here wasn't the true Momma. Just a seed of the source. I saw the true Momma and her history. And it ain't pretty." He tapped the bottom of the cigarette box and pulled one out. "Let that sizzle."

Uriah shook his head. "I should have known it wasn't as simple as it seemed. Nothing ever is."

Ace used some of the burning debris to light the cigarette. "I don't even smoke, but how often do you come across a pack of these? Least I got something out of the deal." He took a long drag, held it a bit and blew out the smoke. "Momma fears you, Evynn."

Evynn bashfully tucked her chin.

"Something about you has her scared. She now knows what you are capable of, and she'll adapt. She's coming. And she's angry."

Uriah turned to Evynn. "Well, where to now?"

"I can think of few places."

"I know one thing. I'm done running."

Evynn stood in her black uniform with her shoulders back. She clenched her jaws. "We'll just have to bring the fight to her, then."

Ace coughed. "I really dig you two."

"We'll find a way to carry the fight on our own terms. Priority now is keeping you and the baby safe. We dig in and create a community of our own. We have the resources."

Evynn rubbed her belly. "You're right…I suppose."

END.

Jack E. Mohr is a guy who loves writing stories.

He can be reached via Instagram or Twitter: @JackWritesMohr

OTHER BOOKS BY THIS AUTHOR:

Journey to the Abyss:

Armed with magic he continually hones, Antiochticus is on a quest no mortal has ever undertaken: he hopes to resurrect a soul that was consumed by the Abyss. On his journey, he crosses paths with a gigantic, bi-pedal ram named Selma. At first, their encounter seems trivial, but unbeknownst to them, destiny is pulling strings behind cosmic curtains.

The bargain is simple, kill the devilish king that exiled Selma, and she will help him get to the afterlife. The only problem is that the Myer Ram King is the most powerful beast that walks the earth — and using magic is not an option.

What started as a grieving boy on a mission to restore his mother's soul quickly becomes a perilous adventure that grows more impossible with each obstacle.

A life for a life is a cruel bargain, and he may not live to see it through.

Mayatte's Catharsis:

The mythical Island of Mayatte was never meant to be discovered by anyone, and its natives are about to find out why. When a ship of foreigners crashes along the coast, everyone but Naña is wary of their inexplicable arrival. While others are suspicious and fearful, Naña is curious and even helpful, especially when one of the outsiders becomes gravely ill. But her goodwill might be a fatal flaw that puts the entire island in jeopardy.

While she grows closer to the foreigners, they discover something that could revolutionize the outside world. A resource so powerful, they're compelled to harvest it at any cost. Naña is now pit against forces that could wipe her people from existence. How can she stop an enemy that's more powerful than any of them can handle?

Mayatte's Catharsis is a bittersweet tale of humanity in all its madness. Follow Naña through mystic battles, political unrest, and acts of kindness with magic leading every step of the way.

Transphobia:

Can one judge a book by its cover? Perhaps the pages within are needed to provide context.

Well… You wake up in a room unsure of who you are or how you got there. The only certainty is you were involved in a car accident.

Now you are being convinced you are a gender you don't identify with.

But why?

How will you discover who you are if your memories betray you?

Who would you be if your life depended on it?

Made in the USA
Columbia, SC
30 November 2023

3374d642-d887-49df-8a44-588da80d061bR01